✳   ✳   ✳

MORALLY GRAY

MORALLY GRAY

A Jonathan West, MD Thriller

WILLIAM J. KENNEDY

Other Fiction by William J. Kennedy
  First Kill
    Previously published as Jonathan West, MD – First Kill

This book is a work of fiction. Names, characters, places, and incidents are the product of the author's imagination or are used fictitiously. Any resemblance to actual events, locales, or persons, living or dead, is coincidental.

ISBN-13: 9780692070420
ISBN-10: 0692070427
Library of Congress Control Number: 2018901836
CreateSpace Independent Publishing Platform
North Charleston, South Carolina

To my dad, a voracious reader who would have loved this.

ACKNOWLEDGMENT

I want to extend my sincere thanks to my "Gray Guys" critique group of the Rehoboth Beach Writers Guild, who continue to help me hone my writing skills, turning a good story into a good book.

A special thank-you to Crystal Heidel for her insights as a teacher and the great cover design.

Chapter 1

Ten minutes ago, I was on the stage, one of ninety-eight newly minted physicians, receiving my diploma from the Yale, class of 1975. Now I was Jonathan West, MD, and sat on a white chair under a white tent on a warm May Monday, uncomfortable in my black gown, the uniform for graduation. The two black stripes down the front and the three chevrons on each sleeve identified me as the holder of a doctoral degree while the green hood was the designation for medicine. Like the uniform and rank designation of the military to the casual observer, we were all the same. But to those in the "club," these uniforms said a lot, just as they did when I wore a different uniform that too green and black, the class A uniform of a soldier in the US Army.

Bored with the ceremony, I looked around trying to find my guests in the crowd. The school gave me eight tickets for the ceremony, including one for myself. I needed a ticket to attend my own graduation! I found them seated near the stairs in a bit of shade—my parents, my wife Monika, Monika's parents, and our son, who also needed a ticket. The extra ticket was given to Gerb Chelebi, a kid from Tehran whose large extended family needed a lot of extra tickets.

My mind wandered as the president of the university performed an ancient rite in Latin. As I scanned the courtyard of Edward S. Harkness Hall, the building that framed the park-like setting drew my attention. The building appeared to be as old as the university itself, but I knew it wasn't—just built to blend in with those that were. A perfect square of grass and trees surrounded by a stone building, four stories high. My mind drifted again to a similar stone building, The Pentagon, also of stone, also perfectly proportioned with walls and stories, five each. That's where my current life had started, not the meeting with Anderson, but having a smoke in the Pentagon courtyard afterward with my CIA handler, Mike Allen. I had traded my innocence and committed to hijacking an airplane in exchange for a place with these men and women who were graduating with me today. Of course, there was the added incentive of $200,000, a fellowship of sorts from the CIA, and the use of the condo in Hamden. Not a bad deal!

While learning to be a physician, the CIA taught me to be one of their operatives, not specifically an assassin but not exactly not. They immersed me in an indoctrination program that exposed me to the intelligence-evaluation programs of the government, intelligence never fully utilized by the highest levels in the White House, Pentagon, and State Department. I learned the dirty underside of international intrigue—a world dominated by radicals seeking to harm Americans and the American way of life and causing mayhem across the planet to achieve their goals. The education was subtle, but in the final analysis, the truth was evident—sometimes the ends do justify the means.

Medical training was an asset in accepting this blunt philosophy. The basis of both was analytical. Evaluate the benefit and the risk. If the benefit to risk ratio significantly favors an action, accept the risk and move forward. At first, this seemed in conflict with medical training, "do no harm." That's not what the Hippocratic Oath says, but it's been considered an adequate summary for many years. As a physician I trained to make those decisions. Amputate a gangrenous arm or leg to save a life. Emergency room triage hardened my resolve—abandon one patient too critical to survive and use those resources to save the lives of those who could survive.

For the month after I put two .25 caliber bullets into the head of Ahmad, Mike Allen had hounded me, concerned I would have a negative reaction to the killing, my first kill. Allen backed off but only after a few carefully chosen words. "Jonathan, it should bother you that you killed. It bothers all of us. You're no different. When you need to talk about it, call me. I'll always be there for you."

Only then did the killing of Ahmad start to bother me. It bothered me because it didn't bother me. I had done a quick diagnostic on my walk back to the apartment that night and concluded I harbored neither psychopathic nor sociopathic tendencies. During my last year of medical school since the kill, I had gone through a psychiatric rotation and paid close attention to the clinical signs and symptoms of these two antisocial illnesses. I spent days in the stacks of the medical library trying to understand the diseases and ultimately myself.

Medicine is both an art and a science, especially psychiatry. I was convinced the working of man's brain would never be fully understood. To do so would be to understand the soul, something God would have revealed to man long ago if he wanted man to know. Medicine's feeble attempt consisted of diagnostic criteria laid out in the *Diagnostic and Statistical Manual of Mental Disorders*, or DSM II. Careful examination of these diagnostic criteria revealed significant overlap and gaps. If I took the test as a presumed psychotic, I failed and fell toward the sociopath scale. If I took the test as a presumed sociopath, I failed and fell toward the psychopath scale. So I was neither and both. Adding to this was the growing body of evidence collected from returning Vietnam veteran snipers who fit the definition as serial killers. These brave men confused the psychiatric community, who classified them as "benign situational psychotic sociopaths." In other words, they were normal. I was neither brave nor a soldier anymore and preferred to think of myself as *morally gray*. Yes, morally gray, like most of humanity. Monastic priests occupied the thin white portion on the far right of the scale while true psychopaths like Hitler and Attila were on the black left. The middle, the gray area, was for those who were basically good people who when asked to step up and fight for their country, or challenged to protect their lives, could make the move to the dark side of gray.

At the back edge of the courtyard, an ordinary-looking man watched the graduation ceremony from the shadows of the century-old oaks offering some relief from the midday sun. The man stood rather than sat, preferring not to challenge the neat creases of his trousers in the humidity of the warm day. He was bored but not from the mystical Latin ritual being performed by the tam-doffed faculty. He listened to the reading by the Yale president and cringed at his syntax and accent. Mr. Anderson studied Latin while preparing for life as a Franciscan and spoke the language perfectly.

From his vantage point, he could see West, who also appeared bored, looking around toward his wife, child, and family. Anderson smiled as he recalled the call from Mike Allen ten months earlier. As Anderson started to leave, his eyes followed the movement of his head but then with that unerring sense he forced the eyes back while the head continued to lead the body away from the ceremony. He spied Jonathan's head turning in his direction. He averted his look and turned away, sure he had not been spotted.

Anderson replaced the phone on the receiver, spun his chair around, and looked out the window at the parking lot four stories below. While small compared to the complex at Langley, "The Farm" in Northern Virginia was still vast by anyone's standards. He felt more secure here than at Langley. Was there a rationale for this? No. Both sites provided the highest standard of security anywhere in the world. Perhaps it was because "The Farm" was less well known. Regardless, he felt more at ease.

His reaction to the news from his trusted agent, Mike Allen, had first been annoyance and surprise. He had chosen Allen as mentor for Jonathan West to help the CIA awaken the US government and public to the potential for airline terror. His daring hijacking of the Northwest Airlines flight three and a half years ago on Thanksgiving eve had accelerated necessary changes in airline security. The carrot for his involvement: a guaranteed place in Yale Medical School. Anderson had concerns the reward wouldn't be enough. West was a brilliant young man. His try at professional hockey and time in the army matured him well beyond his years. He would have gotten into Yale on his own, and West must have known that. Yes, he knew. But he also had doubts if he could pay the tuition. The money made the carrot sweeter. It was his sense of duty that the hijacking uncovered, driven by a clear understanding of right and wrong.

Since then, Allen had carefully cultivated West into the man, or "Company Man," Anderson felt he could become. From the first time Anderson saw his file, he knew West had the discipline and sense of justice required to do the job he had in mind for him. He also knew, or hoped with a high degree of assurance, that West's medical training would prove to be an asset and not a liability. It would hone the skills of making quick life-or-death decisions, seeing everything as black or white, good or evil. Once he decided, West would move ahead in a straight line to the end he had chosen. Allen had spent the last three summers "educating" West to understanding good and bad using the definitions the "Company" did.

He had smiled after only a millisecond of furrowed eyebrows at the news. West had taken Allen by surprise. Even after the casual frisk in the restaurant, West had produced a gun and without hesitation put two bullets in the head of Ahmad, the lone wolf Irani agent of SAVAK. He did it in a calm, professional manner but had personal reasons that erroneously overrode the mission. Still, even with personal motivation, he had stayed cool before, during, and after the execution. Allen would have to work on that with West. He could not let his personal feelings interfere with his mission.

West became more vulnerable with a pregnant girlfriend whom he would no doubt marry. A man with his moral fiber could not contemplate terminating the pregnancy. From what he knew of Ms. Monika, it would be a distasteful decision for her as well. Yes, they would marry, and Jonathan West would present his own new set of complications. It would be an interesting test for him, and for Allen.

I felt uncomfortable, a sense I was being watched. My eyes continued to wander after a pleasant pause on my family. To the right, opposite my family, a lone figure was turning, unremarkable in every aspect except one. All the others in the crowd were still, but he was moving, moving away from the yet-to-be-completed ceremony. But it was more than the movement that caught my attention; it was his manner. The manner of a meek, mild bureaucrat or a Mormon missionary leader. Why was Anderson here? Was he checking up on me? Was Allen here too?

Allen was there, watching from the top floor of Harkness Hall in a dorm room vacated two days earlier by a graduating senior. He had no reason to be there other than to celebrate this occasion with Jonathan in a distant and discreet manner. Jonathan could hardly explain his presence to his family. His familiarity with the campus from his years of using it as a recruiting ground for "Farm" hands and handler of contractors such as West, after graduating himself ten years ago, made access easy. He had spotted Anderson, who wasn't hiding from anyone other than Jonathan, but why was he here? Why was he taking such an interest in this one man? Yes, West was unique to the CIA. He was a physician now who already had an impressive résumé. He had faced danger in hijacking the airplane and killed Ahmad, but there seemed to be more in Anderson's interest. When he had told Anderson of the Ahmad killing, he got a neutral response.

West had surprised Allen by pulling the trigger-twice, and Allen expected condemnation from Anderson for not being more vigilant. He had suffered several lapses that evening. He had failed to detect the .25 caliber Beretta West had secreted upon his person and had failed to anticipate the shot. It was only a second but enough time for Jonathan to put the first bullet in Ahmad's brain. As he moved to take the gun, the impact had forced Ahmad back, making Jonathan take a half step forward to keep the gun in place. That half step had given him time to pull the trigger a second time, another lapse by Allen. Not that it made any difference; Ahmad didn't survive the first bullet. He had been surprised by this young man who was proving to be full of surprises. West had remained calm throughout it all. Dead calm. The apt description "clinical execution" was even more meaningful when applied to West. There were no shakes or sweats after, none during the hour they spent together. Allen was more upset than West. Now he was dealing with Jonathan West who had made his first kill.

Anderson had told him, "Carry on, and keep me posted." Was that a neutral reaction, or was Anderson hiding his surprise? Was he here to get another look at this young man whom he had personally picked for training? Whatever the reason, Allen would have to be very wary in the future of what Anderson expected and what West was doing.

I stood with the rest of my classmates, still wondering about the disappearing figure I took for Anderson, unaware that Allen had been watching both of us. The dean of the medical school approached the microphone. It was time. Time for the ultimate step and final ritual of the graduation ceremony, the administering of the Hippocratic Oath. The oath was one of the biggest misconceptions about the medical community. Television and movies had condensed the oath to five simple words, "Above all, do no harm," words that didn't exist in either the original as written by Hippocrates or the newer version conceived a decade ago by the esteemed medical educator Louis Lasagna. It was the misconception that Allen struggled with when I killed Ahmad. I had done harm, and Allen felt there should be a conflict between what I did and what I wanted to be—a healer, a physician.

The dean asked the class to raise their right hand and repeat after him, "I, Jonathan West, swear to fulfill, to the best of my ability and judgment, this covenant: blah, blah, blah." Thank God, Yale had gravitated to a modern process, and there weren't ninety-eight new doctors trying to repeat Latin—a language some had never heard spoken, and those who had, gratefully burned their Latin II textbooks, thankful they didn't have to take Cicero, the mandatory third-year high-school Latin curriculum.

"I will respect the scientific gains…" No conflict there.

"I will apply all measures for the benefit of the sick…"

"I will remember medicine is an art…"

"I will say 'I don't know' when I don't know…" West was paraphrasing even as the dean spoke.

"I will respect the privacy of my patients…" and then the first challenge between his two new lives. "Most especially must I tread with care in matters of life and death. Above all, I must not play at God." Yes, he had killed, but he had not played at being God. If anything, he had played at being Mike Allen, who would have killed Ahmad if he didn't. And he did tread with care. It was a quick, painless death, no suffering. Certainly a lot less fear than if the others had done it. "No conflict here."

"I will remember that I treat a sick human being, not a disease or a growth…" Ahmad was sick. He was more than sick; he was a plague on society.

"The illness may affect a family of the patient, and I must include their problems." Ahmad was infectious to the greater family of humanity as well as a direct threat to my new family, Monika and our unborn child.

"I will prevent disease whenever I can, for prevention is preferable to cure." There it was. I had my mandate from the Hippocratic Oath to prevent the spread of Ahmad's disease. As I felt my spirits lift, the next part of the oath reverberated in the confined space of the courtyard. The sound system squealed to add emphasis.

"I will remember that I remain a member of society, with special obligations to all my fellow human beings, those sound of mind and body as well as the infirm." The words echoed off the granite walls, emphasizing this segment. I heard three distinct echoes. It was like the voice of God was saying, "Jonathan, pay attention. I want to make sure you hear this." I knew I had potentially saved thousands or maybe hundreds of thousands of lives by eliminating Ahmad. The armed conflict that would have erupted with the deaths of the Shah and the Ayatollah could have been felt all over the world.

I had eliminated Ahmad, a cancer attacking the body of humanity. No different from excising a living, growing cancerous tumor from the body of a patient. The cancer must die for the patient to live. Was it mainstream thinking? Probably not. Did many physicians feel this way? I don't know. It wasn't a question that came up in the classroom or study group discussion. I was confident though physicians would more likely understand my rationale than the rest of society. It didn't matter, did it? It was what I believed and what guided my moral compass. Besides, I had much more in the near future to be concerned about than what happened in the recent past.

West looked to the heavens, then to his family. In a whisper he said, "Thanks, God, I understand. I got it. I'm good now."

Chapter 2

‎ ✳ ✳ ✳

M y young family, the Wests, now three with me, Monika and newborn son, Erik, had a month to settle down before I started my new job at American Pharmaceuticals. We signed a lease for a two-bedroom apartment on Roosevelt Island, visited friends and family, and eased into the transition from medical student to young executive.

Roosevelt Island was a compromise between Monika's need for the big-city life and nearness to her family, and my dislike of the big city life and the need to be close to work. A real island in the East River, it served both our needs. It was close to work—a short tram ride and walk down First Ave—and close to Monika's family in Queens. Monika was still in "the city" and could see the East Side skyline from our apartment, yet the uniqueness of the neighborhood could trick me if I let myself think of this as an oasis off the coast of Manhattan. We could keep the lime-green Javelin, a luxury in New York City, albeit not on the island. Cars weren't allowed except for the pick up or discharge of passengers, or to unload. Cars were parked in a covered multistoried garage just off the island, a short walk across the bridge to Queens.

The month also gave me time to reflect on the previous summer and the future, a future that took me into the business world and further from the healer I had trained to be, not to mention the unknown as a contractor for the CIA.

Nixon resigned the presidency two days before I exterminated Ahmad. The news continued to be dominated by Watergate for months and then shifted to the deteriorating situation in Vietnam. The United States abandoned the embassy in Saigon at the end of April 1975, just a month before my graduation. Some claimed Nixon was distracted by Watergate and lost the opportunity for an honorable peace. After over a decade, thousands of American lives lost, not to mention our South Vietnamese partners and those supporting the North Vietnamese, and millions more whose lives were disrupted or changed forever, the war was over. A decade that seemed a waste now—a disgraced country with a disgraced president. Perhaps now the healing could start. The war took a toll on the nation's economy. While the war business had profited, the national debt rose to over five hundred billion dollars. Billion! If Congress didn't exercise care and caution, the debt would climb to a trillion dollars, from which the nation couldn't possibly recover.

The nation survived the oil embargo, the long lines, and rationing and grew accustomed to higher gas prices. The only visible concession was the introduction of smaller cars from Detroit and an influx of imports from Japan. This was the result of the action of the oil-producing nations in the Middle East and the reaction by the Shah—all predicted by Allen more than a year ago.

My last year at Yale brought an unexpected introduction. Yale had a very impressive faculty dedicated to molecular biology and the new discipline of recombinant DNA. They enjoyed, both by interest and location, close collaborations with researchers in Boston and New York, also heavily involved in this new science. One of the major scientists of the time was David Baltimore, the discoverer of reverse transcriptase, an enzyme essential for all the breakthroughs in this new science. Dr. Baltimore was a professor at MIT but in 1975 took a sabbatical in New York City. He enjoyed close collaboration with the Yale faculty while at MIT and continued it from New York. I met Baltimore both before and after he won his Nobel Prize in Physiology in 1975, and through those meetings, I was able to meet influential scientists from around the world. It would prove important to my work as a CIA contractor.

I knew my two worlds would collide, someplace, sometime, in circumstances yet unknown, and with that collision, the secret I kept from Monika would be exposed. My secret life would make our life together difficult and maybe dangerous.

Allen visited me in New Haven twice that last year. Because my schedule now included "rounds" in the morning, he had to make an appointment. He couldn't just show up at my table when I was having breakfast. Two reasons for that: the "rounds" made for an early start, if not in the wards then in preparation with my team beforehand, and Eric wasn't sleeping through the night, often rising for a feeding at the time I arose. Monika was breastfeeding, a growing trend fostered by the La Leche League. I couldn't help with that, but I could make coffee. After she nursed Eric, we'd sit and have a little quiet time before I headed off for a long day.

When Allen appeared, he was cautiously observant, watching for signs of mental meltdown he was sure would come. None had. He didn't push for me to monitor the Middle Eastern students' coffee club for dissidents and Irani government spies anymore and didn't present me with any new assignments. Rather, he focused on the immediate time following graduation.

I had previously indicated I wanted to go straight into the pharmaceutical business, preferably at American Pharmaceuticals, using my knowledge as a physician but not my skills. This surprised many of the faculty and my classmates. It was unusual to forego the internship and residency programs, but not unheard of. Every year or so there was a graduating student who went direct from medical school into law school, specializing in medical malpractice. Sounds great but I don't know if the doctor or lawyer brought anything special to his clients other than a bedside manner better than an ambulance-chasing attorney. His working knowledge of medicine would fade if not practiced, as I expected mine would. There was even a story going around of a medical student in Buffalo who, burned out from the rigors of his last year, wanted nothing to do with medicine. When he graduated, he enrolled in a long-distance truck driving school and got a license to drive eighteen-wheelers across the country, the "last true American cowboy" he declared. He had business cards made up, giving his name and the grandiose declaration "Doctor of Medicine, Teamster." Bet his mom was proud!

Life on Roosevelt Island settled into a routine, learning our way around this oasis in the middle of metropolitan New York. The first four apartment buildings had just been completed in the middle of the two-mile-long island. At the north end of the island, the hospital and insane asylum remained from its former days when it was known as Welfare Island, and still active. The relative quiet of the island broken occasionally by the sound of an ambulance transporting the sick from Queens to the hospital. Initially, the sound of the ambulance in the middle of the night triggered the doctor in me. My training kicked in, and I wondered what the emergency was and what skills would be needed to treat the patient. Was it a traffic accident, a mother in labor, or a gun shot? With time, I adjusted both to the noise of the city and the ambulance and the doctor thoughts. I either slept through it like most New Yorkers or rolled over and went back to sleep.

Stores on Main Street opened offering the bare necessities: a dry cleaner, a pharmacy, and a photo shop. There was a grocery store that became better stocked as residents made their wants and needs known to the owners. There were two restaurants, a pizza place and a Chinese restaurant, both with active takeout counters. Neither was a place where the diner would want to linger. They were more of a place where young residents stopped for takeout on their way home after a busy day.

The biggest problem I faced in the first six months was the commute to work. The tram running underneath the Fifty-Ninth Street Bridge wasn't scheduled for completion until after the first of the year. Until then, I had to walk across the parking garage bridge to Queens and take a cab into Manhattan. It was a small price to pay for the ultimate convenience I would enjoy. This temporary inconvenience allowed us to take advantage of an unusual, one-time-only, low three-year lease projected to double when the tram came into service. Life at home was good.

Not so my life at American Pharmaceuticals and my life as a contractor for the CIA. Allen was watching me and figured out my morning routine, stopping at the Chock-Full O' Nuts coffee shop on Forty-Second Street. He waited a decent amount of time and didn't approach me until I had four weeks of coffee acquisition under my belt.

"Good morning, Jonathan. Not bad weather for July in New York, but it's going to be a scorcher this weekend. Do you and the family have plans?" he shouted in the crowded coffee shop, not unusual, everyone shouted, but while the others shouted orders, he attempted a conversation.

"Michael," I said with both surprise and apprehension, moving closer to avoid shouting, "it's not like you to make with the small talk. But in the spirit of cooperation, yes, it is a nice day, and scorcher is relative. Now, what do you want?" My response drew a smile from Allen as intended. I wasn't going to be confrontational with him. He was my handler and the only contact I had with the CIA. A friend? I couldn't say, but he knew things about me even the closest of friends wouldn't. He knew things Monika didn't know!

"Right to the point. Sometimes that's a good thing." That left a lot to be said. That meant there were times when I shouldn't be so direct. I nodded.

Allen continued. "You remember Gerb Chelebi," he said as a statement, not a question.

Gerb joined our class as a second-year student, transferring from a medical school in England. He was quiet and avoided everyone. Came off as either a snob or a very serious student. I had mentioned him to Allen when he asked me to become friendly with Irani students at Yale. Allen waved him off as a nobody from a nothing family. When I became involved with the Arabian Coffee League in East Haven, even I forgot about Gerb as an Iranian. He was just another guy in my class.

"Yeah, I remember him. The guy from Tehran. I gave up an extra ticket for graduation, and he got it."

"That's the guy."

"We talked about him as a possible contact for me before I joined that coffee group, but you said I shouldn't bother." Allen was about to speak but paused, looked around, and nodded his head toward the exit, an indication we should go outside. On the noisy street, we could talk, confident no one would overhear us. When we stopped, I said, "I'm going to guess and say he was more than a nothing. I'm going to say you wanted me to stay away from him. Was he toxic?"

Allen took a sip of coffee, looking comfortable with the paper cup, his preferred container of the beverage. Black, no sugar. When I was in the army, I noticed a lot of career soldiers took their coffee black. I asked a veteran command sergeant major in our office if it was a macho thing with them. He answered bluntly they learned to drink it that way. Two reasons: they rarely had sugar and cream in the boonies. The packets of sugar and artificial creamer that came with the C-rations were better traded to the newbies for the four-pack of cigarettes in the C-ration pack, and if you made coffee from canteen water, the bitter taste of black coffee masked the plastic taste of the water.

"He wasn't toxic. We thought we might use him, but we couldn't." He took another hit of the coffee and pulled a pack of Parliaments from his pocket. He shook one out and took it between his lips. Replacing the pack, he took out his old stainless-steel Zippo, flicked it open with a twist of his wrist, lit up and snapped it closed, the distinctive crack of the Zippo ending the cigarette-lighting ceremony. As he inhaled, he looked up and down the street. "I didn't offer you a smoke because I know you're not smoking anymore, again," he said with a smile, emphasizing the "again."

"Seems the right thing to do being I'm in the healthcare business."

"And Monika doesn't like it," he added.

"That too. What about Chelibi?"

"Chelibi's old man was a doctor in Tehran and on the inside with the Shah's people. He was on the Islamic Republic of Iran Medical Council, the IRIMC, almost from the beginning in 1964. It had a goal like our Department of Health, Education, and Welfare but theirs is a nongovernment agency, so it doesn't have any teeth. So IRIMC focuses on education and welfare aspect, you know, a lot of the prevention stuff for the patients, but there's not much of that either. The senior Chelibi rose through the ranks by dint of his political connections. I'm not saying he wasn't a bright or dedicated guy, but to get ahead in Iran, it's who you know, not what you know. The top job has had four different heads in the last ten years, and even though Chelibi should have gotten the job, he didn't."

Allen continued to ramble on, and I wondered where this was going and how long it would take to get there. I looked at my watch, a clear signal to Allen to move along.

"The old man was a lot smarter than people gave him credit. I don't think they passed him over for the top job, but rather, I think he made sure he didn't get the top job. In those positions, in Iran, it only takes one mistake, and you're gone. And by 'gone,' I mean with the capital G, in the most permanent of the past tenses."

"A player in Tehran?"

"I don't know what you mean by player, but the old man knew what to do and what not to do and lived a good life in between those boundaries. He manipulated others to take the risk without them knowing. And he taught his son to do the same, especially to keep a low profile."

"All of this within the health ministry?"

"Power is what you make of it, and it knows no home. Through the ministry, he had access to every aspect of life in Iran except the military, and even they weren't exempt from his touch. Access to medical gave him a lot of opportunities to do good or do evil and win the hearts and minds of the people. Same holds true for the role he defined for the welfare component of the ministry. He was a master and built quite an empire."

I looked at my watch again, wanting Allen to move this along to what he wanted from me.

"His family was well provided for. The Chelibi family was small by Irani standards, just Gerb and his mother. The extended family was close, and it too was small, just an uncle and his daughter. In the 1960s, the trendy thing to do was to send children off to England for education. Gerb was sent to the UK and enrolled in a medical program at Nottingham. It wasn't like it is here in the States. There's no undergraduate school and then off to medical school; it was straight into a program that resulted in a medical degree—five years, I think. When he got there, he did the first three years of the medical program, but then he saw what was available and craved knowledge. The kid wanted more of an education than just medicine and switched to the most general college education in the UK at the time, geography. The old man was furious. Tried to call him home, but the kid was adamant."

Allen field-stripped his Parliament, letting the shredded tobacco drift to the ground, and pocketed the filter. It was another habit carried over from his days in the military. A man of his tradecraft should be more careful to hide his military background, but it wasn't necessary. Every man who had been in the military during the past decade did the same thing, and there were a lot of veterans of Vietnam.

"Gerb came home in 1970, kicked around, trying to make something better in Iran based on what he learned in the UK. The old man's lessons of keeping his head low were long forgotten. Then he woke up to reality when he saw how the zealous religious right was looking at him. He got religion, pardon the pun, and went to his father, full of contrition. The father pulled some strings with our man in Tehran, who did the same in Washington, and the kid was off to New Haven. They gave him one year's credit for the three years he did at Nottingham. He was bright enough but not on par with his classmates. He knew everything he had studied quite well. Problem was, the standards his educators had worked against in the past were below the standards at Yale. That first year in New Haven, he had to hit the books hard to catch up. Worked fine for me because I wanted a low profile for him."

"He was one of yours at Yale?" I asked.

"Did I say that? I don't think so. I think you misunderstood me."

No misunderstanding, the message was clear. File it and forget it.

We had been strolling east on Forty-Second. As we approached the entrance to my office building, Allen slowed, touched my arm, and moved me toward the curb, out of the early-morning rush and out of earshot of anyone who might be listening.

"The father became uncomfortable in Iran and started making plans to leave. Again, he contacted our man in Tehran, began transferring assets into offshore accounts, and learning English on the side. He also talked to his brother and convinced him it was time to leave. The father and brother left Iran within a week of each other—the father to visit the son in New Haven and the brother and his daughter off to a convention in Paris. There was a snafu in Paris, and the French authorities detained the brother and niece for over two years before we could get them over here via Canada."

"So everyone lived happily ever after?"

"No, everyone *is* living happily ever after, and it's my job to make sure that continues as long as it suits my needs."

"And that's where I come in."

"Yes, Jonathan, that's where you come in. It never ceases to amaze me how quickly you grasp the essence of a situation."

"Yes, a lot quicker than it took you to get to the point."

Chapter 3

I turned east and walked toward the office. Allen followed my lead, still talking, but not yet telling me where I fit in.

"Where *do* I fit in? Do I strike up a renewed long-distance relationship with
Gerb, try to get him involved in a clinical trial? Or is it the father? He's here in
the States you said." Allen was walking on the street side of the sidewalk, so I had
to turn to my right to see him and any reaction he had. Directly across the street
from him was the Daily News Building, not as imposing as the Washington Post
Building had been. Still, the iconic home of New York's most popular newspaper enjoyed a large fan base. Virtually every commuter read the *News* before
arriving at work in the morning. The art deco lobby was a favorite for tourists,
boasting a large model of the earth, rotating every ten minutes. Fascinating the
first time you saw it and maybe even the first couple of times. The thrill wore
off after showing it to visiting family and friends a dozen times. Lucky for us
that Monika's family were locals and my immediate family had seen it already.

"No, we've had people working with them since they arrived in country."

"Who then? Not the uncle? I'd have to start from scratch? What does
he do?"

"No, not the uncle. The niece, his daughter."

Allen's answer surprised me. "The daughter? That's as bad as the father. I'll
have to start from scratch, and what is it you want me to do with the daughter?

Take her to coffee clubs?" As I said this, I had all kinds of thoughts running through my head. Women in the Middle East were second-class citizens. They were kept out of every aspect of life except having babies and cooking food. What could a woman, a young woman, offer that would be significant? I felt a bit of embarrassment, thinking of myself somehow in the presence of a burka-clad woman, maybe walking down the streets of Manhattan, drawing stares and snickers. But wait, that couldn't happen. Women devout enough to wear burkas can't go out in public with any man who's not a relative. What then was the value of this woman? Or, maybe she had no value. Maybe this represented a demotion for me. Was she keeping an eye on me? All this negative thinking resulted from a thought that began to fester several months ago.

I hadn't heard from Allen much during my last year in New Haven. When he did show up, he kept the conversation neutral, congratulations on the wedding and offering to help find a job for Monika in New York when she decided to go back to work. There was no doubt the CIA had done a full background check on Monika as soon as we became serious, a deeper security check than when she worked at Energy. Allen's casual comment triggered a nerve, and I told him in no uncertain terms he shouldn't approach Monika to work for the agency in any way.

I'm sure the thought crossed their collective minds to enroll her as a consultant or contractor. She was intelligent and useful, having relatives still in Europe, most in West Germany but some in East Germany. When I cut short any approach to her, had I made myself less an asset?

Allen must have seen something in my expression. He stopped walking, turned, and faced me. "The daughter, the niece, the cousin—her name is Helen, and we can use her." The message "we can use her" was immense, but to anyone who overheard him, it sounded like another round of office politics.

"How?"

"I don't have time to explain everything to you now. Can we meet for lunch today?"

"I have a meeting with an investigator at Mount Sinai Hospital."

"I'll cancel it and meet you there. Same place, same time." And then he was off before I could say yes or no, before I could ask him how he knew the where or when of my to-be-canceled meeting. He didn't have to wait or provide an answer. All I needed was the ten seconds it took for him to turn and walk to the corner and the answer was clear. He was Allen, and he knew everything about me he wanted to know.

I arrived at Ottomanelli's on York Avenue at one o'clock. Before I could speak, Giovanni, the nephew of the owner, smiled and said my guest had already arrived and was waiting for me. At the back corner of the narrow dining room off the bar, Allen was sitting with a mixed drink in front of him and a Peroni at the empty seat across from him.

"How did you know I'd want a Peroni and not a Bushmills?" I asked.

"The Peroni is the right drink for a man in your position to have at a business lunch. Bushmills might be a flag for a drinking problem, and martinis would be an affectation for someone your age. Besides, I know you'll only take a few sips, and then let it go warm without finishing it," he said raising his glass in a welcoming toast. "You don't like to drink."

Giovanni had lingered to pour my Peroni. Unaccustomed to seeing me drink, he paused when the glass was half full—a question in his eyes. A signal with my hand and he left the glass partially filled. I met Allen's toast halfway across the table with a clink from my chilled glass.

"So what about the daughter, niece, cousin?" I asked.

"Helen."

"Yeah, Helen. What about her?"

"Before we talk about Helen, let's talk about Monika. How is she, and how are the two of you doing? Is married life all the poets write about?"

A curious question. "I don't know what the poets have written about marriage. Monika and I are doing fine. We seem well suited for each other and have become good friends. I think there's nothing we don't share..." I said, pausing, both of us knowing what he would say.

"Almost everything. Probably everything except the fact you work for the CIA and killed a man."

Was Allen challenging me? What was the purpose of this discussion? "Yeah, except for that. I often think about that discussion which will eventually come."

"That discussion may come, and when it does, all our resources are at your disposal. We've dealt with it before, sometimes successfully, sometimes not so much."

"Whose definition of 'successful' do you use, the couple's or the CIA's?"

"They're the same, Jonathan. By now, I would hope you understand that." He shifted in his seat and leaned forward in the conspiratorial manner I had seen before. His voice lowered even more. "Does she trust you?"

"What do you mean?" I asked, again not knowing where he was going. It seemed he had changed the subject, but I had no idea what he meant.

"In your job, you interact with a lot of young, attractive women. You travel, often for days at a time, sometimes even with these women. Does Monika get jealous, or do you think she'll get jealous with time?"

I had a better idea of where he was going now, but just the general sense. "Do you mean does Monika have the potential to become the jealous housewife because of my job and perhaps jeopardize a mission?"

"Sort of. What do you think generally; then we can go into specifics?"

"No, I think she's intelligent enough to know I wouldn't do anything stupid and so shortsighted to hurt our marriage. I can't explain it, but it's something we both felt from the beginning." I smiled and added, "She won't be packing her bags and running home to her mother."

"You're smiling, Jonathan. Why?"

"Her parents made it clear, in a joking and loving manner, that if she ever thinks about leaving me, she shouldn't come home. They say if anyone was to leave and go live with them, it should be me. Monika and I had a minor tiff I ended simply by saying, 'If you continue to be angry with me, I'll leave and go live with your mother.' That brought a smile."

Giovanni approached with salads. Allen paused and switched subjects. "I took the liberty of ordering before you got here—salads and veal piccata."

"Beer with veal? Shouldn't we have white wine?"

"You drink your beer, I'll drink my Bushmills, and I'll go back and write a letter of apology to Ian Fleming and all the spy-masters at CIA for this breach of Spy 101." He smiled. I returned the smile. The tension gone, for now.

"What about Helen?"

Allen took a forkful of salad, shook off some of the oil and vinegar dressing, and ate it. As he chewed, he looked at me as he composed his answer.

"Helen is Gerb's cousin, the only child of her uncle."

I had to interrupt Allen. I had a question, and I'm not very good at receiving information if there's a question rattling around in my head. "Is Helen her real name? It doesn't sound like an Irani name."

"No, it's not. Remember her mother is Syrian, not Iranian. She was named Hila when she was born, but she started going by Helen when she went to university in England."

Allen continued where he left off. "The uncle's name and background are not important, only Helen. The father, like many from his background, wanted a son, but his family was completed with just the daughter. He and his wife had no other children. He worshipped her. As she grew up in Iran, the Shah was making changes. Women no longer had to wear face coverings. Western wear and customs were introduced and women offered the opportunity to get an education, albeit limited. We've analyzed this family from many angles, and it hasn't gone unnoticed that her uncle, Gerb's father, was the minister in charge of education. Appears that a lot of different forces were in play that allowed this woman to blossom. She excelled in what we would call high school, both academically and socially. She even took an interest in badminton and volleyball, not official high-school team sports, but at the time, very daring for a young woman in Iran."

Giovanni reappeared, cleared the salad plates, and replaced them with the veal dishes.

"Here's where it gets interesting. The father was an important man in Iran. As is the custom, many other fathers came to him to arrange a marriage when Helen was still a young girl. The old man saw a better life for her. He didn't know what it was yet, but he knew she was special. Being privileged, she was seldom seen in public, confined to the family estate. When it came time for her to go to school, the proposals for an arranged marriage started. The old man at first said it was too early or rejected the suitors as unworthy. He knew someday, the right suitor would come forward, and he would be put in a corner, and his daughter's fate sealed by custom. Here's where he became very clever. He had her wear full-face cover and changed his story. With a certain amount of theatrical shame and humility, he said his daughter had been marked by Allah. That she had a harelip, was unworthy to be the wife of someone of high birth, and would spend her life only receiving the love of her father."

"Wait a minute. You said she was active in school, participating in sports. Surely she didn't wear full head cover when she played badminton and volleyball?"

Allen smiled. "This is where the old man got brilliant. He enrolled her in a boarding school away from Tehran, close enough to see her often, but far enough away that the elite of Tehran wouldn't see her. His search was made easier because his brother was the Minister of Education. Helen enrolled, not as Helen Chelebi, but as Helen Aboudi, using her mother's maiden name, a Syrian name. Helen became used to this dual life. At first, it was a game she was playing, but as she got older, she understood what her father had done for her and embraced the dual identity. So we have an Irani woman schooled from an early age to live two identities. Identities established by her father with the help of her uncle to protect her from customs her family thought were not in her best interest."

"So how did that work out, and where do we come in?"

"Helen grew in her role over the years. I've already said she was an exceptional student and a gifted athlete. When she returned home during school breaks, she donned her full head cover and acted the humble daughter when she had to leave the family home. Having no siblings made the charade easier—no friends of brothers and sisters hanging around. Her family was small, just the uncle and his son, Gerb, and they were in on it. It was perfect."

When Giovanni came to clear the plates, we passed on dessert and settled for coffee.

Allen resumed. "When it was time for college, there was no problem. Most girls didn't go on to college, so the formal application process with letters and recommendations could be ignored. Instead, the uncle stepped in again, used his contacts on the international stage, and got her into Nottingham with her cousin. She was a year behind him, and by the time she showed up, he had switched to the geography program, which she enrolled in. She was smart, and the program was a snap for her, leaving her a lot of time to absorb everything else that was going on. A lot of social unrest in England at the time. Not like the anti-Vietnam protests but a lot of things. The first year, she, like everyone else in the country, got involved in the Guy Fawkes celebration. She loved it, but more important, she studied the history. Helen was fascinated a common man could have the courage to make such a dramatic statement against the government. She became more involved in school politics and became a woman of the world, no longer having her horizon limited by the boundaries or customs of Iran."

"And that's when you noticed her?"

"And that's when we noticed her!"

Chapter 4

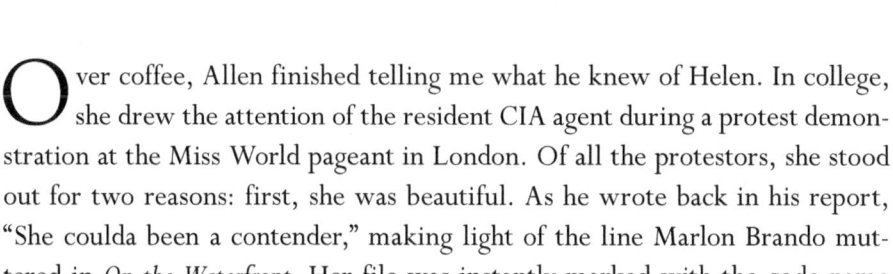

Over coffee, Allen finished telling me what he knew of Helen. In college, she drew the attention of the resident CIA agent during a protest demonstration at the Miss World pageant in London. Of all the protestors, she stood out for two reasons: first, she was beautiful. As he wrote back in his report, "She coulda been a contender," making light of the line Marlon Brando muttered in *On the Waterfront*. Her file was instantly marked with the code name she would be known by, "Terry," after the boxer Brando played in the film. The second thing was she was from the Middle East; her features, black hair, and olive skin were not unlike Italian or Greek, but different. Her accent when she spoke was the giveaway.

"Why was that so unusual? Why would he generate a report just because she was a Middle Eastern student protesting?"

"One protest was organized by the London Feminists Network, and the pageant was being run by the Mecca organization, Mecca LTD to be precise. The company was described as a leisure company with many different businesses, all aimed at entertainment. But—and here's where fate can have interesting consequences—there was another protest. The big news before the pageant was that South Africa was to have two contestants, one black and one white. With the civil unrest being a Communist-fueled problem in South Africa, the CIA covered the event. The agent at the event was new to England and didn't know about the Mecca Leisure Company and nothing about the feminist protests until they happened. When he saw the Middle Eastern girl protesting a Mecca event, he put the wrong two and two together, assuming an Arab woman was protesting Mecca, the holy shrine, and wrote the now-famous report."

"Is he used as an example of what not to do in training new agents now?"

"Wish we could, but it would give up Helen's identity. It would be a worthwhile lesson." Allen finished his coffee and signaled for the check. "After we determined Helen was not an Arab woman protesting the Muslim holy city, we looked into the feminist protest to see if there was anything else of interest. That's when Helen became interesting to us. The feminist organizers had a pamphlet printed with a list of grievances, all directed at men and male-dominated industries and the pageant. Their list was extensive and, in some places, vulgar, one phrase, 'using the *c* word to sell deodorant.' Women in general don't like the *c* word. I've been told that so many times, I don't use it anymore either, but here is a protest group bold enough to use it, and an Arab woman, bold enough to be part of that group. We looked into her past and ran into a dead end. Couldn't find anything about her before she entered elementary school. Remember, she used her mother's maiden name. It made her more interesting. At her college, we found the recommendation from her uncle and worked from there. Then it all unraveled with the connection back to Tehran, her father, and her uncle. The CIA team in Tehran was assigned the case and approached both the father and uncle. By now, the uncle, Gerb's father, was looking for a safe and financially secure exit strategy. We helped."

"That's crazy. It defies everything I learned about the careful analyses you taught me during my summers in DC. Just pure dumb luck and an inaccurate report."

"Yeah. Sometimes, it's just shit luck. You have to know when to take advantage of it. It would have been easy to dismiss the report as an error due to a new man, but we didn't. That's the value of the human element in intelligence gathering. Curious people dig a little deeper to find the mother lode."

"And Helen is the mother lode?"

"Yeah. Helen and her family here, the family in Canada, and the remaining extended family members still in Iran."

Giovanni returned with the check, and Allen paid in cash. We left with things still unsaid. I had to say them.

"What's my connection to Helen, if there is one?"

"She'll be your partner," he said, saying good-bye over his shoulder as he rushed to grab a cab unloading at the curb. He didn't offer to share a ride or drop me off. Instead, he said, "We'll talk again next week, after."

"After what?" I said to a cab door closing.

I returned to the office knowing Allen had something dramatic in store. The smile as he added "after" while pulling the cab door closed convinced me.

It didn't take long. The next morning, I answered the phone.

"Jonathan!"

"Yes."

"It's me, Gerb, Gerb Chelibi from New Haven." I knew this was the "after" Allen had smiled about, but I didn't know it was the beginning.

Gerb was an Intern at Columbia Presbyterian Hospital, one of the most coveted and prestigious internships available. He told me he just learned I was working at American Pharmaceuticals and had to touch base. This put me on high alert. It wasn't a secret I had passed on the opportunity for both an internship and residency and instead opted to go straight into the business world. It seemed everyone in the class was talking about it, so it came as a surprise when he said he just learned of it. I challenged him on his statement.

"Oh no, you misunderstand me. Of course, I knew you had elected to go into industry, a brave move, one I couldn't imagine doing. Leaving the practice of medicine for the unknown of the business world scares me. I couldn't do it. I admire you for having the courage to do it. What I meant was I just learned you were in New York, in fact, just down the street, so to speak. Perhaps it is because English is not my native language I said that wrong."

Gerb had a better command of English than most native-born Americans, but it was an attempt at an apology or something else, something perhaps Allen had a hand in, so I accepted his apology graciously.

"By down the street, I mean we are renting an apartment on east Fiftieth Street between First and Beekman, just down the street from your work."

Actually, it was "just up the street," eight blocks north of Forty-Second Street where I worked, but I wasn't going to get into a geography lesson. I had more pressing information to glean from Gerb, like why was he calling less than twenty-four hours after Allen and I had spoken about him, and what would happen "after" I talked with him.

"We're almost neighbors, an unusual occurrence in a city of eight million people. What are you up to?" I asked. Gerb and I had not been friends in New Haven. In fact, neither he nor I had many friends while we were going to school. I was older and had my "part-time" job with the CIA to eat up any free time I had, and he always had his head buried in his books. Now, after talking with Allen yesterday, he probably had some nonmedical school activities as well.

"Jonathan, as you can imagine, I have very limited free time as an intern. What time I have is full. I would like to stay in touch with you. We weren't close friends in New Haven, but perhaps we could find some common ground, maybe favorite restaurants? My point is, my wife and I are hosting a small dinner party on Friday evening for some family and new friends. I don't know when we'll be able to do something like this again and would like it very much if you and your wife could join us. Can you make it?"

If Allen hadn't mentioned Gerb yesterday, I would have found an excuse to duck the party. Monika and I had little free time, and the little we had, we were drawn to activities with people from work or her family. But I sensed if I passed on this invitation, Gerb or Allen would force the issue. At least there'd be others around, and I'd have Monika with me. "I think we're free on Friday night, but let me check with my wife to make sure she hasn't scheduled us for something else." He seemed happy I agreed so readily. He gave me his phone number and the address, closing with "And you don't have to bring anything, just you and your wife. Dress is casual, not suits or ties."

Gerb's house was a brownstone, built in the thirties on one of the more fashionable streets north of the United Nations. The street dead-ended at its east end at a promenade that looked over the East River. I could see the southern tip of Roosevelt Island almost straight ahead. Unlike our place, it wasn't an apartment but the entire house, three stories. His intern's salary probably only paid the electric bill in this neighborhood. Either he or his wife came from money, or he was spending his CIA consultant fee more freely than I was.

Gerb greeted us at the door dressed "casually"—a blue sport jacket, a tie-less light-blue Oxford shirt, and tan khakis. He was genuinely happy to see me and fussed more than necessary over Monika. Inside, the expensively furnished town house shouted money. Even if he had gotten his entire consultancy fee at one time, he couldn't afford this place. Had to be family money, or maybe US aid money the family stole from the people of Iran before they left.

He introduced us to everyone, me as his old friend from his days at Yale and Monika as my lovely wife. She cringed. She was beginning to have an identity problem not working anymore and resented being identified only as my wife or Eric's mother. As we made the rounds of introductions to the others, it occurred to me the men in the room lacked imagination in choosing their clothes. The majority dressed like Gerb, the exceptions being those who wore corduroys. It shouldn't have surprised me; their style models were the faculty members at Yale and now Columbia. With time, I would come to recognize this as the academic business dress, just add a club tie, preferably red.

We settled into the conversations. Our backgrounds gave us common ground, and my venture into the business world was a curiosity they wanted to explore. One woman asked Monika what she did, giving her the opportunity to first say she was a stay-at-home mother and then describe her job before we got married. Monika immediately became the center of attention when she turned back to the Monika I met that first day at the Energy department in Washington. All the knowledge and outgoing charm with strangers she had that day burst forward. The rest of the evening would be easy. Then "she" came in, offering delicious-smelling appetizers on a silver serving tray.

"I'm Helen, Gerb's cousin," she said. "Gerb pointed you out when you came in. You're his friend from Yale." She turned to Monika and whispered, "We have something in common." Monika stared at her. "The only person we really know is Gerb. The rest are strangers." And with a wink to Monika, she was gone.

Monika took one of the appetizers on a stick and put it in my mouth saying, "Now you can close your mouth, Jonathan."

I closed my mouth but started talking right away. "Did you see that? I couldn't believe it. She looks so much like you only with dark hair."

Monika laughed with a "Yes," exclamation point added, while she did a slight head bow. "Dark hair and a good suntan. I've never had a tan that nice. I would look terrific, don't you think?"

"So you know why my mouth stuck open. The hair and the skin are different but everything else is the same. Same body, same mannerisms, same ease and self-confidence. Even the same stance as you, like a racehorse, a thoroughbred. And when she walked away, the same walk."

"Different nose though. Do you think I should get my nose fixed?" Monika was referring to a little bend in her nose, the result of breaking it as a kid and never having it set properly. It made her unique, and I loved it. It was particularly attractive when she spoke. She favored speaking out of one side of her mouth, the side her nose pointed. It sounds very unattractive describing it like this, but it was very sexy and uniquely Monika.

"No. I love your nose the way it is. In fact, it was the reason I fell in love with you. If you changed it, I don't know," I teased.

She smiled, leaned in to give me a little kiss, I thought, but instead used her finger to wipe either real or imagined drool from my lip. "Jonathan, it was strange. I just met that woman, and I feel an immediate bond to her. I'm so glad we came tonight. I think I have my first new friend in New York." A strange thing for her to say, seeing as how she was born and raised only a few miles from here. But, strange as it may seem for her, I felt the same.

"So, what did you think of Helen?" Allen said as he swiped at mustard around his mouth with a paper napkin and took another bite of the corned beef on rye.

The phone rang this morning as I entered the office. Before I could say hello, Allen said, "Lunch today. The Blarney Stone on Second Avenue around the corner from your office. Noon. My treat." And then, before I could say anything, he hung up.

Now, I sat across from him, my pastrami on rye untouched, holding a pint of Boddington's, feeling the cool wet of the glass as I held it cupped between my hands. It was not untouched. I had already taken a few giant gulps, cautioned by Allen that drinking too fast might give me hiccups.

"You're enjoying this, aren't you? You knew the reaction I'd have when I saw her, and you said nothing. I'll bet you smiled to yourself all weekend."

"I told you we became interested in her when we looked into her activities in London. What I didn't tell you was *I* became very interested in her the minute I saw her picture. From a distance, she could be Monika's sister. With the right wig and makeup, she could pass for Monika at a closer distance. Yes, I saw the possibilities for her immediately. That's why she's your new partner. She's the perfect cover for you, not to mention, you provide the same for her."

Chapter 5

Twelve months passed. I embraced everything in my new life with enthusiasm: the new job, married life, and fatherhood. I had little interaction with Mike Allen other than the occasional lunch. I traveled more than I would have liked, but it provided the opportunity to hide a day in my schedule for intensive training that Allen and Anderson thought necessary for my work with them. Purely academic training I could do on my own time, usually in the last window seat on a plane to avoid the possibility someone would peer over my shoulder. None of the material I had was classified, but it was sensitive if that makes sense. Training that required someone to show me how to do something was more difficult to schedule, and that's where the hidden days came in.

I learned how to follow people on foot in San Francisco—a test of my endurance—up and down hills, trying not to be seen on Lombard Street. I learned how to avoid being followed in a vehicle in Los Angeles with the added bonus of learning how to cuss traffic and other drivers in Spanish. In Denver and Fort Collins, I learned how to follow in a car, an especially difficult trick on Interstate 25, a straight line drawn between these two cities with only one intentional jog left, jog right in the middle to wake up the driver. The secret proved to be easy as long as the car I was following wasn't the fastest on the highway. I remained three cars back and let the normal progression of speeders on this piece of highway provide the distraction and cover for me.

In New York, Monika and I took some martial arts courses together with an instructor recommended by Allen. The training was part of the program he and Anderson had for me. Including Monika was a nice touch after I was convinced it wasn't an attempt to recruit her.

She was a fast learner and enjoyed it. And, as Allen put it, if by some chance I got a black eye or a broken arm during martial arts training, it was better to have her with me than try to explain it if it occurred on one of my hidden training days. Living in the city made it almost impossible to carry a weapon, but I managed to get away to a private shooting range in Connecticut for additional training.

About once a month, Allen arranged for Helen to have work assignments in some of the cities I had meetings. Sometimes we'd just meet for dinner to get to know each other better, but other times we trained together.

Allen asked us to become familiar with the Salma Dam project in Afghanistan. The dam was a huge undertaking that would modernize the area, but the Iran government opposed it. Why? No one knew, but we were asked to get into the details and see if there was a reason. I think the assignment was only to have Helen and I work together and to get us talking, exchange ideas, and learn how the other thought and reacted to criticism. That wasn't the case when Allen met with us for lunch in early August.

Chapter 6

✳   ✳   ✳

The "us" came as a surprise, a surprise I realized when I approached the table Allen shared with Helen. Other than social occasions with our families, I never met Helen in New York. The only exception being when our joint CIA training required us to work together as a clandestine team.

"Jonathan," Allen said, "you know Helen." Taking my seat, I nodded at Helen, who looked as bewildered as I was.

Allen continued talking. "For the last year, you two have been getting to know each other. Yes, you've taken training together, but mostly, what you've been doing is learning about each other. How each other thinks, and how to get along when you're on an assignment. In other words, you've been learning to work and play well with each other. That changes today."

Allen was different, all business. The friendliness and camaraderie we had developed over the past five years was gone, replaced with a down-to-business manner I had only seen with the serious businessmen of American Pharmaceuticals. Was his change due to the presence of Helen? I looked to Helen but got no clue from her; she was staring at Allen, absorbing every word.

Allen continued, "There's a situation that needs your help. We've been following an Irani national, most likely a SAVAK agent, who's listed as an economist on the Trade Mission to the United Nations." Allen took a photograph from the tan folder on the table and passed it to us to examine. "He's easy to follow, so he either knows we're on to him and doesn't care, or our people are doing a good job. The problem is, we're only following him, and can't get ahead of him. When he comes to New York, he does the normal Trade Mission things, meets with US business people for ten days or two weeks, and then abruptly heads for the airport for the evening flight to Tehran. The decision to travel to Iran is made at the last minute because he goes from a routine meeting or activity straight to the airport, always without luggage. Our agents have watched the passenger lists, and his name never shows up on the manifest until he's at the airport. Most times, he arrives for the flight with only minutes to spare, and one time, they held up the flight because he was late, tied up in traffic. Even with this late arrival, his name didn't show up on the passenger list until he arrived at the airport. Everything about this guy raises a flag."

Helen looked at me for the first time, a question in her eyes. A question probably the same as mine, which I verbalized. "So where do we come in?" A slight nod from Helen confirmed my thoughts.

"We have to get ahead of him. We've watched him here in New York and in Tehran. None of the people he's meeting with is on any of our lists. There seems to be no connection between any of the people he meets with and any activity we're monitoring. Even in Tehran, he only meets with international business people. We've concluded he knows we're watching him. The only thing we haven't watched is the contacts he makes on the flights, who he sits with, who he talks to. There's not enough manpower to put someone on every flight to Tehran. The airline is an arm of the government, and we think our people would be spotted, and we'd lose our advantage as soon as we gained it. So we need to know when he plans to travel. That way, we can have someone on specific flights without raising as much suspicion."

"Again, I ask, how do we fit in?" Then I added, "Do you want me to find out which coffee club he belongs to?" As soon as the words were out, I knew I was out of line. I had referred to another action, I had mentioned it in front of Helen, and I said it in a manner that bordered on sarcasm. Allen let me know I made a mistake with an even icier stare.

Allen held his stare long enough to make me feel uncomfortable and then continued in the same businesslike manner. "Jonathan, you played a lot of squash in Boston and continued playing in New Haven. When you played regularly, I understand you were pretty good."

I didn't recall ever talking about squash with Allen. Once again, his knowledge of me knew no boundaries. I played squash in college. It was a fast-paced game requiring good hand-eye coordination. Many of the hockey players played it. The sport was primarily at colleges and universities, and every Ivy League school had several courts. It was a cold-weather sport with courts being unheated and stuck off in an abandoned corner of a basement. The only heat being the players' body heat. Different temperatures necessitated the development of different balls, balls for warm weather and cold weather. Once, I played at McGill University in Toronto with a ball that bounced like a tennis ball in the locker room but barely bounced on the unheated court of a Canadian January.

"Yes, I enjoyed the competition, and it was a good way to stay in shape."

"Our man considers himself a world-class player. He's played on the Iran National team in several International competitions. In New York, he plays at the midtown facility on Forty-Second Street, across from Bryant Park. Do you know the building?"

"Yes, it looks like a Chrysler standing on its rear end, the fins touching the ground and sloping up. It's a racket club: handball, squash, and racquetball." Allen nodded; a smile started to form, got as far as his eyes, but didn't make it to the rest of his face. "Am I to seek him out?"

"No. Don't make any play for him. Just get your game in top form, and he'll seek you out. He looks for the best talent to test his game. If you're good, he'll find you."

"Then what?"

"Then see if you can figure out his routine. Let him schedule matches. Whatever he suggests, be unavailable due to travel. Offer an alternative. Whether he accepts or rejects, we'll have an idea of whether he'll be in town and can act accordingly."

Helen spoke up. "What about me? Am I to be the squash partner when Jonathan isn't around?"

"No. You don't play, and we don't have time to wait for you to become proficient enough to play at his level. Besides, his religious and cultural background wouldn't let him play the game with you—a woman, not a relative, in shorts and a halter top. Not his way. No, instead, I want you to focus on his wife. She's taking a pottery class in one of the schools on the Upper East Side."

"Oh, Jonathan gets to have fun, and I get to play the Manhattan version of the *Stepford Wives*."

Allen smiled to himself; his head went down, and he shook it a little like he was trying to decide something. He decided, and he lifted his head, the smile now a grin. "No, I'd like to you play the Manhattan version of the *Tehran Wives*." Not exactly the correct thing to say to Helen, who wanted to forget the cultural restrictions her former life and country placed on women while she pursued the life of the liberated American woman.

Seeing her disappointment, Allen continued, "Helen, neither of you will be having fun. Both of you will be working, and the impact you have could be more significant than what Jonathan learns from his squash matches. The two of you will be the only women from the Middle East in the class, the only Muslim women as well. The wife, her name is Saphari, spelled with a *ph*, not an *f*, is a devout Muslim, but she doesn't wear the typical Muslim burka here in the States. Maybe she feels it would bring too much attention to her, but she does wear a hijab, and she looks very stylish in it. I'd like you to consider wearing one too for the classes."

Now, it was my turn to smile and Helen's turn to not smile even more. During our training time together, she told me she was distancing herself from the outward signs of the repression of the Muslim faith, particularly as applied to women, even though she considered herself to be a devout Muslim. This would be a step back for her, a regular reminder of what she was trying to overcome.

"Before you voice your objections, let me tell you how your part has the potential to add more value. Saphari has no friends in New York." Allen played with his napkin as he spoke. I'd seen him do this before when he was ready to convince me what I was being asked to do was critical. He did this before when he asked me to introduce Lance to the coffee club in East Haven years ago. He continued, "If it's obvious to her that you're a Muslim woman, she'll probably seek you out, perhaps seeing you as a potential friend—her only friend in this foreign land, a land of unbelievers. You will not only be her friend, but you may represent her freedom. She's driven to the class by her male cousin. Whenever she leaves her apartment, she is in the company of her cousin. That could change with you, allowing her to travel around the city with you as her companion, something her religion and her husband would allow."

Helen had been looking at Allen while he spoke with bored curiosity, perhaps planning her arguments why she didn't want the assignment, but her face and manner changed. She listened to him with purpose now. "How does that help with the husband and the work Jonathan is doing?"

Allen could see the interest now in Helen's face and the tone of her voice and responded with an increased enthusiasm to match hers. "I'm sure she has to be home most evenings to prepare the evening meal or at least to eat with her husband. With time, you may be able to suggest afternoon excursions that would go late into the evening mealtime. If you become friends with her, she may share her schedule with you, days she's available for trips around the city. Days when she has no obligation with her husband. When these days coincide with days he's not available to play squash with Jonathan, we'll have increased confidence he's traveling and can put someone on a plane to Tehran."

"That's it?" she said, looking to Allen and then me. "That's all you want us to do is become friendly with these people to find their schedules? What about all the secret agent stuff I thought we'd be doing? What about the training to follow people? You just want us to walk up to them and be their squash partner and pottery throwing buddy?"

"Yup. I'm sorry you're disappointed, but that's a big part of the work we do, collecting information, direct or indirect, it doesn't matter. This is a unique opportunity to collect directly with little risk to you, the target, or the government."

Helen and I agreed. Still, I didn't know how to feel about this. I was relieved I wasn't being asked to set someone up like I'd set up Hamadi, but then, when I started with Hamadi and the coffee club, I didn't know how it would end. If I had learned anything from Allen over the past four years, it was to expect the unexpected when I least expected it. Should I share this thought with Helen? No, if Allen wants it shared, he'll find a way.

For the next few weeks, I got court time when I could. In New York, I added a few meetings at Columbia to my schedule, using my position as an adjunct professor of medicine there for entry. It may sound glorified, but American Pharmaceuticals got these titles for all company physicians who wanted them. An endowment makes these things possible. Columbia, one of the eight schools in the Ivy League, paid token homage to the squash tradition, with one court in a subbasement of the medical school. I reserved an hour midafternoon. For the first two sessions, I did easy volleying by myself, yet was winded halfway through each session. The second week was better. I felt the moves and the shots returning, finding the skills I had as an A-level player in Boston. I decided I had enough proficiency when an A-level player, after watching me for a while, asked if I'd like to volley with him as a warm-up for a match he was having in the next hour. The friendly volley turned to a friendly match and then competition that only comes from two players in any sport who both feel they outclass their opponent. I lost but attributed it to playing at the end of a vigorous hour workout while my opponent was still fresh. In the cab on the way back to the office, I concluded my opponent was a better player, but I was good enough to attract his attention, and that meant I was good enough to attract the attention of…Mr. Saphari. What the hell was his name anyway? Allen hadn't told us, just his wife's name.

The company encouraged the medical staff to lead a healthy life, encouraging exercise and discouraging smoking. I took advantage of the liberal policy and the company's membership at the racket club across from Bryant Park and headed over when Allen told me Mr. Saphari was likely to be there. Without a court reservation, I hoped I could fill in for someone who didn't make it. I did this deliberately to avoid having my name on the court scheduling sheet, using the company membership. If my target was interested, I wanted to make it a little more difficult for him to find out who I was. Seems the less you know about a person, the more you want to know.

After changing into my gym clothes, I hung around the scheduling desk and got a game within minutes. With the hectic schedule of many of the members, it was common to have "no shows," what with meetings running overtime or unscheduled appointments. I played in a doubles match, not my favorite format.

The court was small enough without having to avoid two additional people. The group were B-level players, adequate, but I outclassed them, a lot. We played a "round" where I changed partners after every game, giving me the chance to play three games. I won three games, and the others each lost two. During the match, I caught sight of Mr. Saphari watching through the rear glass wall and then later, in the open deck above the rear wall. After the customary shaking of hands at the end of the match, I made my way to the refreshment area, which offered only water and fruit juices. As I was finishing a cold apple juice, my target approached.

"Apple juice is a better pick-me-up than coffee, did you know that?" he asked as he motioned to the counter girl for an apple juice, pointing to mine. "Can I get you another?" he asked before I could answer his first question.

"That's what I've heard, but I don't think I could get going in the morning without my coffee." The thought raced through my mind of another time and place, an Irani target, a coffee club in East Haven. Was it a coincidence, or were all my contacts going to have a coffee connection?

"Ah yes, that first hot cup of fresh coffee in the morning. What could be better?"

"A friend of mine once said, 'Morning coffee doesn't have to be hot. It doesn't have to be good. It only has to work.'"

He laughed and nodded his head in conspiratorial agreement, acknowledging the bad habit of the occasional over sleeper. "Yes, even cold, stale coffee. I don't know if it's the caffeine of the cold coffee or the terrible taste, but it wakes me. I'm Jafar," he said as he extended his hand, a callused hand with a firm grip. Not the hand of a workman but the hand of someone who played a lot of racket sports.

"Jonathan," I replied.

"Jonathan, you've a good game. Shouldn't waste it with B-level partners. You've played a lot?"

"I used to play a lot in college. Just trying to get back into it. Today was my first day here, and I was fortunate to get on the court at all. They were missing one of their group and took me in."

"Maybe we can play sometime." An invitation? A challenge? I couldn't tell. Maybe just someone looking for some different competition.

"Sure, that would be nice." I looked at my watch and said, "I've got to run. Nice to meet you. Hope to see you again here. Do you play on a regular basis?"

"Not as often as I'd like. Travel keeps me moving, but when I'm in town, I'm usually here."

"Good. Maybe I'll see you here." And with that I left. I could see his reflection in the glass wall of one of the courts as I headed for the locker room. He watched me and then leaned over the counter and said something to the counter girl. She shook her head with a negative answer. Fish on!

Chapter 7

HELEN

Helen left the luncheon meeting upset. While it wasn't anything like the oppression women endured in her birthplace and all over the Middle East, she felt diminished—her role in the assignment was less than Jonathan's. Assuming a docile feminine role irritated her. The time she spent away from the confining culture of Iran, especially the last two years in the United States, had made her a card-carrying feminist. Yes, she thought as she clutched her purse that contained a laminated membership card from the National Organization of Women (NOW), and the latest issue of *Ms. Magazine*. While neither Betty Freidan nor Gloria Steinem held views completely compatible with Helen's, she could support both. Joining NOW was a major step forward for her. To openly belong to such an organization that criticized male dominance was unheard of in her youth. She cherished the membership as much as she enjoyed being able to read *Ms.* openly as she rode on the subway. What a great country to allow such freedoms!

As she walked past the newsstand at the entrance to Grand Central Station, the headline of the *Daily News* caught her attention: "Indira Gandhi Resigns" it read in bold print. As comfortable as she was in her new surroundings, she found herself troubled that this powerful symbol for women everywhere had stepped aside, even more so today when she was told she must assume the role of an oppressed woman.

After returning to the office, she called the main number for PS 198 on Third Avenue to find the schedule for the pottery classes. Not that she didn't trust Allen—he was always right—but she wanted to initiate her involvement with some action.

"The class you'd be interested in has already met once, last week," the helpful voice on the other end of the phone informed her. "However, you're in luck. The first class was just an introduction with a lecture, a little hands-on work but no pottery wheel work. There is still room for one more student if you'd like to join this session. If not, I can put you on the list for the next class that starts in September."

Helen gave the woman her name and thanked her for making the exception. The woman responded, "It's not a problem, dear, but you still have to pay the full fee for the course. It's the rule."

"Of course. I wouldn't expect any different. Thanks again for your help."

Helen usually worked until seven o'clock each evening when she wasn't traveling. Most of the others left on time, and she could enjoy two hours of relative quiet. A still settled into the area. The whisper of the air-handling system and the buzz of fluorescent lights replaced the ringing of phones and the din of dozens of conversations. A peaceful time when she often accomplished more than she did during the workday without its intrusions and interruptions. It served her well. Without a social life or boyfriend, it occupied the time and made the loneliness of evenings more tolerable. The walk to her flat in Chelsea took a casual thirty minutes. When she arrived home, changing, eating, and doing the few household chores before she settled down to watch television or read had become routine, her routine.

Today, she left with the others. As she waited for the elevator, she got curious looks from those unaccustomed to seeing her leave with them. Maria, one of the Katherine Gibbs secretarial school graduates, asked if she had plans for the evening.

"I'm going to learn how to throw pots."

Before anyone had a chance to comment, Jason, the young Bohemian-type from the department's mailroom, said, "Hey, if you have any extra, throw some my way. I can always find a use for some extra pot." The reference to his social drug of choice only got stares.

Maria continued, "I've heard a lot of people are doing that. They say it's soothing, the wet clay spinning between your hands, the rhythm of the wheel. Where are you taking it?"

"PS 198 over on the West Side. I just signed up for it today, so I have to go home and change."

The elevator reached the ground floor, and any attempts at casual conversation ceased as everyone rushed for the street exit to begin their commute home, a ritual in New York City more of a contact sport than American football.

Helen arrived home in twenty minutes, her brisker pace this evening due to purpose. Tonight, she had something to do, and it had a timetable. She changed and had a light meal, some cold lamb and fruit. She avoided the American diet with its emphasis on beef and carbohydrates, feeling it wasn't healthy. The simple meals of her youth also gave her comfort of sorts. She found her hijab and put it in her bag with a notebook. As she looked around her apartment, readying to leave, her eyes were drawn to the pictures of her homeland. Each year in America brought mixed emotions. While she enjoyed her new life, she missed the simpler life of her youth. Yet, at the same time, the reminders she had, the pictures of familiar areas in and around Tehran became dull and two dimensional. The color and vibrancy of New York was a stark contrast to the drab that peered out from her pictures. New York, even with the corridors of concrete, seemed brighter than the monotonous shades of tan the sands of the Middle East provided.

The walk from her Chelsea neighborhood to PS 198 was too far, so she took the subway, the E train at Twenty-Third and Seventh, and at Fifty-First Street, transferred to the Number 4 train to Ninety-Sixth Street and Broadway, and then a short walk to the school. She put on her hijab as she approached the entrance, feeling conspicuous. It had been five years since she had worn it, this being the first time in America. A handwritten placard on a stand in the hallway announced the pottery class—and several other adult education classes—was being held in the basement.

As she made her way down the stairs, she noticed the odor, a smell unique to schools all over the world, as least the worlds she had been part of. The sweet garbage smell, she concluded years ago in college, was from partially eaten, rotting apples. Whether she was correct, she didn't care, but here, in an elementary school, she imagined most lunch boxes had the obligatory apple, which, even if eaten, had the core tossed into the garbage to rot with all the half-eaten apples. Funny how smells can conjure up images like that.

Helen found the room and spotted Saphari right away, the only other woman wearing a hijab. The room was a combination classroom and lab with student desks that could be moved to a typical classroom setting or moved to the sides and replaced with equipment along the walls. The room was set up for both tonight: a dozen desks in one corner near a blackboard and pottery-making equipment arranged around the room, ready for use. There didn't appear to be enough pieces of equipment for each student, so they would be sharing. Helen took a seat in the middle of the room.

"If we can all take our seats, we can get started," said the young woman who now took charge. "I know it seems like you're back in school, but we must take attendance. Let me assure you, we will not be sending a note home if you play hooky." She paused and received the expected thin laughter and giggles from the women present. "Rather, it's a requirement of our insurance company and the fire department. We must know how many people are in the building at all times."

Once the roll was called, the teacher announced we would work with clay during this lesson. She apologized to the new students and told them she would provide them with the notes from the initial class. Helen was the only one to receive a package. The teacher then assigned each of the students to a team, pairing Helen with Saphari and another woman who didn't seem pleased with her new partners.

Absent from the room were pottery wheels. Helen would not be throwing a pot but rather learning the basic skills of working with clay, basic sculpting, and the use of glazes. Her project would not be a fine Grecian urn but more likely an ashtray. Only she was disappointed today; the others had learned of their limited objective during the first class.

Saphari was a quiet person, seldom contributing to the idle conversation as they added water to the damp lump of gray clay and began molding it, getting to know how it felt. When the teacher announced a break at eight thirty, Saphari walked off to a corner by herself. Helen was pleasant to the others, but she didn't want to form any alliances with them that might make Saphari feel an outsider. She had time; she could wait to socialize. Instead, she walked into the hall, up the stairs to the entrance.

The sun was setting, reflecting off the upper west-facing windows. The contrast of the golden reflections of light and the growing black of the shadows was magical. A calmness came over her. She couldn't get this effect from her south-facing apartment in Chelsea. She enjoyed it, momentarily dismissing the urge she had for a cigarette, another American habit she picked up.

After class, Helen found Saphari walking next to her as she ascended the steps. Saphari, shy and self-focused during class, said, "You did not miss much last class. If you need anything explained, I am happy to assist."

Helen was grateful that Saphari had made the first approach to be friendly, or at least helpful. Not being seen as the pursuer in developing a relationship was to her advantage. "Thank you. That is kind of you. I got the notes from the teacher but have not had the chance to review them yet. If I have questions, then I would appreciate some help. All of this," she waved her arms around, "the American way of doing things is still new." Helen was aware that she had changed her pattern of speech. She used a more formal English, copying the tone used by Saphari and avoiding the contractions that only came with years of practice. Her response was a smile from Saphari, which disappeared when they reached the entrance.

At the entrance, a tall dark man who seemed to be of Middle Eastern descent, features familiar from her youth, dressed in a black suit, white shirt with collar buttoned, and no tie, was waiting for Saphari. He inspected Helen, not with the curiosity of the oversexed American male, but with the eyes of a protector measuring someone who might pose a threat to his charge.

Without another look or word, Saphari got into the car and left.

What a curious life that must be, never out of the sight of a male relative, thought Helen, but even as the words formed in her head, she remembered she had lived such a life in Tehran as a young girl. She realized the strangeness was only due to time and location. In Tehran, it was natural. It was all she knew.

Here, as it had been in Europe, she became used to being on her own, making the ancient religious custom awkward in modern Western society.

During the next two classes, Saphari became friendlier, inquiring about Helen. For the most part, Helen was honest, telling of her cloistered childhood, attributing it to a medical condition more than an attempt at evading the scrutiny of the authorities. She became more animated as she told of her schooling in the West and eventual move to the United States. If anyone checked her background, it would be true except for the CIA connection. She confided her growing comfort with the ways of the West.

Saphari interrupted her, pointed to her hijab, and said, "But with the comfort you express for the West, you still wear the hijab. Even in Tehran, it is not necessary except for those who practice the moderate form of our religion. Why do you wear it here?"

"While I am comfortable with many of the customs of the West, I need the comfort of my roots regularly. I dress in the Western fashion for work all the time, but there are times when I am doing something for my inner being, like taking this class. It is at these times I feel the need to return to my roots. I am not ashamed to wear this symbol of my religion; in fact, it is an honor. I enjoy the looks I get, like tonight on the subway. In America, there is a respect for beliefs, especially those that are not in the mainstream."

"Yes," Saphari responded. "I see that, although I don't see respect. I see tolerance."

"Yes, Saphari. That is a better word, 'tolerance.' You have a better knowledge of the English language than I do. How long have you been here?"

Saphari gave a little of her background, her education, schools, and the neighborhood she had grown up in. Her marriage was arranged when she was a child. She described her husband as a good man who doesn't beat her and allows her a degree of freedom she wouldn't have in Tehran, like taking the pottery class. She went on to say her husband had a job in Iran's Trade Mission to the United Nations, a responsible position. The description she provided sounded like it had been memorized. However, she added a bit that wasn't part of the script, telling Helen he would work in New York for ten to twelve days, and then he would be off to Tehran for up to a week.

"Two weeks here with me and then a week away from me. Perhaps he has another family or wife." She said this in a matter-of-fact manner. It was common for men like her husband to have several wives, and there was no shame. It was a right, and they seldom hid the fact, often bragging and comparing one wife to another, often beating one wife because she was not as good as another. Saphari ended this aside by saying, "If it is so, then I will find this out when we return to Tehran at the end of this assignment."

Helen seized the opportunity to ask a powerful, yet innocent question. "I hope that is not too soon. I think we are becoming friends. My only friend who understands and appreciates my culture."

Saphari beamed. "No, it is not too soon. We arrived only three months ago and should be here for at least three years. And I too think I have found a friend in America I can share things only we can appreciate." She giggled and took Helen's hand in hers. "A friend who can be my companion when I leave the house. My cousin is the man who drives me here and takes me home. If I go out during the day, he must accompany me. Now I have a Muslim friend to walk with me and tell me all the things she has learned about being in America that I long to know."

They hugged a conspiratorial hug and shared another giggle. Yes, they would be friends, and yes, Helen would tell her the things about America she wanted to know. Helen had a twinge of guilt, knowing she was using Saphari to gather information. She seemed such a sweet, innocent young woman, barely into her twenties. She would unwittingly provide information that may put her husband or her country in jeopardy. Poor Saphari might grow up quickly, only to die young, or be a young widow.

Chapter 8

During my first year at American Pharmaceuticals, I took on new responsibilities. A promotion to director removed me from the drudgery of visiting sites to examine study files and gave me a more strategic role in the planning and execution of programs for all the antibiotics in development by the company. In this new role, I became exposed to the international aspect of drug development with travel to the company's research headquarters in England west of London.

On my first trip, I fell in love with the English, their customs, and their country but hated the travel. Colleagues always referred to England as being "across the pond." In just one trip, I learned to detest the term. How could seven hours in a plane, across five-time zones be considered a trip across a pond? The irony of complaining about security delays at check-in wasn't lost on me. My hijacking of an airplane was the cause of this wait. I thought I could save a day with my family by traveling on Sunday evening, sleep on the plane, arrive around seven in the morning, and go directly to work. The jet lag punished me severely, causing me to make such bad decisions on the first afternoon that I had to revise the second day. Not an effective way to start.

Yet, I found the people fascinating; bright, well educated, versed in the classics as well as current events. Some had a better grasp of American politics than I did. As they had done in school, during meals, they would follow a heated discussion of world events by challenging each other to recite poems they had learned in school. Not little ditties like I had but epics like the Don Marquis classic "Freddie the Rat Perishes" and "Kubla Khan" by Coleridge. I realized these recitations were as common among the university educated as the recitation of major league batting averages in the taverns of America. I also learned that the "garden" was merely the backyard, and a "holiday" only a vacation, not the grand images the terms suggested.

Allen was pleased when I began the international travel, especially to England. The research facility in Marlow was only thirty miles from London with the rest of England and Europe within a few hours by air. But he was not pleased when he learned of a potential future transfer for me to England to gain international experience. That possibility disappeared as quickly as it appeared, no doubt through intervention by Allen.

I made three trips to Marlow the first year, gaining experience in the international nature of the business and learned to adapt travel to suit my needs. After the initial jet lag disaster to my system, I tried the Saturday-evening flight, arriving early Sunday morning. While refreshed when I arrived in the office on Monday, doing nothing for most of Sunday bored me and cost me a full day with his family. Even the Sunday British Air day flight, leaving JFK at 10:00 a.m. and arriving at London's Heathrow only eased the tiredness on Monday but still robbed me of a day at home. I resolved both problems by settling for the Sunday-evening flight, taking a four-hour nap when I arrived at the hotel in the morning and starting my workday at 1:00 p.m.

Each time, I stayed at the picturesque Compleat Angler Hotel in Marlow on the banks of the Thames at the weir, a small dam used to regulate the height of the river. The hotel was an English country home, elegant but conveniently in town on the river. A large well-manicured lawn ran down to the river where the hotel maintained a dock, complete with an excursion boat to take travelers west as far as Oxford with the weir prohibiting travel east to Windsor and London beyond. The boat reminded me of an elegant, polished teak version of the boat Rose and Charlie shared in *The African Queen*. On reflection, the only things the two boats had in common were they were small, and they floated.

I had settled into a routine during this past year: work, travel, family time, and the occasional training with Helen. That changed with my luncheon meeting when Allen handed us a CIA assignment and the unknown it held.

Between us, Helen and I could alert Allen to a possible trip by Jafar. I had become a regular opponent of his on the squash court. Both of us were A-level players, probably world-class level A, and our games similar, making each match more of a challenge. Both of us had busy schedules, so to maximize playtime, we exchanged calendars. He advised me of possible gaps when he might not be available. When compared to dates Saphari proposed for possible excursions with Helen, Allen knew when to have Jafar followed.

Allen called for another lunch meeting with Helen and me at the Blarney Stone on Second Avenue, a block east of Grand Central Terminal. As I walked the short block to the meeting, I wondered if Allen had a thing for Irish food. The fateful meeting with Ahmad had been held at an Irish pub on the west side, the previous meeting with Helen at a Blarney Stone, and now this. Did he order the same thing each time? Was it the food, the location, or an Irish thing?

Allen, already seated when I arrived, had a hot corned beef on rye in front of him.

"I've asked them to run a tab for us. Get yourself something to eat and join me."

No waitresses at the Blarney Stone, self-service at the counter. I never liked ordering at the counter or buffets. I tended to eat too much, choosing everything that looked good. Being distracted today with lunch being a business meeting, I didn't give into my normal weakness. I rolled the choices over in my mind, "Corned beef or pastrami?" Corned beef won, as did a side of fries and a dill pickle, all to be washed down with a Budweiser. While I still preferred Schaefer, I didn't want to suffer the humiliation by Allen of it being a college-boy beer. Helen was at the table when I returned, choosing not to eat.

Allen began between a bite of his sandwich and three fries, which he grabbed from my plate. "We've followed Jafar on two trips to Tehran and back. Both were almost identical. On the trip over, he had no luggage either carry-on or checked, ate a light meal, and fell asleep during the movie. He didn't talk to people sitting next to him, and only polite conversation with the stewardess. Upon arrival, there was someone from the government waiting for him, who ushered him through customs without even showing his passport. A car waited for him outside and took him straight to the office in the ministry."

Helen finished the small glass of water she had, reached over for my Bud, and poured about two inches into the glass. All this she did without looking at me. The familiarity of her move surprised me.

It didn't go unnoticed by Allen, but he continued, "Same thing in Tehran. Nothing special. Of course, we don't know what he did behind closed doors at the ministry."

Helen had by now become familiar with my fries. She grabbed the ketchup and covered them with the stuff. I'm not a ketchup-on-top guy, preferring to squirt a blob on the plate, put a healthy coating of pepper on top, and dunk my fries, refreshing the pepper when I can no longer see it. Sharing them was all the better for me because I really didn't want them but had taken them on impulse, regretting it as soon as I put them on my tray.

Helen added, punctuating Allen's description of Jafar's activity in Tehran, "And we don't know what he did inside his home."

Allen was a ketchup-on-top guy. He grabbed a handful of fries and transferred them to his plate. He was also a pepper guy, shaking a lot of the spice on them. Smiling, he said, "Not exactly. We don't know what he did in his house because he didn't go there. He went to the apartment of a young lady he's been seeing for almost a year since before he and Saphari left for New York. We have an idea of what he was doing but no 'eyes on' for every night, all night he was there."

"Saphari suspects he has a girlfriend. In fact, she's hinted he may even have another family. Many Muslim men have multiple wives or a wife and several girlfriends. She's surprised he's keeping it a secret. Most men brag about it, feel it's a sign of their virility, or a sign they're fulfilling the command of their religion. It's not the woman who bothers her, it's the secret. Maybe it's the girlfriend we should be looking at."

"We had the same thought when we followed him on the first trip, but she's clean, at least as far as we're concerned." Allen took the rest of his sandwich in one bite and wiped his face with a handful of paper napkins and then wiped his mouth and chin. After a mouthful of beer, he continued, "No, our curiosity about the girl lasted only until his trip home. On the last morning of his trip to Tehran, he took a car to the ministry, emerging thirty minutes later, and then straight to the airport. Remember, when he traveled over, he had no luggage, not even a briefcase. That remained the case during his time in Tehran. When he got out of the car at the airport, he was carrying a briefcase. He didn't have one when he left the ministry; the briefcase was waiting for him in the car."

I leaned forward. "That's interesting. Who put it there?"

"Don't know for sure."

"How long was it in the car before the driver picked him up in the morning?" Helen asked.

"Don't know for sure."

I asked, "Is there anything you know for sure?"

"Yes, let me finish." Allen continued, "He took the briefcase onto the plane. On the trip over, he flew first class, presumably because it offered better sleeping accommodations. On the flight from Tehran to New York, he flew business class, exposing him to many more people, including American and European businessmen, like the cover being used by our agent. He was much more outgoing on the return flight, even engaging in extended conversations with the man traveling in the seat next to him. They weren't friends, just two people stuck next to each other for nine hours. You and I have both done it. You don't remember what you said two hours after you land. That's the impression we had. Except..." And then Allen paused.

"Except, the man sitting next to him had the same briefcase as Jafar."

"What are the chances of that?" I asked.

"I forget, Jonathan. Is that sarcastic or sardonic?"

"Sardonic, but I said it in a sarcastic manner, so you can take your pick." Amused that Allen still referred to the friendly banter they had on these words, I was reassured Allen tried to keep the stress level down.

"When they left the plane, they didn't acknowledge each other. There was someone from the Iran delegation waiting for him inside of the secure area. After going through the diplomat line and avoiding customs and immigration, Jafar sent the delegation guy ahead and went to the first snack area, got a coffee, and sat, watching the exit from the secure area. When his travel companion emerged, Jafar ditched the coffee and made straight for the men's restroom even though he had been in the lavatory just before landing. The other guy came in; then Jafar emerged, followed a couple of minutes later by the other guy, both still carrying the identical briefcases."

"Did they switch?" Jonathan asked.

"We couldn't tell, so on the second trip, we put a man in the restroom when the flight landed. Both came in as before. Jafar stood at the urinal, his briefcase against the nearby wall. The other guy came in, placed his briefcase next to Jafar's, and started doing his business. Jafar zipped up, went to the briefcases, and took the other guy's bag and left."

Helen asked, "Didn't he wash his hands?"

We both looked at her. She was serious when she asked, caught up in the moment. Allen ignored her question.

"So they switched, but why?"

"Don't know. Jafar has diplomatic immunity, so he was carrying something in it that would have raised questions if customs found it with the other guy. The question is, what was it? Once we know, then we'll need to ask why."

"Any ideas?"

"We have a good idea of what it wasn't. It wasn't guns. Guns are easier to get here than in Iran. It wasn't pornography or booze; that traffic goes the other direction."

Jonathan asked, "So what do they have a lot of that we don't?"

Helen responded, "Sand and oil."

Neither of us responded to her answer. She seemed distant, not totally engaged. Her mind somewhere else.

She snapped out of it. "Sorry, that was unnecessary. I was thinking about the last time I was there, two years ago. I had been at school for most of the previous four years and was startled by the changes that had taken place while I was away. There was an undercurrent of political and religious unrest that invaded every aspect of everyday life. It was below the surface, and I got a sense people were just waiting for it to burst through and overtake everything. People were making plans to leave, quietly. My father among those concerned."

Allen now took Helen seriously. "So what do you think was in the briefcase?"

"Revolution!"

Chapter 9

"Revolution?" Allen and I said at almost the same time. Almost the same time. The effect was like that of an echo chamber.

We were both looking at Helen when she responded, "Yes, a revolution. Close your mouth when you're eating."

Speaking first, I asked, "A revolution. Please explain."

Helen handed Allen a napkin and began. "The briefcase has to contain something that would raise a red flag if customs saw it, so it had to come in with diplomatic immunity. You're correct he's not bringing in guns, drugs, or pornography. There's more in America than anywhere else in the world. It's a light load, because he didn't seem to struggle with the briefcase, so it's probably not gold bars. Must be something like diamonds or explosives. Maybe phony identification for people already here. I don't think we can guess what it is, just what it isn't."

"So the revolution will be here? Why here?"

"No," she said. "If,—and it's still an 'if'—it's a revolution, it'll be in Tehran. This will be a distraction, either here or someplace that's easy to get to from here. Something to keep the Western world occupied."

Allen finished the mouthful of stolen fries and washed it down with a pull from his beer. "Helen, I'm dumbfounded by this talk of revolution. There's certainly unrest. Hell, that's the reason you and your family fled the country. Also, the increased rise of the conservative religious zealots, but I don't think we'd call it a revolution. Where are you getting your information?"

"Much of what has occurred has been happening for years. The rise has been slow but steady. Maybe, it's not a revolution that's happening now. Maybe it's better termed a political evolution. The West is familiar with revolutions that are quick and violent. Shots at Lexington and Concord, the cannon fire on Fort Sumter, and the assassination of Archduke Ferdinand. The list goes on and on. You forget that other cultures like Vietnam and the Middle East have been in conflict for centuries. One thing it has taught us, that you can't or won't understand, is patience. The West refuses to learn patience, but after centuries of waiting and planning, maybe the Middle East has learned from the rest of the world. Waiting has its value, but the winners of recent conflicts were those who reacted quickly and violently. It could be what you and your analysts see as a slow, steady evolution is what the 'evolutionaries' want you to see."

I sat staring at Helen. She was different, and while I wanted to interrupt, I forced myself to let her finish, to hear her complete argument.

Allen had no such reservation, saying, "Helen, are you saying the militants, or revolutionaries, have studied Western military tactics and were using them, combined with our low opinion of them, to formulate a plan against the West?"

"Michael," she said, looking at Allen and then at me, "you are partly correct, but you're thinking like a Westerner even after hearing me describe what's happening. Immediately you think the military action will be against one of the Western countries. The West thinks we're a backward country, living in an inhospitable environment, in sand deserts and rocky bare mountains and think we don't know better. That we just put up with it. We have adapted to our land. Yes, we are fortunate oil has changed our lives for the better, but in our minds that is the will of Allah. We prospered in the eyes of Allah before the oil. Allah chose to let us have the oil as a gift. Let the West covet our wealth. Make the West dependent upon our gift. To many, it marks the time."

"Time for what?" Allen asked.

"With the gift of the oil, many believe the faithful were put to a test. The lure of wealth and what it can buy, things of the world, drew many away from the faith. Many have failed the test, but the money and wealth have provided the means to return to the will of Allah."

Allen and I remained silent. She continued, "The people of Iran are neither a backward nor ignorant people. We had a culture when the West was still learning to read and write. The region is the birth of mathematics, the written word, and music." At the mention of music, Jonathan cringed, and Helen reacted to it. "You may not like our music but like the music of China, Japan, and India that share the same intricacies, it predates any music of the West by hundreds of years. You don't consider China or Japan to be backward. Rather, you admire those cultures as ancient, yet because of our geography, and the barrenness of the land we choose to live in, you consider us backward and ignorant.

"You underestimated us when they found oil. The West came in, saw people riding camels and living in tents, and they took advantage. They still think of us as ignorant and backward. The only difference now is they say we *used to* live in tents and ride camels. That's as wrong as saying there are people in West Virginia riding donkeys and living without electricity and assuming the whole state is like that." Helen paused to let this have her intended impact.

"The assumption we were ignorant was incorrect. Treating us like we were ignorant was a serious miscalculation. The United States backed the regime of the Shah, ignoring how the people have lived, have wanted to live for the last two thousand years. They assumed everyone wants to live in a democracy." Her voice rose. "You don't understand that democracy doesn't work everywhere. You fight to install it, you fight to keep it, and it fails. And when it fails, the old order is waiting to step back in." Helen stopped, spent from the physical and mental effort of speaking about her culture.

"Helen. Thank you. I'll go back to Washington today and meet with the Middle East team at State tomorrow. I'll share your concerns and get their reaction. If work needs to be done to get a clear answer, I'll make sure they have the resources and time to do it. You've been read in on this assignment, so when they're ready, I'll ask that you join us for the debriefing. You too, Jonathan. The two of you are a team, and I count on you both."

Grateful that Allen had broken our silence, I stayed quiet, thinking of what I had just heard. Helen and I had spent a lot of time together during the past six months. Never had she expressed any allegiance to the life she had left behind.

Instead, her focus was on the future—her future here and the future of the United States, her adopted country. This outburst was a surprise. Did something trigger it? Was it something she had always believed but just now it burst to the surface? If so, what was the trigger?

The remainder of the lunch was quiet. There was no more work talk, and the small talk was very small—the weather and a discussion of the merits of ketchup on top versus dunking. Even that seemed strained. Helen stood and left, but not before giving me a meaningful look, a look that left me wondering what she meant. Allen and I remained, sitting in an uncomfortable quiet, content to let the surrounding noise substitute for conversation.

Allen broke the silence. "Jonathan, I'll take this to the think-tank guys you met at State. I know you respect them as I do. Let's hope there's merit in what she said because if not, she's a liability as we go forward."

This caused me to glare at Allen. What did he mean by "liability"? He must have caught the concern I had, and rather than continue the discussion, he went to the cashier to settle our bill. Following his lead, I got up, stood next to him while he paid, and walked out with him. On the street, a simple promise to stay in touch and we went our separate ways, he west toward Grand Central and me east, back to the office.

As I crossed Third Avenue, some of the late-noon crowd had stopped and looked to the sky. These weren't the tourist gawkers; these were the regular New Yorkers, accustomed to the unusual. I stopped and looked skyward, but almost before I did, I could sense what it was. There was a thump that was barely audible, but I could feel it in my chest and in my feet coming up from the pavement. Looking to the sky, I saw the big white New York Airways helicopter coming in from the east, either JFK or LaGuardia. It was directly above, the canyons of buildings on Forty-Third Street focusing the noise from the powerful engines and the beat of the rotors down. The graceful machine was preparing to land on the top of the Pan Am Building above Grand Central Station. What a sight! A helicopter landing in midtown Manhattan.

I continued to the office, thinking I was fortunate to work so close to the Pan Am Building. Some of the other executives at American Pharmaceuticals had used the helicopter service to the Long Island airports. A short ten-minute flight to JFK, New York Airways advertised a guaranteed connection to any

Pan Am flight leaving from JFK if the traveler left the Pan Am Building forty minutes before the scheduled departure, weather permitting. I made a mental note to try the service that had just resumed on February 1. The service had been established many years ago but was only marginally profitable. The 1973 oil embargo and high fuel prices that followed caused the business to fail.

Helen, annoyed with herself for losing control during lunch, had said far too much, too much about what she carried inside her from the years in Tehran and the years away from home at school. The look she gave to Jonathan allowed a look into her soul, a soul she wished to keep hidden. The look he gave her as she got up and left, a look of concern, yes, but was there something else? She wanted him to look at her. Enjoyed it even, but not that way. Allen called for another meeting with Helen and me one week later. A different Blarney Stone this time, across town on the west side, but still a Blarney Stone. The same routine with him seated already, we got our meal and joined him at the table. I hadn't seen Helen since the last meeting. The uncomfortable feeling we had then continued. She avoided eye contact with me while she forced a serious face for Allen.

"Thanks for meeting on such short notice. I'm glad neither of you was traveling." We nodded. "I've spoken with the analysts at State, in fact, had a couple of meetings with them. They were aware of the unrest in Iran Helen spoke about last week, but had it on a low-alert level, something to come back to and evaluate on a regular basis. When I described how upset Helen was, it raised their concerns. They looked deeper into Jafar's background and opened a file on his travel companion, the one he traded briefcases with on the flight. We already had a file open on him and shared what we had."

The silence and tension at the table was palpable. I spoke, attempting to relieve some of it. "You must have found something to call us back together. I can't imagine you just needed another Blarney Stone fix." It didn't work. The tension remained, and my comment seemed frivolous.

"Yes, Jonathan. We found something. We located him—his name isn't important—in the Brighton Beach area, in a community of other Middle Eastern and Eastern European dissidents. Our agents hadn't noticed him before, but they knew the people he contacted."

Chapter 10

Allen waited a week before calling me. No lunch this time, just a lunchtime meeting without Helen. We met in the park on the east side of the United Nations, between the building and the river. I referred to it as the UN rose garden, for it was here they had beautiful trellised rose bushes extending along the paths. If we were in Washington, the sight and scent of cherry blossoms might have lent some additional cheer to the early-April day. Instead, spring would come to New York a few weeks later and with it the blossoms. Today, despite the warmth and sunshine, the fauna was still winter dormant.

Mike Allen sat on a bench, looking out over the East River, elbows on his knees, deep in thought when I approached. He looked up and patted the seat next to him, an invitation to sit. We weren't going to walk around. The promenade was almost empty and secure from prying ears.

"Are we waiting for Helen?"

"No Helen today. Just us," he said as he sat up, staring out over the water to the docks of Brooklyn on the east side of the river. Turning, he said, "I met with the think-tank guys at State last week, specifically Walt Jackson. Remember him?"

"Yeah, Walt 'Call Me Frank' Jackson. The guy who gave me my final exam at State. Good man. Knowledgeable. Does he still wear a pocket protector?" I asked to see if I could lighten Allen's mood.

"Yeah, he's a good man, and yeah, he still wears a pocket protector except now he wears a suit jacket. Makes it tough to see he's still a geek." A slight smile appeared. "He's been promoted to a section chief, but it's only on paper. The only real difference is the suit, his paycheck, and the dark circles under his eyes. His promotion elevated him above the level of the day-to-day analyst and gave him responsibility for parsing the intel into bite-size digestible bits for the bureaucrats and politicians further up the line."

"Why the dark circles? Too much for him?"

"He can't give up the hands-on analysis. He loves it. So he continues to do it and his new job of writing reports and managing a few people."

"Why doesn't he go back to the old job if he likes it so much?"

"Can't. He needs the money. He's got two kids, and he's saving for college. Plus, he thinks he can make a difference with his reports. He agonizes over them, writing and editing to get the right words into the reports that convey more of the truth than they have in the past. The trick is getting the reports past his boss."

"Sounds like a recipe for unhappiness."

"Nah, he considers it a challenge, a game. He's smarter than his boss and wants to get a stronger report up the line. The question is whether there's someone up there who'll understand it. I talked to him about it. He feels sometimes, it'll be just one word that can make the difference. One word. All that effort for one word."

"That's why we're here today, to talk about Frank?" I asked.

Allen fidgeted, looked around, rubbed his nose, and then stared at me. "No, we're here to talk about the guy with the briefcase and Jafar."

"Then shouldn't Helen be here?"

"Not yet. Let me fill you in, and then we can talk."

"The guy with the briefcase is an unknown, not on any list, here or in Interpol. The Israelis have better contacts in Tehran than we do, so they're looking into him." I gave him a look that said I didn't believe him. He continued, "The Israelis think they have better contacts than we do. It's convenient for us to let them think that. They can do the leg work, and we can check the intel they give us against ours. If it matches, they're still on the up and up with us. If not, what can I say?"

"How long?"

"Don't know but Frank doesn't think anything's imminent, imminent being defined as we gotta know the day before it happens, if that makes any sense. I told you he was working a lot." Allen pulled out a pack of Winston, a switch for him. He offered me one. I declined but took the pack, examining it. "Yeah, different brand. I'm trying to quit. I have to take my annual physical next month, so I've been doing a little running. 'Little' is the operative word there. Lungs and legs aren't what they used to be. Changing brands every day is one way of doing it they say. Get off your old reliable, change every day. Try menthol. Problem is, I changed to Winston last week and found I liked them better than my old brand. Go figure." After lighting his smoke with his old chrome Zippo, he took the cigarette pack from me and put both in his jacket pocket.

When Allen gave me a briefing, he was direct—sharp sentences, punchy prose. Today, he was in no hurry to move our discussion along. I wondered if I should be participating in a dialog with him. Was I not carrying my weight, and that was the reason for the delay?

"There's a file on Jafar. Everyone who comes into the country on a diplomatic passport has one. Not much in it. When I asked Frank to take a look and give me his read, he had some questions. Still has. Seems our Jafar is the agricultural attaché for the Mission to the UN. But—and this is a big 'but'—in Frank's mind, he's been in this country for over a year and hasn't been to a farm yet. In fact, the only time he's left Manhattan, other than trips back to Tehran, was one trip to visit the ponies at Belmont. Seemed strange to Frank he wasn't visiting the farms of New Jersey or Long Island, very strange."

"That's certainly odd behavior for an agricultural attaché."

"Not really. You'd be surprised at the number of staff at the UN who are here as this attaché or that, when the only reason they're here is to have an enjoyable time. The reward for being a good soldier or bureaucrat, or merely for being the third son, the son who won't get the crown when his father dies. And it's not the fact Jafar has a girlfriend back in Tehran who may be pregnant.

Second families are common for these guys too. They're just practicing to be middle-aged men. No, Frank is curious about Jafar exchanging briefcases with a man we have no file on, a man who goes straight to Brighton Beach and the Eastern European community there as soon as he gets the briefcase and is seen with people we do have files on, some of them very bad people."

"What about the revolution Helen referenced?" When I mentioned her name, the loudness and tone of my voice dropped like it was a term I shouldn't be using here today. It was like when we said "queer" or "colored" in conversation, an unnatural softening of a word we were taught was not polite to say. Had I moved Helen into this category of those who shouldn't be spoken of out loud?

"Why did you whisper her name? Do you see her?"

"No, I don't see her. Don't know why I whispered." And that was the truth.

"Jonathan, we've talked before many times about the situation in Iran. It's a powder keg, has been for a thousand years. When I ask the analysts at State is anything going to happen soon, they give me the look and ask me, 'Do you mean relative to the last thousand years?' They know what I mean, but it's their way of responding to what they think is a ridiculous question. It's a place they're constantly monitoring. What is considered a significant event anywhere else is a regular occurrence."

Allen wasn't finished; he paused, giving me time to reflect on previous discussions, and then continued, "That was the first meeting I had with Frank. I got a call back at the end of the week from him." Again, a pause.

"And?"

"When there's something brought to their attention, the analysts cast a wide net, looking at everyone. They paid closer attention to our principals, Jafar and the guy with the briefcase, and all the people they had contact with in Brighton Beach. The net was cast far enough it caught you and Helen." He didn't have to wait for my reaction.

"What? Why would either of us get caught in that net?"

"Helen's comments precipitated the investigation, and you're her partner. It's routine."

Somewhat reassured, I sat back, having reflexively sat up and leaned forward in a confrontational position.

"What he found troubled him. The routine background check on Helen was perfect."

I hated this. Allen was feeding me a debriefing a line at a time. Was he waiting for me to do something unusual? Was he waiting for me to reach the same state of agitation Helen had last week? If so, why? I chose not to take the bait. Instead, I responded, "Perfect is good."

"Sometimes it is. Sometimes it isn't. Remember a couple of years ago when we were dealing with Ahmad? We looked at his background and saw it was perfect? What the boys in the trade call 'amateur perfect.' His persona was created for his mission. Only when he got ambitious did he tip his hand. If he hadn't, he could have remained a SAVAK asset living and working here forever. Who knows what havoc he could have wreaked? It was only when we became suspicious that we looked and saw it was fabricated. We could tell because there were noticeable holes. As a result, we modified our profiling, going deeper into backgrounds to find the truth.

"When Frank looked at Helen's background, a flag went up, not a red flag, more pink. There were no holes. There was a complete story of this woman from the time she was born until the day you met her at her cousin's party. If we wanted to look, we could find a diary she kept with details of every day of her life from the time she could write. Before that there's family photos of her detailing everything she ever did."

He paused again. This time I had to ask, "Why's that so unusual? You could probably find the same thing for my sisters or for most of the women who work for you."

"Precisely. It's the kind of thing common in America, not the thing that's common in Iran, or any country with an intelligence agency like the SAVAK. Families don't record things. They don't keep perfect records. Why? Because with a regime change, it would provide damning evidence. But because it is what Americans do, it was created to look comfortable to an American analyst looking into the background of someone who wanted to fit in as an American. They, whoever they are, learned from us and put together a background like we'd do it. In fact, if you compare her background to the one we created for you, it's superior. Yours has a three-day hole in it before

Thanksgiving 1971, when you were traveling across the country. Hers has no holes."

There was no need for me to comment; my face told of my shock and disappointment. "Helen's an agent?"

"Probably, but we don't know for who. We'll have to look deeper into Jafar and the guy with the briefcase for answers. Even then, the answer won't be clear. Could be she's a member of that group or she's trying to infiltrate them to get intel to put them down. Only Helen knows."

I sat on the bench overlooking the East River long after Allen left. He was clearly disappointed at the news. As devastating as it was, I felt he was holding something back. That would have to wait. In the meantime, I had to come to grips with this latest information, even if it was incomplete.

I sat for a long time thinking about what Allen had just told me, and the time I spent with Helen over the past several months. Helen was working for someone else, but who? The good guys or the bad? She hadn't told us about the guys in Brighton Beach, so we had to assume the bad, or she was off on her own. Even that option, working on her own for our benefit, was bad. Why wouldn't she tell us?

I thought of all the conversations I had with her, trying to remember if I had let anything slip about anything I shouldn't have. I was sure it was all according to the "need to know" instilled in me by Anderson, and everything I'd said to her was operational and current, nothing from the past. But that was just a momentary relief because she had become friends with Monika. Why? Was that part of her plan, or did it just fit better with her background cover? What did Monika say? How could I quiz Monika without making her suspicious? It wasn't like I could ask Monika, "Hey, Babe. Has Helen ever said anything to you that might indicate she's a spy?" Nah, couldn't do that. I never called Monika "babe."

Chapter 11

*　　*　　*

M onika found a calling—politics. Not running for office but working on political campaigns for office seekers. The charismatic Ed Koch had gotten her attention when as a member of the State House he opposed John Lindsay's proposal for a housing development in Queens. The satisfaction she got from doing what was right and winning propelled her to work even harder when Koch ran for mayor of New York. His campaign was already underway in August 1977, when she dragged me to a fundraiser rally the weekend following my meeting with Allen.

I didn't want to go and thought it was a phase she was going through until she explained her motivation. Monika's parents had grown up in Nazi Germany before the war. While not Nazis, like everyone else, they were mandated to show up at all party rallies. These were indoctrination dramas, staged by the government to show the world the might of the Third Reich and the commitment of the German people to retake the place they felt was rightfully theirs on the world stage. No one in her family ever spoke of the War, but it became clear her father had avoided military service. All she would say was that it was honorable. After that, I never pushed the issue further, convinced if he didn't move to the United States until 1950, our government had had plenty of time to look into his background. If they said he was okay, it was okay by me.

After the war, the German people had had enough of remaining quiet while being told what to do by the Hitler regime. They became very vocal, and public discussion of everything became the norm. The favorite place for discussions became the city or village square, the heart of daily commerce for these poor people trying to recover. At first the rallies were protests about the lack of food, medicine, fuel for cooking the food they didn't have, and fuel for the fires in the homes they didn't have. The marketplace had nothing to sell and often closed early. The lack of merchandise led to these markets being open only one Saturday morning a month, yet the people congregated mostly to discuss the lack of everything. When merchandise became available, the marketplace remained the place to congregate on the weekend to discuss and argue politics. The gatherings produced little either in the demands for goods or political change for Monika's parents before they left for the States.

When they arrived in Queens, the availability of goods astounded them. Equally surprising were the political rallies. These were, for the most part, local people arguing for local changes, and unlike Germany, the protests and discussions resulted in change, if only at the local level. On weekends, her parents took Monika with them, and the seed for involvement in the process took root. When she got older, she did a little protesting while in college, but the surge of political unrest about Vietnam and the sexual revolution occurred after she took the job at Energy. Now, back in New York, the ember of the dormant political coal was fanned, and she warmed to it.

The gala was held at the Commodore Hotel on Forty-Second Street, above Grand Central Station. The hotel had been one of the finest in the city but now showed its age. Built before the time when phones, air conditioning, and in-room television were standard, the hotel had struggled to stay current, and as a result routine maintenance suffered at the hands of the upgrades. Overall, it was a big, seedy, expensive hotel occupying prime real estate in midtown Manhattan.

The guests came from both sides of the political spectrum. Koch was a Democrat, who had a conservative streak, making him attractive to nonpoliticians from both parties. The stance he took against Lindsay afforded him celebrity status among the common man while the interest in real estate made him popular with the businessmen and developers eager to profit from the growth phase following the near collapse of the New York City real-estate market earlier in the decade.

Monika mingled easily with the crowd, knowing many more people than I would have given her credit for. Tonight, I was relegated to being Monika's husband, a role reversal that took me by surprise but one I enjoyed immensely. Monika shined again as she did those first days when I met her during my training in Washington.

One developer seemed to be an old friend. He embraced Monika a bit too enthusiastically for me, but when she introduced me as her husband, he shook my hand just as much. He was the talk of the New York City revitalization circles, a young real-estate developer from Queens making his mark in Manhattan. I had heard his name but never realized how young he was until now. He was about my age, maybe a couple of years older. Tall, with a shock of blond hair, he had a gravelly voice, and when he spoke, his lips formed an Elvis curl. The man was something, and he knew it. Yet despite, or maybe because of, his bigger-than-life personality, I liked him.

Helen was there with her cousin Gerb. We waved little finger waves, and I thought that was it. Monika spotted her and headed off toward her with me in tow. She had invited Helen to attend the event, thinking it might be a way for her to meet interesting men.

"I'm so glad you made it. Have you met anyone yet?" Before Helen could answer, Monika continued, "There are so many attractive eligible men here. You're so beautiful; you'll have lots to choose from. I just introduced Jonathan to Donald. He'd love you."

Helen nodded. I think it was just polite. Monika was in her element, and Helen seemed to be as intrigued by the transformation as me.

"Let's mingle," said Monika as she grabbed Helen by the arm and led her away.

Gerb and I followed in the wake. "Now, I have company in my follower's club. You'll get introduced as Helen's cousin to men who will not see you any more than they'll see me."

Monika moved through the crowd, bouncing from one group to another, introducing Helen as she went. Almost as an afterthought, she'd introduce Gerb and me. Before long, Gerb and I moved away to one of the many bars set up along the walls of the vast ballroom. Helen broke away from Monika to get a drink. She got two champagnes, giving one to Gerb, asking him to deliver it to Monika, leaving us alone for a short minute.

"Allen called before I left the house tonight. Wants to meet us tomorrow morning, southwest corner of Bryant Park at eleven fifteen. It sounded urgent. Said to bring your squash gear."

We had never used Bryant Park as a meeting point. I had a quick flashback of that late-Sunday afternoon two summers ago where I paused before meeting Mike and Ahmad. Was this to be a reminder of that day? If so, for what reason? Asking me to bring my squash gear hinted I could use that as an excuse to get out of the apartment on a Sunday morning. Or, did it have something to do with the squash club on Forty-Second Street across from the park?

"Okay. I wonder why I need my squash gear."

"Don't know. Did he give you any sign this might happen when you met him earlier this week?"

How did she know about the meeting? "No. Did he tell you about the meeting?"

"No. You just did," Helen said as she turned with a fresh glass of champagne, passing Gerb as she returned to Helen.

On the way home from church on Sunday morning, Monika made me promise to be back by midafternoon so we could attend her cousin's birthday barbeque. I promised, hoping I could keep it. Allen called for the meeting with me and Helen on short notice.

Helen and Allen arrived as I approached the designated meeting spot, walking across the grass on the diagonal from the northeast corner behind the New York Public Library. A momentary chill ran down my back as I walked through the families taking advantage of the warm April day. A bench near the corner was empty, and we claimed it.

"Thanks for meeting with me on such short notice. It's important, or I wouldn't have asked you." Without waiting for either of us to respond, he continued, "Frank got what we need on Jafar and the others at Brighton Beach. I won't go into the details of what or how he found out, but they're bringing in typhoid."

"Typhoid?" I said. "Why?"

"They want to distract us with a major health emergency while they do something else, somewhere else in the world. What that is, we're working on. The immediate concern is to stop them here. If we do our job, whatever they're planning gets delayed, and we get more time to figure it out."

"Can't we just raid the Brighton Beach location and round everyone there up?"

"Sure we could, but we don't know if they've distributed it around the country yet."

"Around the country? Not just here in New York?"

"No. For it to be a successful diversion, they need a national emergency. They got the idea from a couple of guys in Chicago a few years ago, who were going to put typhoid in the drinking water. The two got caught before they could dump it, but the analyses done after by the various local and federal agencies concluded it would have been a major health problem, not just in Chicago but around the country. Once infected, it can take anywhere from a week to a month for the symptoms to appear. Chicago, being a major transportation hub, would act like a distribution center. Travelers going there on business or passing through would spread it all around the country, perhaps even the world. This will be bigger because all indications are the Brighton Beach group plans on multiple releases in multiple metropolitan areas."

Helen asked, "And we don't know which cities are targets?"

"No, we don't."

"Who does?"

"Jafar, that's where you come in. We have to snatch him, the two of you. Then we can sweat him and find out."

I smiled, a lazy sort of "what the fuck" smirk, and looked around the park. Shrugging my shoulders, I turned back to Allen. "Jafar's a diplomat. Doesn't that mean hands off? Have you ever seen Forty-Second Street when the United Nations is in session? There's no parking spaces. People have to walk out into the street to get on the buses because they even park in the bus stops. We can't ticket them or tow them away because they have diplomatic immunity! You couldn't stop Jafar at customs because he has diplomatic immunity, and yet you want us to snatch him? How do we do that? The Iran Mission will be on us as soon as we pick him up. The press will crucify us. It'll be an international incident."

"They won't come after him if they think he's dead."

"But won't they be coming after the body?"

"Not if they don't know where the body is."

"You're not making any sense," said Helen.

"You're right. I'm sorry, but I was leading you along, waiting for your 'aha' moment when you saw the solution. We don't have time for that, so I'll explain. Let's move over to the kiosk for a coffee. Not good to stay in one place too long."

As we walked to the kiosk on the corner of Sixth Avenue and Fortieth Street, Allen continued, "Jafar and the guy with the briefcase are couriers, bringing in the typhus and whatever else they need to disperse it. Jafar has only been in the country for a short time, less than a year, so it seems he was sent here with that mission. He's usually met at the airport with a car and driver but two trips ago, he was involved in a serious auto accident on the Van Wyck Expressway. Since then, he's been taking the helicopter. It's more secure. He stays inside the JFK perimeter to the New York Airways terminal, and then a direct hop to the Pan Am Building, a trip down the elevator, and a car to the Iran Mission. Very tight security. We must get him in the helicopter."

"How do we do that? And I mean," I asked, looking at Helen, "how do the two of us do that?"

"Jafar's reserving all the seats on the helicopter and just using two of them. We have to make the helicopter crash. Not a crash that jeopardizes the crew or anyone on the ground, but a crash that leaves questions. He's given us some of the confusion we need. By reserving all the seats on the trip, if there's a crash, there will be confusion about what happened to all the passengers. If the helicopter had to ditch in the East River, we get there first, snatch him in the confusion. The Iran Mission will be just as confused as everyone else. We'll isolate the crew for a few days because of their injuries, giving us time to question Jafar and turn him. The crew then tells the investigators there were only two people on board. Then we produce Jafar. Maybe the guy with the briefcase doesn't make it." Allen rubbed his nose. Was he really doing that? Rubbing a nose was a mafia code for "snuffing" someone.

"How do we get the helicopter to crash in the East River? Is one of us going to learn how to fly a helicopter?"

"No. All you have to do is make sure Jafar gets on the right helicopter. He usually reserves all the seats on a flight, but when he gets to the Air New York terminal, they'll tell him they had to cancel his flight because of mechanical problems. There will be another helicopter available, one that your company has reserved to fly a group of European scientists from the airport to the city. When it's ready to leave, there will be a few who have not yet cleared customs who you're waiting for. You see how upset he is and step in and let him take your helicopter but only after an argument with the ground agent and a guarantee that the helicopter will come straight back for you and your passengers. The New York Air agent will give you a hard time, but keep pushing. You'll get what you want."

"Then what?"

"You and the group of people you're with disappear. You're not responsible for them, just yourself. Grab a cab back to the city and go back to work."

"What about me?" Helen asked. "Jafar knows me and knows I don't work for the same company as Jonathan."

"You're not there. Stay at work. Do what you normally would be doing."

"I'm on the sidelines? Why did you bother bringing me to the meeting?" Helen was upset. She was being read into a mission she had no part of. It made me curious too. Seemed to violate the "need to know" creed.

"Just so you're in the loop. I think of you two as a team. You should know the plans. If something goes wrong, I can give you instructions without having to waste time giving you the background. This is important. Don't kid yourself that sitting at your desk isn't part of the team."

Helen sighed and looked at Allen and then at me. "Yes, sir," she said.

"All right, that's it. Take different exits from the park, leave at different intervals. Helen, you first. Head north on Sixth to Forty-Fifth before you turn east. Jonathan, back the way you came. Me, I'm heading south." With parting nods, we left the park.

Contrary to his instruction, Allen didn't head south. Instead, he went east on the south side of Fortieth Street and waited for Jonathan at the corner of Fifth and Forty-second. Jonathan, deep in thought, didn't see him until he approached.

"I thought you might need an explanation for what's going on," he continued without waiting for me to respond. "Let's take a seat on the steps," he said, turning toward the east side of the New York Public Library, the massive steps a congregation point for many people. Some engaged in conversation, some read, while others found it a convenient place to people watch. We could carry on a conversation surrounded by people wrapped up in their own worlds.

When seated, Allen turned and said, "This is all very confusing to you, as it should be because you don't have all the pieces. I'll give you those pieces now, or at least some of the pieces you need to understand."

"I'd appreciate that," I said in a voice that merged pissed-offed-ness and genuine interest.

"Is that sardonic or sarcastic? I can never tell with you. Doesn't matter. Whatever it was, I deserve it. You've been kept in the dark but only because I didn't have all the bits of information yet, and it didn't make any difference about what you had to do." Allen paused, his eyes moved to watch my eyes. He continued, "We got a full picture on Helen. She's Mossad."

Chapter 12

I watched the people around me and those walking on the street. Men, women, and children all dressed more casually than those I saw during the week. The women, all attempting to be individuals were all too similar, bound together by the fashion of the day, none more pronounced than the big hair. Whether dark or light, short or long, it was big, puffed to its puffiest. Was it an attempt to copy the Afro style of the time or an imitation of the big hair popular in Hollywood? What difference did it make? The men, barely a tie present. Some informal in their leisure suits with bell-bottoms flared over two-inch platform shoes. Monika had bought me a leisure suit. I wore it once to please her; it wasn't me and never again. Now she only bought me socks and underwear, boxers not briefs.

My eyes wandered as my mind tried to understand Allen's words. "Helen is Mossad? The Israeli intelligence group?"

"Yes, Jonathan. Are you with me?"

"Yeah, just trying to digest what you told me," I answered. Adding emphasis to my mental state, a cloud passed in front of the noon sun. As I retreated into myself, the sounds of the street faded. The traffic on Fifth Avenue became muted. The sound of car and truck horns, the background symphony of daily life in New York, faded as I went deeper into my thoughts. I recognized the psychopathology. I heard something that shook me, so my brain turned that

sense down. The other senses were heightened. The granite steps, uncomfortable before, were now a pain in my ass. Smells became dominant. Why smells?
I could smell the hot dogs floating in the greasy water of the Sabrett street
cart. Pretzels toasting, perhaps burning. No, not pretzels! Someone lit a joint. I
looked around, back in the present with Allen.

"There's a lot more," Allen said. "And just to put your mind at rest, most
of it's good." He stared at me, eyes sympathetic to the confusion he had caused.
"It's a long story. I'll give you the short version." He leaned forward, taking a
pack of cigarettes from his sock. The army habit came in handy now that clothes
had a trim fit, and the stiff cigarette box would spoil the line of his trousers. He
offered me one, but I declined. I noticed he was back to smoking Parliaments
again. He spoke through the exhaled smoke.

"Everything I told you about Helen before was true—her early childhood,
the cloistered school away from home, her father keeping the suitors away, and
her university time in England. Except the early childhood story was for Helen's
sister and the background of her university days was Helen."

Two guys with a boom box walked up the library steps and sat down six
feet from us. While there were unfriendly looks, no one moved. Everyone just
spoke louder. A New York City cop followed them up the stairs and got them
moving before they got comfortable. Everyone went back to talking in hushed
tones befitting library steps.

"I don't understand."

"Helen and her sister are twins."

"Twins?"

"Yeah. Their father was a brilliant man. He was working to support the
Shah. He thought the future of the country would be better served if it were
more Western than ruled by the religious zealots. To help his country, he
allowed himself to be employed by the Mossad. He fed them information the
SAVAK had on any insurgency that might be brewing. Felt he had the best of
both worlds with two governments working to maintain the peace in Iran. But
he was a realist too. He knew if he got caught by his country, his family was
at risk. That's when he started thinking about defecting to the West. When
the twins were born, he was frantic. Twins, especially girls, were considered

special by the religious right, often taken from the parents to serve the priests, and he had no doubts about how they would serve. The Israelis stepped in and offered to take one of the girls and raise her in Israel. He only had a brief time to decide—give up one of his daughters or lose both. He made the Solomon decision: he split his children."

"So he kept both daughters safe and alive by giving up one."

"Yeah. He gave up Helen. The Israelis took her. Put her on a flight to Tel Aviv and raised her in the Jewish faith, but were honest with her. As soon as she was old enough to understand, they told her the truth. The family that raised her wasn't in the Mossad, but connected to it, doing what was necessary without a link back. They did an excellent job of raising her, and she embraced both worlds, an Irani Muslim raised as a Jew. She saw the conflict of the religions and wanted to do something about it. She trained for the Mossad from an early age. Neighbors and friends may have suspected something but didn't say anything. There were always a lot of war orphans."

Allen paused, looked at me, and asked if I was okay. "Yeah. You're doing a good job of making a complicated story easy to follow. I'll have questions later, but for now, I'm okay."

"When it came time for the sister in Iran to go to college, she and her father chose England for all the reasons I told you before. When she left for school, her father told her the truth as well. All very upsetting, but when she realized what he had given up protecting the two girls, she accepted it. Not only accepted it, but applauded him for what he was doing for the country and for his family. He told her of his plans to move the family from Iran to someplace safer. The clincher came when she met her sister, Helen.

"The plan was simple. Helen would take her sister's place at university, and the sister would return to Israel until her family fled, and then she would join them. Simple. Easy peasy. No one was the wiser. The daughter who returned to Israel took Helen's place. Of course, she didn't speak the language, or know the customs. She wasn't as fit as Helen. So they invented an accident requiring a long convalescence, during which she came up to speed. They said she had a concussion, so her speech, memory, and physical shortcomings, compared to Helen, had credibility."

"And Helen was starting university where no one knew her. What about when she came home for visits, like during Christmas?" I knew what I was saying—a Jew, a Muslim, and the Christian holiday. So did Allen, but he ignored me.

"Helen stayed in England for the first year. Her father visited her twice. He was so happy to spend time with the daughter he hadn't seen in twenty years. As a twin, being with her had a strange familiarity, at least physically. With time, he learned her unique personality. It was also a time to educate her on things she should know when she returned to Tehran. And she did return at the end of her first year. There were differences of course; she was a different person. They attributed these changes to the influence of England on her, not the least of which was an English accent she had purposefully acquired."

"So she pulled it off?"

"Yes, beautifully, as did her sister in Tel Aviv. The sister was at first confused, being dropped into a foreign culture, away from family and friends, but her father visited her, explaining things more fully until she accepted her new identity. She also understood her family would leave Iran as soon as it was safe for them all to get out. That was the most significant thing to comfort her. She began to understand the situation in Iran as her father saw it and agreed life there would change for the worse and it was best to start over again some place safer with more assurance of the freedom they had enjoyed during the good times under the Shah. With time, she became curious about her sister's life in the Mossad, what had attracted her to the organization. For reasons still unknown to us, she began her training and is also a Mossad agent now." Allen paused, drawing the last of the smoke from the Parliament, shred the remaining tobacco, and put the filter in his shirt pocket.

"The thing I don't understand is how you didn't know any of this until just now. I thought the CIA was the top intelligence agency in the world, yet you got snookered by two girls from Iran."

Allen smiled and flipped his hand in a casual manner. "We knew about Helen before she came to this country. I should say Frank knew about her. We had eyes on her in England, and our people in Tel Aviv were watching her father when he came to visit the sister. There were photos of the father and the sister together in the files. Frank saw them. One set of photos was the same time

Helen was involved in the feminist demonstration in England. Easy 'one plus one' for him. Same girl in two places, had to be two."

"So you knew all this and kept me in the dark?"

"Sorry. Had to. While we knew there were two sisters, and we knew about Mossad for Helen, we didn't know much about the sister. We also knew the old man was working a deal to get out of Iran. We had to let it play out. There were lots of potentials in the game: the old man, the sisters, the Mossad, and the SAVAK. If he was so clever to assure the safety of his daughters and also work the SAVAK while he's developing an exit strategy for his family, was he also being clever with the Israelis? Didn't know, especially when Helen shows up in New York to be near her cousin, who just happens to be an old classmate of yours. We didn't bring you in because we didn't want to take the chance you would betray what you knew. A gesture, a look. Remember, Helen is very capable, very clever. If there was the slightest chance she was a double agent, we had to know."

"And now you know?"

"Yeah. She's okay."

"You say so?"

"Frank says so."

Monday, I met Jafar at the racket club. We played a vigorous match, for me more exercise than skill. My mind was elsewhere. When we finished, I asked if he was available on Wednesday for a game at noon.

"No, Jonathan. Sorry, but I have a quick business trip back home. I'm on the evening flight, but I'll be back next Monday, the sixteenth I think."

"Okay, I'll reserve a court for next Monday, May sixteenth."

"I'm sorry. I'm not being clear. I'm returning from Tehran on the sixteenth, late in the day. Probably won't be in condition to play for a couple of days. I don't adjust well to jet lag."

"I'll schedule a court for Tuesday. Exercise is the best treatment for jet lag, and after the drubbing you gave me today, if your travel gives me a little advantage, I'll take it."

Helen confirmed Jafar's travel plans the next day. Saphari called her, asking if she was available for window-shopping and a walk in Central Park on Sunday.

Allen gave the go-ahead for snatching Jafar on the following Monday as he traveled by helicopter from JFK to the Pan Am Building.

Allen met with us at the safe house on Thirty-Ninth Street, the same apartment I had lived in the summer I had interned at American Pharmaceuticals. He included Helen even though she wouldn't have an active role in the mission. It was a big risk, I thought, if there was any lingering doubt as to her loyalty. Then I thought of Frank and his team at State and put those fears aside.

"Jafar's scheduled to arrive at JFK at four forty p.m. on Monday on a direct flight from Tehran, but those big Boeing 747SPs can make up time on the listed thirteen-hour flight. So we'll have our people in the airport an hour earlier. These are the people who will pose as your key opinion leaders coming in for the company medical meeting. They have their assignments and will work from a timetable that begins when his plane lands, gravitating as one or two people to the New York Airways counter. All you must do is wait at the helicopter terminal, act anxious for those who haven't shown up, and then graciously offer your helicopter to Jafar. We'll take care of the rest."

"What about Helen?"

Allen seemed to look off into the distance, searching for something. Perhaps a word, or perhaps more. "She doesn't have a role in this, and as she said, Jafar knows her and would question her presence with you." He paused, looked at me and then at Helen, and continued, "No, she'll be at work, doing her job." Why is Allen talking about Helen as if she isn't present?

With that our meeting was over. It may have been the shortest briefing a CIA agent ever got before a mission. But I had a limited role in the mission. Not much I could do wrong or prepare for in that regard.

I didn't hear from Allen for the rest of the week, nor did I see Helen. On Sunday, I suggested to Monika we spend the day in Manhattan, strolling on Fifth Avenue and maybe grab some hot dogs with Eric in Central Park. She reminded me of the luncheon with her family after the mass celebrating their thirty-fifth wedding anniversary. I had completely forgotten about it. Distracted, but it wasn't the assignment. I was a benign contributor to this, just a facilitator. Less involved than I was when I introduced Lance to Hamidi in New Haven several years earlier. No, there was something else I couldn't put my fingers on.

That night lying in bed waiting for Monday and the mission, I felt Monika beside me. As I looked to her, her head in the shadows making her hair appear dark, I thought of Helen. Reaching for her, I hesitated, not knowing who it was I was reaching for.

Chapter 13

✳ ✳ ✳

Monday morning was uneventful. A cab from Manhattan got me to the Pan Am Terminal at John F. Kennedy International Airport by three o'clock. Wandering around the terminal, I stopped once to check the arrival of the plane from Tehran and then made my way to the New York Airways area, arriving at three thirty. With an on-time arrival, I was more than an hour early. Trying not to be conspicuous, I made my way to the coffee shop across from the Air Iran gate and got a black coffee. I would wait only for the time it took me to drink my coffee at an unhurried pace, not wait for the arrival, but just long enough to see if the arrival time changed. At four o'clock, I got up, tossed my paper cup in the garbage, and walked back toward the New York Airways area on the far side of the terminal.

The area was busy. The helicopter shuttle prospered now, having failed in its first attempt; the new business model was ambitious but doable. Then the 1973 oil embargo occurred. High fuel prices cut into the tight margin together with a general slowdown in the economy, and the convenient hop to Manhattan ended. But all was better now. The economy had turned around and with it a new opportunity to cater to those with big expense accounts in a hurry.

The shuttle was busy most of the day. In the early morning, the "red-eyes" from the West Coast deposited passengers eager to get to meetings in Manhattan after an all-night flight. They avoided the long cab lines and the commuter traffic crawling into the city with the short ten-minute flight to the heliport on the top of the Pan Am Building. Other executives, wanting to avoid the morning rush hour and competition for cabs, waited to take the flight to JFK. In the afternoon, the flights from Europe began arriving at 2:00 p.m. and the cycle continued with more passengers going west from JFK. In late afternoon, the cycle reversed with businessmen ending their day in Manhattan, squeezing the last bit of work time in before taking the helicopter to avoid the evening rush hour leaving the city, much of it east toward JFK.

The late-afternoon crowd made it easy to fit in. If I walked, there were lots of people to mingle with, in any direction. I had to walk with a purpose to fit in. Or, I could just stand around. There were as many waiting as there were walking. Some of those waiting seemed relaxed, taking a break in a hectic schedule to slow down with nothing to do until the next connection in a day or a week or a lifetime waiting for connections.

I chose to appear to be waiting for a trip to the City, for people to appear who might be late and make me late, or waiting for people I didn't know because that was what I was doing, and I must have done it well. A ground stewardess approached me and asked if she could help. "No thanks. Waiting for some colleagues. I have the five o'clock flight reserved for a group that's coming in on different flights."

"Ah yes. Dr. West," she said checking her clipboard and making a notation with the flick of her pen. "Let me know when your group is here. We'll need to check everyone in before we board." With that she moved to others waiting in the area.

At half-past four, two gentlemen in academic business casuals approached me. The blue blazer, khaki trousers, white shirt, and club tie were identical to those worn by Gerb's colleagues at his first house party, sans the tie.

"Jonathan West, it has been too long, my friend." The stranger shook my hand, introduced me to the gentleman with him, and asked, "So how many more are we waiting for?"

I glanced at the arrival board outside in the main terminal to find a status change. The American Airlines flight from Minneapolis was delayed ten minutes. Turning back to my new friend, I answered, "Looks like most of you are on the ground, but the physicians from the Mayo will be late, not much, just a few minutes." As I said this, two more of my guests walked up. I recognized them before they joined our growing group. Both wore corduroy suits, not even the almost acceptable narrow rib, but the wide rib. As I wondered if these were all New York field office agents or they came in from Washington or from nearby offices in Connecticut and New Jersey, I saw Jafar walking down the ramp toward the waiting area. He walked with purpose, not in a hurry, but not a saunter. As he entered the waiting area, he saw me and came to where I was standing.

"Jonathan, I never expected to find you waiting for me," he joked with a broad smile.

"Jafar, what a surprise! Are you just getting in?"

"Yes. This is an on-time arrival direct from Tehran. I love those big 747SP planes. Even though we left a few minutes late, the plane made up the delay. What brings you out here?"

"The company is hosting a Key Opinion Leader meeting on one of the drugs I'm involved with. Many are my investigators, and because they're important, I thought it was the least I could do to shepherd them from the airport into Manhattan." I leaned in. "Besides, it was a great excuse to take the helicopter, something I've not done yet."

"Smart move. It gets the meeting off to an efficient start, taking them by helicopter rather than being frustrated in traffic for an hour." He leaned in and whispered, "It's also a wonderful way to impress them."

Shaking my hand, he said, "See you tomorrow. I'm glad we're playing at lunchtime. Jet lag usually doesn't set in on me until midafternoon." With another smile, he left and went to the ticket counter.

I watched as he began an animated conversation with the young woman behind the counter. The poor woman looked contrite, shaking her head but constantly mouthing the words "I'm sorry." Jafar's frustration seemed to grow with his hands becoming active with wave and gesticulation. I never saw him in this state before, but then again, when I saw him he was playing, not working. He looked like a difficult man to work with, a man used to getting his own way.

I took this as a cue and approached the desk. Seeing me, he calmed a little. Why, who knows, but he did.

Before I could say a word, Jafar spoke. "Jonathan, I'm embarrassed. I forget I am a guest in your country, and I should be more patient and more respectful." As he said this, he looked at a blushing ticket agent. I wonder what he said to her. He let it go at that. That was as close as she was going to get to an apology.

The ticket agent broke the silence. "I was telling your friend we have some delays right now. There are two problems. We have a larger number of passengers than normal, and we have an aircraft we had to take out of service for repairs. This has caused a backup. While a reservation isn't needed, we have two flights that are completely reserved, one of them is his."

I looked around as if looking for his companions, and seeing no one nearby, I said, "Jafar, perhaps they'll have things back to normal when the rest of your party gets here. I have a flight reserved myself, but unfortunately, I too am waiting for some stragglers."

"The travel staff at the Iran Mission always reserves an entire helicopter for my use. I'm embarrassed they do, but they seem to think I should have it. They claim security reasons, so I go along with them. This young woman has told me my aircraft may not be ready for an hour. Under normal circumstances, I could wait, or take a car into Manhattan, but I have a meeting at the Mission at six, and I won't make it."

Turning to the woman I asked, "All my colleagues aren't here yet. Perhaps we could trade aircraft. Jafar can take my helicopter, and I can take his when it arrives."

"No, Jonathan. That is very kind, but I can't impose my problem on you. You have important visitors."

"Jafar, it's all right. I just checked the arrival board, and the last of my guests' planes isn't even at the gate yet. It'll work out fine."

The ticket agent interrupted our discussion. "Gentlemen, I'm glad you worked things out, but the aircraft taken out of service was for Mr. Jafar. I'm sorry, but I can't just exchange it like that. Look around the room. I have twenty passengers waiting to go into the city. I can't let an aircraft leave with one person on it and tell the waiting passengers it might be another hour before there's another flight, and during that hour, they watch another helicopter leave that's not full. That would be your reservation, Dr. West. You don't have a full flight either."

I looked at Jafar and then at the ticket agent. "Let me make a proposal. Jafar, you take this helicopter, my reservation, but take some of the waiting passengers with you. When my group arrives, I take any waiting passengers with me. You get to your meeting on time, the waiting passengers get into the City, and my group gets in a little later. Everybody makes a little sacrifice, a little inconvenience, but no one has a big inconvenience. Hell, if we do nothing, chances are everyone would be a lot more delayed than they will by the compromise."

Jafar smiled. "Jonathan, you Americans are such negotiators. How can I refuse an offer like that?" He turned to the now-beaming ticket agent and nodded his approval. Turning back to me, he said, "I'll think about this tonight. Think about not playing so hard tomorrow. Perhaps letting you win."

"No, no. You're not getting away that easy. If you lose tomorrow, you want to get in my head, thinking you let me win. I'll beat you fair and square. If I think you're going easy on me, I'll let you win." We both laughed.

As he left to board the helicopter, he leaned into me with a conspiratorial whisper. "Don't mention this to anyone. If my security finds out I shared a flight, I'll have to travel with a babysitter in the future." He shifted his eyes to the two agents in corduroy; winking, he continued, "If you tell, I'll tell everyone your company pays its Key Opinion Leaders so little for their expertise, they can't even afford a decent suit." Both of us laughed.

As Jafar got on the plane, one of the guests in my group left and made his way to the bank of telephones outside the waiting area. Two others walked to the front of the line and boarded the helicopter behind him. I stood at the window and watched the big rotors spin up to speed and New York Airways Flight 972 lift off at 5:11 p.m., turn in the air, and move west toward Manhattan. When the flight was airborne, all the men waiting with me dispersed, leaving just me, one blue blazer, and one wide corduroy. None of us were waiting for the next helicopter. I expected them to say something. What? I don't know, but instead we stood in silence. The third man who had gone to the phone returned, and we waited some more.

At 5:35 p.m., all hell broke loose in the New York Airways area. Phones started ringing, agents became frantic, and most eyes were trained on the skyline of Manhattan, less than twenty miles away. Sunset wasn't until about eight, so while the sun was in the west, it wasn't so low in the sky I had to squint. From where I was watching, I couldn't see anything abnormal, just the slight shimmer of heat rising from the concrete heated by the May sun all day.

A voice in the waiting area boomed, not from a loudspeaker, but just from the crowd, "A chopper is down. A chopper is down."

"Where?"

"The news is saying the Pan Am Building." I followed the voice to a man sitting by the window, looking west with the others; he held a small transistor radio to his ear. He was repeating what he heard as breaking news. "They say it was the flight that just arrived from JFK. My God! That's the one that just left here."

"What happened?"

"Is anyone hurt?"

Questions were flying at the man with the radio like he had inside knowledge, more than he was reporting from the news report.

"That's all they're saying. There's no reporters on the roof yet. A blade fell off, hit a building, and killed someone on the ground. Looks like it was bad."

I had mixed emotions. In one sense, the mission was a success. We got Jafar, but it was supposed to be an abduction. Was this another twist in my relationship with the CIA I couldn't figure out? If there was a crash, were the two men who followed Jafar on board sacrificed? If so, did they know? Or was it an accident, and they got caught up in a terrible coincidence?

Anderson appeared at my side. Another shocking surprise! I hadn't seen or talked to him since that first day in the Spring of 1971 in the Pentagon when he recruited me. He looked the same, like time had forgotten him for the last six years. Same tweed sport jacket. Same military haircut. Same Florsheim shell cordovan loafers. Why was my boss's boss suddenly at my side after a helicopter crashed in Manhattan?

"Jonathan, let's have dinner, shall we? Do you like the Palm? I'm afraid we'll have to take a cab. The helicopter service seems to have been canceled for the rest of the day. We should have no trouble getting into the City now. Most of the traffic will be outbound."

Chapter 14

M anhattan is full of great steak houses, and each claim to have the best steak. I've been to many of them, almost always as a business lunch or dinner, most at the request of my out-of-town guest. Of course, I go where they choose, even though I see little difference in the meat. I think what distinguishes these places is the ambience, the service, and sometimes a side dish. All have creamed spinach, deep-fried onion straws, baked potatoes with gobs of sour cream, and chives. All claim to have the best cheesecake in New York, and they do because all the restaurants buy it from the same bakery.

The Palm on Second Avenue is unique to some because of the ambience. The decor is rustic, not in a cowboy sense, but in a minimalistic way. No fancy tablecloths. No ferns. Just basic tables and chairs to sit and eat the food that's supposed to be the star. In contrast to the starkness are the caricatures drawn directly on the walls. Most are of celebrities who have dined there. Others are of frequent but lesser-known diners. Not moved by celebrities, these aren't the attraction for me.

What draws me there over the other places is the tomato, onion, and cheese salad that's simple but elegant. The tomatoes are big, fresh, flavorful beefsteaks, cut in a healthy slice. The sweet Bermuda onion cut to the same thickness, as is the cheese, a fresh *mozzarella di bufala*. There are two of each, alternating layers on top of each other, the stack then toppled and spread across the plate. The salad was topped with a little basil and then drizzled with fresh virgin olive oil and vinegar with fresh pepper added at the table.

The maître d' welcomed Anderson as if he was a regular customer.

"We don't have reservation, Thomas, but I hope you can make room for us." I watched his hands as he said this, looking for the tip to be passed for this favor. Anderson and Thomas made no contact, not even a handshake. I was struck by a thought. I never saw Anderson shake hands. He was conscious of his hands and how they portrayed him. The manicure I noticed the first time I met him attested to that. Yet he didn't offer his hand in greeting.

"No problem, sir. I can always find a table for you. Tonight, I can even offer you a choice of tables. We've had several no-shows and cancelations because of the tragedy unfolding just a few blocks from here."

"Yes, I heard. Tragic." Anderson displayed the correct amount of emotion for an out-of-town visitor, sharing the grief of someone calling New York home. "Is there any news?"

"Nothing that hasn't been on the news. Thank you for your concern. If someone comes in with anything different, I'll be sure to let you know. May I show you to your table?"

Thomas took us down the narrow restaurant to a table in the back corner. He held the chair facing the door for Anderson.

"Thank you, Thomas."

Again, no money changed hands. Very unusual for a New York restaurant— a table with no reservation and a preferred table without a tip given, or apparently expected. But then, both The Palm and Anderson were not usual.

At the table, Anderson explained why he had asked Thomas about news of the accident. "We might get information on the crash before it's available on the news. The restaurant is home base for most of the journalists in the area. The *Daily News* is right around the corner. The *Herald Tribune* journalists were regulars here before the paper folded in 1966. In fact, the caricatures you see started with the newspaper cartoonists who were always short of money, drawing pictures on the walls as payment for a meal."

"That's interesting. I've been here several times on business and admired the caricatures but didn't know the back story. Now, I'll have something to say to impress my guests." I said this to engage Anderson in some light conversation, but he merely pursed his lips, nodded his head, and looked around the room. Not a casual gaze, but a study of the room and the patrons who shared it with us.

A waiter appeared with a chilled bottle of Pellegrino. Anderson had not ordered the Italian water, but they knew he wanted it. Helen always ordered Pellegrino, gassed. Gassed was the European way of ordering bottled water with carbonation. The first time she ordered it that way "gassed," I told her she was being redundant; Pellegrino is only available as a sparkling water. She ignored me and continues to add the unnecessary descriptive. She had to order, but the Palm staff brought it for Anderson without being asked. He was obviously a special guest at the Palm if not a regular customer.

Anderson finished his look around the room. "This is the original Palm, as I'm sure you know. Started as an Italian place in the twenties, about the same time the *Herald Tribune* newspaper started. There's another in Washington, and of course, the Palm Too across the street, but I like this one best. Something to be said for the original wouldn't you say, Jonathan?"

I nodded agreement while studying the menu. Helen had told me the story of the Palm. She was fascinated that the caricatures were not framed pictures but drawn directly on the wall. As a foreigner, she felt obligated to absorb every detail about places or things American she liked. She felt it helped her assimilate quicker. This love of all things American meant she probably knew more trivia about New York City than most native-born New Yorkers.

Anderson had not picked up his menu. He reached across the table and took mine from my hand. "Jonathan, I know you prefer the rib-eye steak, but if you'll indulge me, I'd like to order for you and see if I can broaden your tastes." He signaled with a nod of his head, and Thomas was at our table. Not a waiter, but Thomas.

"Thomas. We'll both start with the tomato salad please. My guest and I will have a petite filet. Cook his the same way you cook mine." A conspiratorial grin passed between them. "I'm trying to show him the beauty of the filet over the rib eye. Creamed spinach for the table, and I called ahead for a baked potato I'll share with my guest. Another bottle of water, please."

I should have been annoyed that Anderson presumed to know what I wanted and even more annoyed he ordered for me. But I was more surprised than annoyed. "I didn't see baked potato on the menu."

"It isn't. The Palm is one of the few steak houses in New York that only offers French fries as the potato. Trying to distinguish themselves from the others. I think it's a shame to have a steak and not have a baked potato. In the Midwest, it would signal the demise of the restaurant, but in the East, especially here in New York, French fries and hash browns seem to work, and the baked potato isn't missed."

A quick flash back to my youth brought a memory that I shared with Anderson. "I had a friend growing up whose mother cooked with a coal stove in the kitchen. She always had hot baked potatoes on the back, staying warm. Of course, we didn't call them baked potatoes, just potatoes. There was nothing better on a cold winter day. Warmed the hands and warmed the belly."

Seeming to ignore my attempt at conversation, he continued, "I made arrangements with the chef here. I call ahead when I plan on dining. He sends a boy up the street to get a single Idaho potato for me. They cook it as it should be, and when finished, they put it on the back of the stove, much like I imagine your friend's mother did. When I order, they put it on the grill for a few minutes. This last little touch makes the skin crisp and a bit charred. Perfection, just like my sainted mother made them."

The story seemed practiced, as if told to every guest he brought to the Palm. Different tonight as I had provided the link to Irish mothers. I wondered if he had taken Helen here and had shared these secrets with her.

Anderson stopped talking about the restaurant and food. He picked up his fork, examined it, and returned it to the table, and began, "On the eleven o'clock news tonight, they will report all twenty of the passengers from JFK had safely disembarked from the helicopter before the accident. The aircraft's manifest will not reflect Jafar or two of my men as having been on board. The initial report will attribute the accident to a tire that blew. Later, after the National Transportation Safety Board completes its investigation, they will cite corrosion of the sponson strut assembly caused the undercarriage to detach from the aircraft. The report will suggest the corrosion was caused by small surface pits of undetermined origin. The investigation will not make any attempt to determine the origin."

I sat stunned at Anderson's directness, not that his hand was in it but that he had all the answers before the questions were asked. "And you know this how?"

"I know this because it is a fact."

At this moment, I felt the power of the man. Physically, he was less than imposing, but his power came from within. His eyes were intense and every word he said delivered with authority. I saw the intensity Allen had described that night so long ago in the restaurant after my first kill. For a moment, I feared him.

Thomas appeared with our salads. After allowing him to grind a liberal amount of pepper, Anderson continued, "Somewhere else in the paper there will be a short article written by a stringer who supplied the piece to the *News*, reporting a government raid on a house in Brighton Beach. It will report that the suspects, all recent immigrants from the Middle East, responded to the call to surrender with gun fire. None survived. Names are being withheld until relatives can be located and notified. Enough information will be provided during the investigation that there will be no doubt to their superiors as to their identity. The news will be false. All the residents of the house were captured and are now beginning intense interrogation. All the accumulated biological weapons were collected and will be destroyed."

"And Jafar, I assume he's alive and undergoing similar intense interrogation."

"No, Jonathan. As a diplomat, he can't be held or interrogated. That's international law." Anderson put his salad fork down and looked at me. "In the aftermath of the tragic accident, he'll be found walking on Vanderbilt Avenue directly under the crash site in a dazed state. The men who accompanied him on the helicopter flight will have removed his wallet, so he'll have no identification on him, and be taken into custody. He'll protest he's a diplomat but won't be able to prove it. The police will take him to a wing of Bellevue Hospital, where physicians will examine him for any injuries and place him under mandatory forty-eight-hour observation in the psych ward for making outlandish claims. I think you might agree claiming to have diplomatic immunity at the scene of a major accident and having no identity papers, at least on the surface, satisfies the broadest definition of such a claim. The authorities will take others into similar custody for observation at the same time to demonstrate a concern for safety and security."

"Our people?"

"Yes, people friendly to us." His meaning was clear. He continued, "and perhaps a couple of street people who could use medical care, a safe place to sleep, a shower, and decent food for forty-eight hours. The street people are a nice touch. None of them will have any identification. One will be the man who frequents the Grand Central Station area claiming to be the prince of spring."

Anderson started eating again as I asked, "And after forty-eight hours?"

"The physicians handling him will release him. Agents from the Federal Marshalls and the State Department will be waiting for him. They'll have documentation declaring him a diplomat persona non grata, ordering him to leave the country within forty-eight hours. Unfortunately for him, the papers were being signed as he was on the ill-fated helicopter, so his forty-eight hours will have expired. The agents will take him back to JFK, where he will take the evening flight to Tehran. At the airport, he will be seen and photographed by SAVAK agents, receiving an envelope from one of his escorts. Also, a surprised Jafar will be embraced by one of his escorts and receive a firm handshake from the rest. On the plane, the SAVAK agents will isolate him from other passengers, and when they search his luggage, which we conveniently had in the trunk of the car, they will find a lot of cash, a Swiss passport, and a coded document to a numbered account in Switzerland. They will have no problem breaking the code."

Anderson put his salad fork down again. He was a slow eater, seeming to savor everything and get the most of it. Taking a package of crackers, saltines, he removed one from the package, held it in two hands, and broke it in half. Next he combined the two halves, one on top of the other, and still with two hands put the split cracker in his mouth. I had seen this ceremony before, up close as an altar boy. He just performed the consecration rite of liturgy of the Mass. Was it a show for me, or a carry-over from his days as a Franciscan student? His daily reminder of the vows he intended to take for life? He finished and picked up his fork again, giving no explanation for the ritual.

My turn to guide the conversation. "No doubt you know of his fate when he returns to Tehran; he'll be interrogated. Intense by our definition would be a gross understatement. Of course, he'll deny any involvement with the US government because there was none, and he'll be executed. Bottom line being, he'll come to the same end as Hamadi when he was taken from New Haven four years ago."

"Yes, Jonathan. That is what will happen. Jafar was an evil man with an evil purpose, who planned to bring death to innocent Americans, not as an act of war, but only as a distraction so more evil could take place in another part of the world. We have thwarted his effort, saved countless lives here and abroad, sent a message to his superiors, and punished Jafar for his crime."

A waiter came and cleared our salads, followed by Thomas, who served the main course. In spite of the prolonged time Anderson had taken with the salad, I hadn't finished mine, my appetite gone. He viewed his filet with eager anticipation.

"I do hope your failure to finish your salad was a sign you were saving yourself for the filet, and the activities of the day and our conversation haven't taken the edge off your appetite."

I didn't respond, but he continued, "The chefs here have been cooking marvelous steaks for years. I, like you, favored the rib eye to the filet until I had a filet in Paris." Anderson went on to describe the cooking process in Paris and how and why it was superior. He recommended this method to the chefs at Palm, but they rejected it. As a compromise, they agreed to cook his to order whenever he came in.

As he went on with his cooking tips, my thoughts shifted again to Helen. I wondered if she had heard the news of the crash and had made the association to Jafar. Was she trying to contact me? If she wasn't read in on the mission, she knew enough to maintain security and keep her questions to herself.

"You might be wondering about Helen."

There he goes with that mind reading shit again. How does he do it? I must have a "tell," the term applied by poker players to an opponent's weakness, something that gives them away. Perhaps a twitch, a look, the way I hold my fork?

"Whether she's in the loop? Helen is very much in the loop. Another deception for which I apologize. I sense there is more between you and Helen than a work relationship. It certainly is the case for her. Of you, I'm unsure how deep your feelings for her go."

That caught me off guard, and I showed it. He raised a question I had asked myself many times. I justified my interest in her as a professional, smart, competent, and bearing a striking physical similarity to Monika. It was easy to look at Helen and realize naked, she would be very similar to Monika. Once that thought entered my mind, I chased down that familiar path of all men, wondering if the experience of making love with her would be the same as what I was used to with Monika, or if different, how different?

"Helen led the raid in Brighton Beach. Not for the US government, but for the Mossad."

Chapter 15

N ow my appetite was gone. It left me and walked out the door. No doggie bag. No dessert. No coffee. I put my fork and steak knife down, staring at Anderson. "Mr. Anderson, I think it's time for me to display some righteous indignation. For several weeks, you have deliberately kept me in the dark, feeding me bits and pieces of information by Allen, presented as complete, only to find there was more being kept from me. I'm doubting where I fit."

"Dr. West, you are exactly where I wanted you to be when I picked you six years ago. I like your description of being fed bits and pieces for it is now time for you to feast on all you need and want to know." He chuckled at his ability to remain in the food analogy I started. "That's why you're having dinner with me rather than Allen. I'm going to lay out the master plan for you, the plan for which you were selected so many years ago."

He signaled for Thomas to have the table cleared. I had barely touched my meal, and he wasn't finished. Thomas didn't inquire if there was something wrong with the meal as I would expect with neither meal finished. Thomas hovered as the waiter he summoned cleared the dishes. Anderson ordered coffee for us both and waited in silence until it was poured. He asked they leave the pot, a signal he didn't want to be disturbed.

"First, let's address the elephant in the room, or more precisely, the brunette in your head. We've known all there was to know about Helen, her family, her twin sister, and her involvement with the Mossad for years. Allen already told you this. Despite this, or rather, because of this, we made you partners for this mission. She is a seasoned agent. Has had multiple assignments with the Mossad in the Middle East and Europe. If there was a flaw in you as an agent, she would have detected it, and we would have become aware of it. She made no bad reports on you to her superiors. We also used her to see if there was a flaw in your character. Helen's trained to seduce men. She tried to seduce you, albeit in my estimate, she was much too subtle. Too subtle, I think because she has feelings for you, but that shouldn't matter."

I attempted to object, but only got the chance to lean forward a little and open my mouth before he put his hand up and told me he wasn't finished.

"Your future with Helen is now up in the air because her future presence in the United States is an unknown, a foreign agent who conducted a mission on our soil." He waved his right hand in dismissive manner. "Yes, it happens on a regular basis. We do it too. But—and this is a big 'but'—there's a courtesy among allies where we let each other know something is afoot. Yes, we know what's happening without being told, but it's the courtesy thing. We were watching them, they knew we were watching them, yet they didn't tell us they were conducting a mission, nor did they tell us after the mission was completed. The bodies left in Brighton Beach to take the place of the Iranis they are interrogating are a mystery, probably undesirables from Iran who presented a threat to many countries, but we still must go through the trouble to identify them. Courtesy would dictate they tell us."

He refilled his coffee, looked at my untouched cup, shrugged, and put the pot down.

"The coffee here is quite good. I didn't have to make any changes at all."

There was no need to respond. I didn't want coffee. I wanted him to keep talking.

"Let's talk about you. When I saw you back in 1971, I saw a man who had the potential to be of service to this country for years, not short term but long term. Everything you've done has been calculated for the mission I'm about to discuss with you."

Now he had my interest.

"It was not an accident your first assignment was directed to strengthening the security of our airports and air travel. The threat was real, and because of what you did, airport security is tighter now. It's also been no accident we've focused you on targets in the Middle East, specifically Iran. That country has been a threat for many years. I won't go into the history. You're aware of that. The threat is now becoming a reality. It's getting to a point where we'll have to act, where you'll have to act."

He let this sink in for a measured count, all the while looking for a reaction from me. I had none because he hadn't defined the threat, nor had he told me my role. I didn't ask but let him stare and waited. It wasn't time yet for dialogue.

"The Shah will be overthrown by the religious zealots. When? I don't know, but it will happen within the next two or three years. The Shah is aware as are the members of his government. You only have to look as far as Helen's father to see them preparing to leave the country. The Shah is preparing to leave the country."

"Why don't we step in like we did in the fifties and strengthen his government? Lend him support. Stand by him. Didn't we set him up and establish him as a friend in the region?"

"Yes, we set him up, but times were different then. We had the support of the Brits and most of Europe. Through back channels, we even had the support of the Soviets. Oil was the name of the game, and everyone wanted to play. Even the Israelis were playing. They sent thousands of their people to work in Iran, skilled workers who could have contributed greatly to the needs of a growing Israel."

"So what's different now?"

"In many ways things are the same, just at a different level. We always saw the country as basically unbalanced but at equilibrium, if that makes any sense. What I mean by that is there were always three factions in the country: the religious zealots, the people seeking a democracy, and those in the middle who wanted the best of both worlds. Unfortunately, it was never that simple because of the cultural difference between the Sunnis and the Shi'ites, a difference that extended to most aspects of life and government in Iran. The balance has shifted, and the result will be an overthrow of the Shah's government and establishment of a theocracy led by the religious zealots."

I'd heard this story before. Then, the words came from the mouth of Ahmed, a madman who had wanted the CIA to help him assassinate both the Ayatollah and the Shah, leaving a void he felt only he could fill as the new leader of Iran.

"Sounds like the world described by Ahmed if we didn't join him and make him the leader of the new Iran as he saw it."

"Ah yes. Ahmed, the man you assassinated because he threatened your sense of family."

Was he goading me, trying to provoke me? As I attempted to control my response, I looked around the restaurant. The early after-work diners had departed, being replaced with a more social crowd, mostly couples in contrast to the earlier business dinners being shared by middle-aged men trying to see who could drink more martinis, close the better deal, and still catch the 7:45 train home to Katonah.

"I believe I merely performed an act that was already planned. I moved the timetable up and changed one of the participants."

Anderson changed character. No longer the superior, he adopted the character of a friend and older uncle. "Jonathan, you're correct. I'm sorry if I've given you a reason to doubt the high regard I have for you. It is precisely that confidence I have in you that propels me to discuss the next assignment with you. Me, rather than Mr. Allen. He knows, but I want to impress on you how important the role I have for you is."

"Thank you, Mr. Anderson. I feel you haven't been honest with me for the past few months, and it's made me a bit testy."

"Straight shooting from here on. I'll get to the bottom line, and then we can work backward on the details. Your next assignment is to assassinate the Shah."

I was dumb struck. No, he knocked me off my seat. Not literally, but figuratively. Literally, I knocked over the water I was holding.

"You have got to be shitting me. Assassinate a head of state? I thought the Constitution, or the Bill of Rights, or something forbids that?"

"It does. You won't be able to assassinate him until he's out of office. And the word is 'forbade.'"

"That makes no fucking sense at all." I was beside myself. My voice rose just a little, and I caught the eyes of the nearest diners looking our way. I forgot the Russian cuss words Allen had taught me. It wasn't like I was fluent and they just popped in my head. Mine was a spontaneous reaction and had no time for the nicety of translating.

"Jonathan, please, you know I dislike vulgarity. You're an educated man. You don't need to talk like that."

"But the Shah is an ally, one of the strongest in the region right up there with Israel."

"Yes, he is one of our strongest allies in the region." He paused and then added, "For as long as he is the Shah of Iran. When he ceases being the Shah, he becomes a liability. A liability can't be an ally."

It was impossible for me to calm down. Anderson saw that and called for Thomas to bring him the bill. He merely signed for it—no cash, no credit card. Then we left, he leading the way.

Out on Second Avenue, sunset had the west side of the street in long shadows. The tops of the buildings on the east side were still bathed in light, a golden color at this time of day. Anderson had explained my assignment in more detail, not enough for me to make the "hit" anytime soon, but as much detail as I needed now. The final details were mine to work out. He and Allen and any resources I needed within the CIA would be made available to me, but the planning and execution, weird term now, were up to me.

Still trying to digest what he had told me, I walked north on Second Avenue toward Monika and home, a sanctuary of sanity I needed. He explained with certainty the Shah's regime would be overturned within the next twenty-four months to thirty-six months. He couldn't be more precise than that. With time, events in Iran would dictate a date, but for now, I worked off the twenty-four months. The Shah would fall to the religious zealots, most likely the exiled Ayatollah Khomeini. The coup would be bloodless, the Shah getting advanced warning and able to flee. His flight would serve the new ruler well. He would show the Shah fled with vast wealth stolen from the people of Iran, wealth he had taken from the West, principally the United States. The Ayatollah would use this to clamp down on all things Western and install Sharia law, the law of Islam, not the law of the West, not the law of the Shah.

The Shah was not an old man, but the rumors would be started that he was in poor health and gave up his throne because he was too ill to rule. He would seek asylum in the West under the ruse of needing advanced medical care. It was my job to make that illness real and fatal. I was to assassinate the Shah and make it appear he died of natural causes.

Anderson would initiate my assignment by taking advantage of the unique positions cultivated for me, namely, my consultancy with the CDC, and my position as an adjunct professor of medicine at Columbia. In addition, I would be invited to work on a joint program with the World Health Organization (WHO). This new responsibility with WHO would require significant international travel and elevate my status as a government and private-sector physician, giving me access to cutting-edge medical advances. American Pharmaceuticals would be asked to allow me to spend more of my time in this role and would readily agree. Any prestige that fell on me would reflect on the company.

There were lots of questions, questions Anderson chose not to answer. Rather, he told me he had decided for me to meet with Walt "Call Me Frank" Jackson. Walt had been my mentor at State Department during my CIA indoctrination several summers ago. The time spent with him convinced me the mission of the government, especially the CIA, was noble, and decisions based on well-grounded facts, facts that often got distorted by politicians seeking a fifteen-second headline on the evening news. But still, assassinate the Shah of Iran?

The Palm was just around the corner from my office, and I had gotten used to the one-mile walk from Forty-Second Street to the tram that would take me to Roosevelt Island and home to Monika. In fact, I preferred to walk and only took a cab between the office and the Fifty-Ninth Street tram station in inclement weather. My mood dictated the route I took. I'd take Second Avenue with all its frenetic New York City hustle—the shops, the people, and the cabs—most of the time. It was vibrant and connected me with the city. When I needed to decompress after a hectic day, I preferred the more residential First Avenue with fewer shops and fewer people. It even seemed to have fewer cabs, or at least cabbies who didn't practice full-body contact horn blowing. Tonight, after dinner with Anderson, I needed the tranquility of First Avenue.

Anderson had given me another assignment, one that promised to have profound consequences around the world. I had yet to be briefed by my mentor in State Department but knew in my heart the rationale for the assassination of the Shah of Iran would be based on sound facts and reasoning, and the world, or at least the United States, and the people I loved would be better off for it. That didn't bother me. What bothered me was the smiling face of Monika I would see when I arrived home.

I had a history of deceiving Monika. From the beginning, I hid my involvement with the CIA from her. Of course, I rationalized, it was a matter of national security, and she didn't have the need to know as defined by the government. But she had the "need to know" from a higher authority, our marriage vows and the love, trust, and honesty she thought we had. A love I shared for her. A trust I might lose.

The walk to the tram station near the Fifty-Ninth Street Bridge would take twenty minutes. At this time of day, the tram ran multiple cars to accommodate the commuters from the island to Manhattan. A quick three-minute ride followed by an even quicker descent to street level on the island and I would be minutes from home and Monika even if I walked and didn't take the "Red Bus," which provided free transportation to island residents. I would be home in less than thirty-five minutes, not enough time to resolve my problem.

When I got home, Monika was bubbly with all the news of her day and the latest of Eric's "firsts." I had gotten used to listening to these achievements of his, even looked forward to hearing about them. Tonight, it was different. Tonight, they seemed trite in the grand scheme of things. Today, he saw his first robin, smiling when his mother retold the story. Whether he was smiling because he remembered the bird or because of his mother's animated antics that accompanied the retelling of the adventure, it didn't matter. I wanted to shout out, "Hey, I had a first today. It was the first time I've been asked to kill a head of state. Yeah, the Shah of Iran." I didn't of course, but it put things in perspective. I was having a challenging time separating my three lives: pharmaceutical executive, loving family man, and CIA operative.

Chapter 16

It took but three days before my boss at American Pharmaceuticals called me to his office and informed me I was being loaned to the World Health Organization, not on a permanent basis, but for some consulting work. He couldn't control his pleasure the company had been selected for such an honor. Of course, I'd be expected to keep as many of my projects on schedule as possible, but he also made it clear that failing in the WHO assignment wasn't an option.

He gave me a letter of invitation from the WHO, directed to the company president, and a memo from the president, congratulating me on the assignment. All I had to do was say yes, and he would respond on behalf of me and the company. With my agreement, he told me a preliminary training session had been arranged on short notice for me in Washington beginning the following Monday.

On Monday morning, I arrived at the reception area of the State Department at ten o'clock, having taken the seven o'clock Metroliner from Penn Station in New York. The leisurely ride even included time for a light breakfast of coffee, juice, and a bagel in the dining car. The bagel wasn't very good considering the train originated in New York, home of the best bagels in the world. Mine tasted like it had been made in Denver four days ago.

I announced myself and waited for an escort. As I waited, memories of that summer five years ago flooded my mind. I had started the CIA indoctrination program at the Department of Energy, where I met Monika. When I moved to State the following week, the contrast between Monika and my escort there was dramatic. Walt "Call Me Frank" Jackson came to pick me up and sign me in, just as he had done five years ago. He hadn't changed much. Maybe a little more gray in the hair, although it could be he sorely needed a haircut and there was just more gray in more hair, or perhaps the greasy nature of an unwashed head made it seem that way. The ovoid body was a bit more ovoid than I remembered. The pocket protector was still there. His shirt looked like he washed it with the rest of his wash and wear clothes, but it wasn't wash and wear. It was a short-sleeve cotton thing that pleaded for an ironing. If we had met on a college campus, I would have thought him the typical absent-minded professor, more interested in things of the intellect than the material world.

Frank told me we were going to meet in a conference room he had reserved for a couple of days. As we walked the hallway to the room, I asked him why he preferred to be called Frank when his name was Walt.

"It's a long story, and we don't have time. If you want to call me Walt, feel free. Of course, I might not answer the first couple of times, but if you say it often enough and shout, I'll probably get the message."

I decided I'd call him Frank.

Once in the conference room, Frank settled into our work right away. There was the briefest of small talk—an inquiry about the trip and what I had been doing for the last five years, but no inquiry about Monika, someone he knew, or at least knew of. Nothing. There wasn't any coffee or water. In fact, there was virtually nothing in the room, just a large room with a large government-issued conference table in the middle, gray metal with a gray Formica-like top, a vestige from the fifties when it was one of the newest buildings on the Mall. Old gray metal chairs matched the institutional table. The only color in the room came from the rug, a green, short-napped synthetic fiber, worn by foot traffic and the occasional vacuum cleaner. The walls were bare—no pictures, calendars, or blackboards, just windows, holes that let some additional colors into the room. On a gray day, this room would be gloomy beyond gloomy. The only adornment was utilitarian—a black telephone, unique in that it had no rotary dial and no push buttons, intended for incoming calls only.

Frank began, "Jonathan, I'm going to review a lot of material you already know. By going over it, I'm not insulting your intelligence, your memory, or your understanding of the Middle East. I want to put you in a mind-set to accept the material I'll go over on Tuesday and Wednesday." Pausing only long enough for my nodded agreement, he continued, "In some ways, things in Iran haven't changed much since we spoke last, but then if you look closer, things have changed a lot."

I looked at him, my expression transmitting my thought. If things haven't changed much, why am I here being briefed for three days?

"There's always been turmoil in the Middle East, and the same can be said of Iran, but we've not had a serious interest in what's going on there until about seventy-five years ago. Why? Oil. That's when the West got interested and started paying attention."

Frank settled in, seeming to get more relaxed. He took a deep breath and looked around the room, seeing the nothingness we occupied, nothing to distract us. "Sorry, Jonathan. I know you've been through this before. So have I. I was in my Iran, Middle East, basic course mode I have to do for new members of Congress every year, who've just won an election and think they know everything. The briefings I give are a race to see how quick I can get through it. None of us want to be there, but protocol requires they get briefed. So I brief them. 'Brief' being the operative word."

"Understood."

"If you remember your history, Iran is one of the oldest countries in the world, an empire that goes back thousands of years. Persia in the older texts." Frank continued about their proud history, not that you'd know it today. "The people were bound by a common culture and, more important, a central ruling figure throughout that time. Like other countries, they had their problems; rich and poor, war with their neighbors. The whole region changed with Mohammad. A dynamic figure as profound as Christ in the impact he's had on world history. In a sense, he was the first unifying figure in the region beyond Iran, encompassing the whole of the Middle East. When he died, things changed. A split in the religion brought about the current schism between the Shiites and the Sunnis."

He shifted in his chair—slouching, sliding down, looking for a comfortable spot. He swung his left leg up over the arm of the chair and continued.

"Then the real problems began with the Great War, World War I. Before the war, cartographers had a hard time keeping up with the boundaries of the countries in the region. Hell, they had a hard time keeping up with the names of the countries. There were always wars, more like skirmishes, one sheik against another, multiplied a dozen times over. One would win, the other would lose, and the boundary changed. A marriage contract and lands would change hands. Didn't seem to make much difference to us watching them. Just exchanging one pile of sand for another. We couldn't understand the sand swap, but they sure as hell did. More important, we didn't understand the boundaries weren't national but tribal, or sometimes religious."

He went on about how the Germans brought the area into play when they sent the Ottoman army down and later got involved themselves. The Russians, English, French, and later the Americans saw the potential for a dangerous situation. If the Germans controlled the region, they'd have access to the rich petroleum reserves upon which Europe, and to a lesser extent, the Americans were becoming dependent. The Brits were more alarmed because they saw the Suez Canal in jeopardy and, with it, their colonies in India and the Far East, especially Hong Kong. The Germans weren't making direct attacks on India, but with the Suez Canal in their hands, cargo from India—including native soldiers England was depending upon—would be forced to sail around the tip of Africa, adding months and money to the trip, having a profound effect on the economy and their ability to wage war.

Frank was telling me the same story he had five years ago but adding a flavor to it I hadn't been exposed to then. This rendition was friendlier, nonacademic. It was Frank talking and me listening in fascination. He held my attention through something I thought would be a boring reiteration of the previous discussions.

"When the Allies realized what was going on, they came in and courted the local tribes, formed a big confederation to fight the Germans, and told the tribes if they didn't fight the Germans, they'd lose everything, and if the Germans didn't take over, the Ottoman Empire would. Remember our previous discussion about Major T. E. Lawrence and the role he had? Not just that they made that movie *Lawrence of Arabia* about him, but his ability to understand the region better than any man before or since. He gave the Allies the solution to land distribution after the war, and they threw it away. Instead of using boundaries respecting tribal ways, cultural differences, and natural-resource distribution, they took a ruler to the map and gave us most of today's problems. All those fancy diplomats were fucking amateurs compared to him. History doesn't do him justice, even today."

Frank had already made known his strong feelings toward Major Lawrence. He had instilled an admiration for the man during our first training sessions. The Arabs trusted him and fought for him against the Germans. Having read the works about Lawrence, I became convinced his role in the Allied victory in World War I was pivotal and greatly underestimated. Certainly not given the credit he deserved in the ultimate victory.

We talked for another hour, mostly about the boundaries Lawrence had drawn for the countries of the Middle East at the end of the war. Frank addressed each country's existing border and cited multiple examples of conflicts, big and small, that would have been avoided if the boundaries defined by Lawrence had been used.

At precisely 11:25 a.m., Frank stood up. "Lunch," he said and walked to the door. I hurried to join him. It didn't take more than getting up and following him because I had nothing to gather up. Frank provided no handouts, and I wasn't allowed to take any notes as was protocol for meetings with him.

"The cafeteria opens for lunch at eleven thirty," he said. "Today is Monday, so the egg salad is fresh this morning. They'll have it on the menu tomorrow, but it'll be left over from today. Doesn't taste as good. They put it in the refrigerator next to something that gives it a funny taste. Not funny ha-ha, funny peculiar. No egg salad on Wednesday, but they have it again on Thursday, but I think they make it Wednesday afternoon because it has the same funny taste on Thursday."

I didn't know what to say, so I said nothing. It didn't stop Frank from continuing my education on egg salad.

"I get there early, first in line at the sandwich station. The lady there knows I like egg salad and that I like cold egg salad, not warm. So she makes my sandwich from the top layer in the bowl, doesn't go deep into it. She can still make a thick sandwich just using the top layer." I nodded, imaging the poor lady suffering through endless lessons on the correct way to make an egg salad sandwich for Frank. Did he eat her mistakes and just gave more precise instructions the next week, or did he return an unacceptable sandwich? I let that question go unasked.

The doors to the cafeteria were opening just as we got there. With me following, Frank stopped at the tray rack and grabbed an empty one, some napkins, and eating utensils. I followed suit. Next he moved to the sandwich station and ordered an egg salad on white, not toasted, with three strips of bacon, crisp but not burned, a little mayo, a little lettuce, no tomato, sliced on the diagonal. The lady behind the counter was the sweetest looking grandmotherly type I could have imagined. Central casting in Hollywood couldn't have done better. Her gray hair in a net, starched white uniform crisp, she smiled as Frank recited his sandwich order. She waited until he finished before beginning the assembly. He watched as she applied a thin coat of mayo on one piece of white bread, looking up to gain his approval. Then several scoops of egg salad, evenly spread across the other piece of bread, again gaining his approving nod. Three pieces of bacon, each selected and approved by Frank before she placed them on the sandwich, followed by the joint selection of perfect piece of lettuce. Once assembled, she selected a knife and carefully cut the sandwich on the diagonal. I've done this myself and always squeezed a lot of the sandwich filling out. She didn't. Placing the sandwich on a plate, she lifted the plate to the counter and passed it to Frank with a smile. Did I hear Frank's salivary glands do a Pavlovian slam as he accepted the sandwich, or was it my imagination?

Frank moved aside but stayed at the counter, waiting for me to place my order. I'm not stupid, and I do like egg salad, so I said, "I'll have the same, please." The sweet angelic smile faded for a fraction of a second before she assembled my sandwich, looking to Frank for approval at each step.

She finished, but before she lifted the plate, she asked, "Pickle?"

Before I thought, I responded, "Yes, please." Her smile broadened as she placed a kosher dill spear on the plate next to the sandwich.

As I brought the plate down, Frank handed me a napkin saying, "Don't let the pickle juice get on the bread, or the sandwich will be ruined." Accepting his napkin, I placed it on the tray, removed the pickle spear from the plate, and placed it on the napkin. While he didn't smile, his frown became neutral. The sandwich lady smiled and winked at me.

Chapter 17

⁂

After lunch, we returned to the conference room. The twitching that had marked Frank's behavior in the morning was gone, replaced with a quiet satiation. He sat comfortably at the table, up straight, a gleam in his eyes. I attributed his earlier fidgeting to his anticipation of lunch and his beloved egg salad sandwich. During lunch, there was little conversation, Frank more interested in his sandwich. Frank might be quirky, but God knows I'd be too if I had his job. All things considered, an obsession with a sandwich once a week was a small price for our country to pay to have such a talented man working for us.

Frank dedicated the afternoon to a continuation of the refresher course he began in the morning. He covered the relative peace in the region following World War I up to the start of the Second World War. During the interim years, there were tribal skirmishes, no less and no more than before the artificial boundaries had been drawn. There was a difference. These new conflicts were more purposeful, trying to regain ancient lands, favored grazing land for the nomadic tribes, or water. Oil was a factor, but to the mostly poor wanderers who inhabited these countries, they needed to feed their herds and families.

Frank began, hands at ease in front of him, "War didn't come to the Middle East in 1939, when Hitler began his conquest of Europe. In fact, except for a German presence to the west in Algeria and Libya, the Germans weren't much of a factor in the Middle East. The Allies thought the area would be a major target like it had been in World War I. The spoils were the same and thought to be even more important: the Suez Canal and the oil of the region. In anticipation of a major campaign by the Germans, England, and later, the Americans deployed large forces in the area. The Germans never came that far east. This may have been Hitler's plan for an easier conquest of Europe. With a large force in the Middle East, England had little to offer for the defense of Western Europe."

I enjoyed this renewed Frank. He was the man I'd come to admire when he first indoctrinated me years ago. He sat erect in the chair, shoulders square. Even his shirt was less wrinkled, probably due more to the warmth of the day and the humidity of Washington than anything he had done. I suspect part of his enthusiasm was due to the subject matter having a more direct impact on current events.

"Mussolini sent planes on bombing missions, but he wasn't a match for the Allied forces waiting for him. Hitler had planned to invade the area from the west, get control of the Suez Canal, and then move north through Palestine as a back door to the Russian oil fields. But for all intents, the war in the Middle East was over in 1943 when Rommel's forces were defeated. If Germany had been successful in Russia, things may have been different." This last statement, Frank punctuated with a shrug of his shoulders and a look that said, "But who knows?"

Frank's brief description of the area during World War II was an eye-opener. I had been a fan of *The Rat Patrol* on television in the midsixties. The show chronicled the fictional exploits of American and British soldiers raising hell with the German troops in the desert, often taking on tanks with machine guns mounted on Jeeps, doing their damage, and retreating over the nearest sand dune. I incorrectly assumed sand was sand and had no understanding of the limited area of combat action in a limitless Sahara Desert. So much for learning history from television action shows.

"After the war, there were a lot of areas where things got worse before they got better." He was getting closer to the time frame and events he enjoyed. "Berlin and Korea to name two." Pausing, he waited for me to say something. A question maybe. "In the Middle East, and again I'm including Iran in this, even though it technically isn't part of what's described as the Middle East, things didn't get worse before they got better. Do you know why, Jonathan?"

"Probably because the war had such little impact on the area?" I responded.

"Wrong. Because things in the Middle East never got better. Do you know why?"

"No." I was here to learn and wasn't going to keep guessing if I didn't know the answer.

"Once again, after the war, the winners got to divide up the conquered lands. The Jews wanted and deserved a homeland. They wanted to live in Palestine. I don't blame them; it was the land they lived in before everyone started persecuting them centuries ago. The Romans started it, and they'd been homeless ever since. Problem was the Palestinians already lived there." Frank stopped, looked around the room, and then said, "There's no water in here. They should have put water in here." Looking at me, he asked, "Do you want some water?" I nodded yes. Maybe talking about the desert made him thirsty.

Frank left the room and came back with two bottles of Nehi orange soda. He leaned across the table and gave me one. No explanation for the soda rather than the water. No question of whether I like Nehi orange. Frank liked it, and that's what mattered. He sat down, the soda bottle in front of him, looking around for something. He thought for a minute. Standing, he took the soda and placed the lip of the cap against the edge of the metal conference table and gave the top of the bottle a sharp rap. The cap flew across the room. I smiled and rose. Handing me the opened bottle, he said, "You looked amused when I did that, like you've not done it. Practice on your own time." With that, he repeated the move with his soda and sat down. A long pull of the cold drink and he started talking again.

"It wasn't like the Jews just decided to go there at the end of the war. No, it started long before then. At the end of World War I, the British promised the Jews a homeland in Palestine in writing. It was a weak document that made the promise, but it was a start. As weak as it was, it pissed off the Palestinians, who were already calling it home. Between the wars, the Brits allowed the Jews to settle in Palestine. The numbers were small, just a dribble." Frank leaned forward, a finger pointed at me, and said, "You'd think if the Jews were so intent on making Palestine their homeland, they'd be buying up the land, wouldn't you? Well, they didn't. By the end of the 1930s, they had about twenty percent of the population but only six percent of the land. I've not been able to find out why. This discrepancy always bothered me." As he said this, he scratched the side of his face and had a brief moment where a far-off look crossed his face. It struck me this was a problem for Frank, he didn't have an answer. It showed vulnerability I hadn't seen before. Not the fact that Frank didn't know something. I'm sure there were lots of things he didn't know. Rather, seeing it bothered him if he didn't know something. His fingers drubbed a few times on the table; he leaned back again and continued.

"In 1939, the Brits wrote what became known as 'the White Paper.' This allowed the Jews a specific number of immigrants into Palestine each year, ten thousand. It appeased the Jews who now had a number to work with, and it appeased the Palestinians to a degree. They thought of the Jews as infiltrating Palestine, sort of illegal immigrants. This put a cap on the immigration."

He sat up straight. Seated, he appeared less ovoid. Getting more interested in what he was saying, I guess he was out of his "brief the freshman members of Congress" mode. "Here's where it gets interesting. The Brits had set Palestine up as a kind of protectorate. They called it a Mandate, but, you know, it was a colonial thing for them, making the Jews and Palestinians feel they were incapable of governing themselves. Same thing they did in India. This made both resent the Brits, and they both did their share of sabotaging the British contribution to the war effort. Not to the point where victory was in jeopardy, but more like they were trying to keep Palestine in a state of flux. The Jews and Palestinians never aligned with each other, proving the adage 'An enemy of my enemy is my friend' wrong. There were enough enemies around for everyone."

I had to ask "But the Jews got the bigger piece of Palestine after the war. What did they do to win that concession from the Brits?"

Frank looked to the window, not looking out the window, just toward it. He was pondering something. He got up, walked to the window, and looked out across the courtyard in the direction of the mall he couldn't see, just the dome of the Capital Building off in the distance. I don't think he was looking at that either. I don't think he was looking at anything in particular, just walking and thinking. He turned back, his face a dark blur, a silhouette, the bright sun of the late-spring day behind him.

"Jonathan, that's a great question. The answer's not necessary for us to continue, but still a great question. It's something you should perhaps consider on your own. Come to your own conclusions. We can discuss it later if you want. Not this week but…later. Okay?"

"Sure," I said. A strange response from Frank. Frank did everything for a reason. When I had the answer to the question, I'd talk to him. More importantly, I'd find out why he wanted me to come to my own conclusion and not give me the "company" answer, or his answer. Perhaps, they were different.

Frank continued going over the establishment of Israel as an independent state. Up to the point of independence, Frank said "Jews," but from that point on, he said "Israelis." What a well-ordered mind he had. As a physician, my mind wandered, wondering about the wiring of his neurons, the structure of the cells, the synaptic neurotransmitters, the number of glial cells, the density of the neuronal sheaths, and any of the other complex anatomical or physiological differences that could account for his well-ordered mind and superior intellect.

Following an explanation of the beginnings of the State of Israel, he went over the history of Israel to the present day, including the numerous conflicts and the major wars, but was less detailed than five years ago. No doubt this was because he probably remembered every word he said then and didn't want to bore me or himself with another recitation of the same material. While he spent less time on the Six-Day War and the Yom Kippur War, he added information on the first war the Israelis fought after gaining their independence. It was an extension of the civil war against the Palestinians that gained them their independence. It continued for another year, formally ended in 1949 with a peace accord that existed only on paper, but continued for almost a decade with skirmishes. His brief oral history took the rest of the afternoon, with one break for the men's room and another round of Nehi orange soda.

Frank ended the day. "That's it for today. Between what we talked about five years ago, and what you got today, we're up to date on the region and ready to talk about the Shah and Iran. We have two more days on the books, but I'm hoping we can wrap it up in one. Then we can both get back to work." A pause, a telling look, and he continued, "Of course, if you need more time, you've got it. I haven't been read in on your mission, but based on what I've been asked to cover, I think I've got it. So I'll do the best I can to prepare you for it. Okay?"

"Yeah. Thanks. How will we know if I know enough?"

"I'll know." And with that, Frank took me back to the reception area. "Early start tomorrow. Be in reception by eight."

"Got it." I said good night to the back of his head as he disappeared down the corridor.

Chapter 18

✳   ✳   ✳

E xiting the State Department building on C Street, I hailed a cab to the Mayflower Hotel. It was a beautiful late-spring day, and I would have preferred to walk after being stuck in the oppressively stark conference room all day, but I didn't know where the hotel was. When my secretary was making my travel arrangements and asked me where I wanted to stay, I paused. During my previous summers in Washington, I stayed at the house over by the Capitol, and I only knew three hotels: L'Enfant Plaza, because it was next to the Energy department where I had met Monika; the Shoreham out by Rock Creek Park, where even if it wasn't too far away, it was the place I had gone with Brooke Thanksgiving weekend in 1971. That left the Mayflower, where I had lunch with Mike Allen once, and I didn't know where it was.

The driver headed toward the Ellipse, past the White House to Connecticut Avenue. Traffic was heavy. Washington at quitting time. The streets were full of cars, buses, and cabs. The sidewalks were full of people. At intersections, pedestrians and vehicles competed for the same space—vehicles squeezing into an intersection just as the light changed, blocking pedestrian crosswalks. Roles reversed when the light changed, with pedestrians running against the light. A small-town budget could be filled in just a week with fines for blocking inter-sections and jaywalking.

Entering the Mayflower's cool lobby, I experienced the elegance that has been greeting guests for decades. The dark wood, bright brass-and-marble floor, which had welcomed kings and presidents, welcomed me. The liveried staff, friendly, gracious, and helpful treated me like one of those past dignitaries. I looked around the elegant lobby, expecting to see someone important, but I didn't recognize anyone. The clerk at reception verified my reservation for two nights and gave me the key. A bellman took my small bag, led me to the elevator, and showed me to my room on the seventh floor, room 700.

Room 700 was a two-room suite on the corner. Moving the curtains aside, I looked down on the traffic on Connecticut Avenue. The living room was comfortably appointed with a sofa and several chairs, one with a pedestal lamp beside it. No mistaking that chair, perfect for reading. The television was a new twenty-five-inch Sylvania color unit, set in a bookcase that took up most of one wall. The bookcase sagged from a full load of books, a decent mix of classic literature, and a few new releases. The bedroom was elegant—dark furniture, a queen-size bed, another television, and another reading chair. The bathroom was a typical hotel bath, the only exception being a pair of white terry cloth robes hung on hooks behind the door.

I decided I'd stay in for the night. A phone call home to Monika, room service, and a fluffy robe in front of the television seemed perfect.

In the morning, a cab back to State had me in the lobby at seven fifty-five, where Frank waited. At first, I didn't recognize him. As I was signing in at the reception desk, he approached. I looked up, thinking someone wanted my attention. Only when he said my name did I recognized him.

"Jonathan, you're early. Good. Let's grab a coffee before we start."

I stood staring. The voice was familiar, but that was all. Before me, Frank had changed from the sloppy man I had known into a middle-aged, middle-management businessman. From top to bottom, he stood transformed. His hair, still long even for the style of the day was clean and combed. A dark-blue suit stood in contrast to a gleaming white shirt that looked like it had just come out of the store wrapper. A conservative blue-and-gray striped tie accented the rest of his outfit. Black shoes were like the Florsheim Imperial loafers I wore.

Frank let me stare for a long minute and then said, "I have a meeting with the DCI later today," and turned with a nod for me to follow.

DCI was a term I had heard before, "Director, Central Intelligence." It was used in two ways as the person and as the office. I didn't know which way he was using it. Grabbing my pass from the receptionist, I ran to catch up with Frank.

"When I meet with the DCI, I do a lot less explaining if I dress the way they do. Seems a disheveled exterior means a cluttered mind." He looked at me for a sign or agreement. "I, on the contrary, find their minds are cluttered most of the time with things I don't find important. Things like budgets, politics, the party in power, the next promotion. What's important are the facts."

We got coffee from the cafeteria and continued through the other side to an elevator.

"I apologize for the conference room we used yesterday. It's one used for visitors, hence the bareness of the room. We leave nothing in there that may be of use. The starkness of the room, combined with my basic lecture on the Middle East may have been responsible for a few lapses in your concentration. Today we're going to a different room." He stopped in front of a room near the elevator we had just exited. "Today, and if necessary, tomorrow, it's critical you absorb every detail I tell you. No distractions." With that, he opened the door and entered.

What a difference. While not the boardroom back at American Pharmaceuticals, it was several steps up from the one we used yesterday. The conference room table was well polished oak with comfortable high-back chairs on wheels. The walls had the obligatory picture of President Carter and Secretary of State Cyrus Vance. An American flag stood in the corner, next to a podium. The windows had drapes that could be drawn, making the projector and roll-down screen at the far end of the room more effective. There was a sideboard with a coffee service and a tray of Danish. The room also had a white-board and an easel. Carpeting, while worn was clean, the marks of a vacuum still visible. It even smelled different, not musty but clean.

Frank went to the sideboard and took a cheese Danish. "I forgot they automatically set this room up with coffee and Danish when reserved. Help yourself."

"I'm good," I said, holding up the coffee from the cafeteria.

Frank had been standing, and now he sat, his coffee and half-eaten pastry in front of him. "The Shah, his name is Mohammad Reza Pahlavi, is an enigma. As a kid, he was one of eleven kids. Had a twin sister. His old man became Shah after the First World War. He was a big guy, and by all accounts a prick. Didn't seem to have a close relationship with his son, even though he was the presumed Shah. The kid was short and timid, raised mostly by his mother and the women of the court, but still had an attitude because he was the Crown Prince of Iran. The father sent him to a French high school in Switzerland, first time that happened for the ruling family in Iran. Mohammad got beat up there and wasn't aggressive enough for the school's football team. While there, it seems his only friend was the son of the gardener, a homosexual who became kind of a bodyguard. The kid brought him back to Iran when he finished school." Frank looked up from his coffee cup to see if I had a reaction. I raised my eyebrows, not at the fact he made friends with a homosexual, but because he brought the guy back to Iran.

"Make of that what you wish. That's part of the enigma. The old man was a macho guy, and the kid known to be something of a ladies' man, and yet he did that. Can't figure that one out. Maybe he just wanted to piss the old man off. Anyway, the guy, his name was Perron, remained with him, living in the palace, a major influence on him."

I had to ask, "Was the Shah a homosexual?"

"No one can say either way for sure. He married in 1941, had a daughter, but divorced in 1945. The whole time he was married, he chased other women openly. He married again in 1951, and this one lasted until 1958 when he married his third wife soon after, and they're still married. A lot's been written about whether he's a homosexual, but it's all conjecture. It doesn't seem to make any difference in what he did or didn't do, just part of the enigma. He may just have felt more comfortable around this guy, having been raised by women." Frank shrugged. It really didn't make any difference to him.

"The kid was short, and wore elevator shoes. Don't know if it was to be more like his father, or he wanted to be taller. Most of the women he chased were tall. Maybe it was as simple as that."

He continued, "As a young man, he had three passions: flying, women, and the history and culture of his country. He loved planes and was qualified on jets. Doesn't fly like he used to, but he still has the interest in planes. I don't know if he still chases women. It doesn't make any difference for you. Just background. Neither planes nor women will help you get close enough to him for your assignment."

There it was. Frank knew I had to get up close to the Shah for my assignment. He showed no emotion. It was just a statement of fact.

Frank reviewed the history of Iran during the fifties and sixties, touching on the nationalization of the oil industry, the coup, and the assassination attempts. He reminded me of the involvement of the United States with the Shah, supporting him in regaining and retaining his throne.

"The Shah's other passion, the history and culture of his country, may not seem germane, but I think it explains a lot of his behavior and may even account for the changes in recent years. Even though his family was only in the Shah business for two generations, he took his cultural heritage seriously. He considered himself more of a Persian than an Iranian. You may not think of them as different, but it's like an Italian thinking about the glory days of the Roman Empire and considering himself more of a Roman than an Italian. Hell, in 1971, he put on a massive celebration of the twenty-five-hundred-year anniversary of the Persian Empire." Frank paused and looked to me for understanding of the distinction.

I nodded acknowledgment of my understanding, and he continued, "Seems he embraced this to distinguish himself from his father. You see, he looked at Iran as merely the modern name given to Persia, and when he looked at Persia, he saw the oldest continuous empire in the world. An empire thousands of years old, older than the Romans, and greater than any empire had ever been. And he was right. His goal, and everything he did, good or bad, was to make Iran a world power again. He began a modernization program on the good side, and he used the SAVAK to secure the country from any obstacle to achieving that goal. He had a plan he didn't share with anyone in any detail. It was probably a plan that had another twenty years to reach completion. By the early 1970s, he had already transformed the nation and proven himself a world-class leader if not a world leader. And then things changed. He accelerated his plan and, in doing so, alienated the religious right and the moderates in his country as well as the other member states in the region."

Frank paused here, stood up, took his jacket off, and draped it across the back of the chair next to him. He brushed off something he saw on the shoulder of the suit jacket. I could see his shirt was new. It still had the fold marks. He had no pocket protector.

He remained standing and continued talking. "This acceleration of his plan started in 1973 with the OPEC oil embargo. When you think of accelerating a plan that requires lots of money, it makes sense. Oil prices were skyrocketing, and he figured he'd take advantage of it by ignoring his OPEC partners and sell at the inflated price, filling the country treasury and lining his own pockets. Of course, this pissed off his OPEC partners, who had voted for the embargo, but he didn't seem to care. He was driven to achieving his objective."

I felt Frank was leading me to question the reason for the acceleration of the plan. "Frank. Right. That was just a few years ago. Iran was powerful. They had stood up to the Middle East oil producers, and sided with the West, providing oil, even at inflated prices to avoid an even worse economic crisis. The press hailed him as a hero of sorts. Didn't the Brits get a big loan from him to get them through the tough times?"

"Yes, Jonathan. He was, and he extended credit not only to England but to other European countries that needed a boost to their economy. The Shah was on the verge of making Iran the world power he dreamed of. Some say, he had achieved it. But he wanted more."

Frank walked to the window where a large spider plant hung in a macramé noose by the window. He played with the "babies," holding them against the breeze from the air-conditioner vent in the ceiling.

He turned back and said, "I think at this time he realized he was sick, really sick, and didn't have the twenty years he needed to complete the plan he had for Iran. It was his legacy, and he didn't want to leave it unfinished, or to be finished by someone else."

"He was sick?" I asked.

"Yes, but let's begin that after lunch. I'm afraid my meeting this afternoon won't allow us to finish today. Just as well. It's important. We'll use the time well."

With that we went off to lunch. Frank was quiet during our meal, explaining he needed the time to run through his presentation for the DCI in his head one more time.

Chapter 19

After lunch, back in the formal conference room, Frank began, "The Shah has cancer. There's been no announcement, and there's no speculation out there, but that's what I think. It would explain the acceleration of his plan, and I believe his treatment would explain some of his erratic behavior. I'm not a physician, let alone a cancer specialist, but that's my gut feeling. I've discussed my suspicions with cancer docs, not telling them why I'm asking them of course, and they've said nothing contrary to change my mind. Comments?"

"Well, Frank, I'm not a cancer specialist either, so I'm not sure I can help you. What's your diagnosis based on?" Diagnosis was not the proper term to use with Frank, but it was the vocabulary I knew as a physician.

"Hardly a diagnosis, Jonathan. More of an educated guess. Let me take you through the process as it unfolded for me. Can't tell you why I was watching the Shah. Just know the things I'm describing evolved over the course of the last five years."

Was it just coincidence my indoctrination with the CIA, specifically Frank, began five years ago? Has Frank been studying the Shah and Iran in preparation for my assignment, the assassination of the Shah, for the last five years? Is this the reason the CIA wanted me as a physician?

"When I began studying the Shah, I did a lot of the background stuff on him. Very detailed examination of his early life. Much like we went over yesterday, just more detail. Thought I had a good handle on him and figured I knew his long-range plan: a return to glory for Persia on the world stage and a place in history for him right alongside Cyrus, Alexander the Great, and Julius Caesar, maybe bigger. Then the oil embargo thing. So unlike him because he had become an accomplished diplomat, and this was not diplomatic. This was a power and money grab. Why?"

Frank hadn't sat down yet, or taken off his jacket, but paced at the end of the table, reliving the process as he told me.

"I went over everything I had on him. Just the current stuff, the last four years. That's where the answer was. I was sure of it. Took me a while to find it. The Shah was a traveling ambassador for Iran, going all over Europe and the Middle East on a regular basis, and all that time he traveled with his wife. Except beginning in early 1973, he stopped taking her on his monthly trips to France. That was it. He must have had a girlfriend there, or maybe even a boyfriend. He had taken a lot of heat in his youth from the religious leaders in Iran when he was running around. Figured he was screwing around again, drinking, and gambling. After all, it was the rage for a lot of Muslims in the early seventies. I had the hook now, but I had to figure out how it was responsible for his change in behavior. So I sent one of our men in France to tail him on one of his monthly trips." Frank stopped pacing directly across the table from me.

I was fascinated with his performance. I was seeing Frank's analytical process, taking me through the steps he went through to reach the conclusion he shared with me. Unlike his other presentations that were just a recitation of detailed facts, he was excited and animated.

Frank continued pacing and talking. "The trips were always to a hospital in Paris. Always the same hospital." He stopped again and looked at me and pounded his fist into his open hand. "Thought I had it. Visiting a foreign doctor without his wife. Figured he had a venereal disease—syphilis or the clap. But when I checked into those diseases, I found out he didn't need to see a doc every month. Could've gotten some pills. What else could it be? So it wasn't just the hospital; I had to find out which doc he was seeing."

Frank had reached the far wall, turned, and started back toward me, his face pensive. "The Shah saw a doc named Jean Bernard, a well-known hematologist, who was also a bacteriologist, a guy who treats infections." He looked at me and got a look that said I knew what a bacteriologist was.

"Sorry. Forgot for a minute. Of course, you know, but at the time, it confused me. I asked around and connected the two. Figured he had a blood infection, maybe malaria or something. Got me sidetracked for a while. I checked further into Bernard and found he had left that world far behind. So much for looking things up in old reference material. Bernard had moved on. He had become a specialist in cancer, specifically leukemia. One of the leaders in this field."

By this time, Frank had walked around the table and stood alongside of me. He pulled his chair out and sat down. "I was close. It was his spleen. It was enlarged." This time he paused before he continued. Looking at me, he continued, "Of course, you know an enlarged spleen is usually a sign of something else. The trips to Paris stopped, but Bernard started going to Tehran. Bernard wasn't a young man. In addition, he had a full plate being an expert in his field. He couldn't be at the beck and call of the Shah, so he brought his assistant, Dr. Georges Flandrin. They did the tests they do in these things and concluded the Shah had chronic lymphatic leukemia or CLL. The Shah's doctors convinced the French doctors to tell him he had something else, serious, but not cancer. Seems the Shah feared the word. The French docs told him he had Waldenstrom's disease. He had been on prednisone, so they increased the dose and added a cancer drug."

I interrupted Frank and said, "Ah, the prednisone would account for some of the abhorrent behavior. It causes mental confusion and mood swings in some patients."

"Yes, I learned that. Just forgot to mention it now." He continued, "The Shah's wife never knew. She and everyone else in the palace were led to believe the docs were discreetly treating someone else, probably his friend Perron for something. So the cancer was a big secret. No one knew, not even the Shah."

Frank moved toward me, sliding the chair closer in a conspiratorial way. "You'll understand this better than I did. The charade was a dangerous game they played because it kept the Shah from getting proper medical treatment. A fear of seeming weak to his subjects was the reason his docs gave the French docs. Anyway, the Shah, convinced it wasn't a fatal disease wasn't very diligent in taking his medications and skipped a lot. In 1975, he had a crisis, and they told him he had to take it more seriously. They increased his meds, limited his activities, and Flandrin made the trip from Paris to Tehran every month or so to do blood tests and monitor the Shah's condition."

Frank stopped talking, looked at his watch, and said, "Jonathan, I'm sorry, but I have to leave. We should stop now, give you a chance to think about what I've said, and finish up in the morning. Then we'll have time to talk in detail about anything that's not clear. That okay?"

"Sure. I think that's a good idea. There's a lot to think about. What time do you want to start in the morning?"

"How about nine?"

"See you then."

With that, Frank grabbed his suit jacket from the back of his chair and walked with me to the front desk. He left me to sign out, leaving through the revolving door for his trip to the DCI. When I got outside, he was nowhere to be seen.

The afternoon was still young, and the weather was delightful, warm, sunny, a slight breeze, so I decided to walk back to the hotel. There was no hurry as I had nothing to do until tomorrow morning. Frank's history lesson was still ringing in my ears. When he started, I wondered why we were doing it again, but his manner and subject matter were spot on to help me understand the situation and get me back into a positive frame of mind. The world was even more dangerous than it was five years ago. The mission I was preparing for would be as important as the hijacking; of that, I was sure. I would kill again, but this time it wouldn't be personal.

The weather was pleasant—light fluffy clouds and warm. The temperature hovered around eighty degrees, but unlike summer in Washington, the humidity was low, so a leisurely walk wouldn't drench me in sweat. I followed the route the cab had taken yesterday, pausing near the Ellipse, just to take a rest, not to enjoy the oasis of green in this city of stone buildings and monuments. Only one detour on my way back to the hotel, a turn to the right onto

Pennsylvania Avenue at the Old Executive Office Building for a look at the front of this venerable old building. Up close, it wasn't as majestic as when seen from the back seat of a cab. The stone walls, a light-gray granite when new, were dark and dirty. A disappointment.

To wash that image from my mind, I continued on Pennsylvania Avenue to the White House. The building was striking as I imagine it will always be. Gleaming white, windows sparkling in the afternoon sun, all sitting in a park of green accented with flowers of red and white. On the grounds, the shade looked cooler than it was. Certainly cooler than the heady business being conducted inside by President Carter and his staff. As I stood in front, I wondered if anyone in the building was working on problems of Iran—or were Anderson, Frank, and I the only ones? If we did our job, maybe there wouldn't be any Iran problems for the Carter administration.

The next morning Frank met me at reception—no suit, no tie, but no wrinkled shirt either. His hair still had the sheen of yesterday, not the shine of Monday. The pocket protector was back. There was no small talk as we walked down the corridor. As we walked, I tried to determine his mood. If we went to the cafeteria, could I expect the animated personable Frank? If we went straight to the Spartan-like conference room of Monday, my expectations for an enjoyable day would diminish—still informative, but more tedious.

Frank didn't stop at the cafeteria. Rather, we went straight to the bare conference room, but to my surprise, a coffee service had been laid out, complete with pastries. He motioned me to join him at the coffee. I freshened my cup and took a small raspberry Danish. As we moved to the table, I asked how his meeting went yesterday. He gave me a questioning look.

"With the DCI?"

He answered only with his eyes and a nodding of his head, indicating it went okay. Nothing verbal. Curious or cautious?

We spent the rest of the morning going over some of the things on which I needed more detail to help me see the mission better and help me formulate a way forward. As we broke for lunch, I asked if I would have any contact with him after today. Frank smiled.

"Jonathan, this is more important than the hijacking in 1971. You were trained for six months before that event. There's a lot you still have to learn, but I'll leave that for discussion over lunch."

As we left the conference room, Frank ran his fingers through his hair, took the pocket protector out of his pocket, and left it near the coffee service. We walked to the cafeteria in silence, following the noon crowd. Instead of queuing up in the cafeteria line, we went left into a private dining room, where Mr. Anderson was waiting for us.

"Jonathan, I thought we'd have a little quiet for our lunch. Here, sit next to me." A strange request as the round table was set for three, equidistant from each other. Anderson neither stood, nor offered his hand, just the seat. I chose the one on his right. As I pulled the chair out, my religious upbringing kicked in. I thought, seated at the right hand of the father. Did I really think of him as a god?

He continued, "I've ordered for all of us. A simple meal. Soup and salad. Navy bean soup. The same soup they're serving up on the Hill today as they have for about the last seventy-five years. The secret is the mashed potatoes, they say."

With that, a side door opened, and a navy steward emerged, rolling a serving cart. On it was a large soup terrine, three modest bowls, three salads, and assortment of rolls. After serving us, the steward left.

Anderson started on his soup. After the first spoonful, he asked me to summarize the situation in Iran and with the Shah as I now understood it.

I began while he and Frank continued eating, stating simply the Shah was ill, probably with terminal cancer. Iran was in chaos even though it was not apparent to the outside world, and the Shah was likely to be overthrown within the next two years and replaced with a conservative Muslim theocracy.

Anderson wiped his mouth with his napkin and asked, "Should we intervene and save his government from being overthrown?"

"No. His usefulness to us as an ally is gone. He was a balance in the region. A Muslim country we could support. We can't continue to support him because his reign is doomed. There's no one to replace him who's friendly to our interests. We must distance ourselves from him, or those who come to power will take their revenge on Israel."

"What will happen if he survives his cancer?" Anderson was staring at me now, head tilted slightly, examining me.

I looked to Frank, who was concentrating on his soup, and answered Anderson, "It makes no difference what happens to the Shah. Whether he lives or dies, his rule is over. If he lives, there will be supporters who will fight for his return to the throne, but it's likely they'll be hunted down and eliminated by the new government. It would be best if he didn't survive his cancer. With no one to replace him, there'd be no opposition. The transition would be seamless, with the violence directed inward, to remove the modernization he brought about."

Anderson looked to Frank and said, "Well done, Frank. You've taught him well." Then a question to me. "How's your French?"

"I don't know. I took the basic courses in high school and college, but I've never used it outside of the classroom. Why?"

"We're sending you to WHO headquarters in Geneva for a month or two. Consider it an orientation meeting. It's already been cleared by your company in New York."

"A month or two?" Seemed like a long time to be away from the job and even more so from Monika and Eric. He answered part of my concern by telling me the company had already given the okay. But the family, that's a different story.

Anderson once again demonstrated his amazing skill at reading me. "Of course, you can bring your wife and son. I understand your wife has relatives in Germany whom she visits every few years. She's due for a visit, so it should be welcomed news for her."

He was right; Monika had talked about a trip to Germany.

"But let me continue. At WHO, everyone speaks English, so you'd get by, but if you spoke French, it would separate you from the other Americans. Make you more acceptable. During your secondment at WHO, I'd like you to spend some time in their Paris office. After an introduction to Drs. Bernard and

Flandrin, regular visits to Paris would give you the opportunity to get in the inner circle of the Shah's medical team. I have every reason to believe you'll be a welcome addition to the people treating him." This last statement was made with a twinkle and a smile. I'd bet the time and place for my meeting with the Shah had already been put on his calendar. "The Shah prefers to speak French with his physicians, so…"

I nodded understanding, and he continued. "Because I sense you're not comfortable with your working knowledge of French, I think it would be appropriate to send you to the DLI school in Monterey, California, for an intensive one week refresher course to start, and then more as needed until you feel comfortable. The Defense Language Institute at Fort Ord is one of the finest in the country, maybe the world. You should take Monika and your son with you. She may enjoy spending a week with her sister in San Diego rather than remain alone at home in New York." The twinkle appeared again as he shared his intimate knowledge of my extended family. "If additional training is needed, either in French or current cancer therapy, it'll be provided before we send you to Geneva."

It was settled. I would get a refresher course in French, take Monika and Eric to Europe for a month or two, and begin planning the death of the Shah, either by accelerating the natural course of his disease, or by intervention where I would directly cause his death.

Chapter 20

When I returned home Wednesday evening, I took Monika to dinner at Piccolo Trattoria, the little Italian place on Roosevelt Island. She had fed, bathed, and tucked Eric in by the time I got home. The lady on the floor above came down to watch him, disappointed he was asleep already. She was a grandmother, but her children lived in Tucson, and she saw them infrequently. Eric had become a surrogate for them.

I was tired, my mind full of competing thoughts I hadn't resolved on the three-hour Amtrak ride from Washington.

The pleasant walk to the restaurant invigorated me. Living on Roosevelt Island was easy, and we had grown fond of the small-town feel of this community. The noise and the congestion of the city were just across the river, but the surrounding sounds were almost pastoral. No taxis blaring horns or any vehicular traffic because of the car ban on the island. As we walked to the restaurant holding hands and talking, I was content for the moment.

After the hostess seated us, Monika told me her news—Eric's newest discovery, events at her parents', and the neighborhood gossip. Then she asked about my trip. She had gotten used to me being brief and abrupt about my work, and she accepted my simple answers of "good," "okay," and "the usual" without pressing for details. This time my response was different.

"The trip was good. Busy. Part of it was getting the necessary paper work filled out. Despite this being something sanctioned by American

Pharmaceuticals, its sponsored by the US government. So I'm going over in my capacity as a consultant to the CDC, and needed to get training in the dos and don'ts of a government employee working in a foreign country."

Monika reached across the table and took my hand; a smile formed on her lips. "My husband, the diplomat. God, Jonathan, how quickly things have moved for you these last few years. When we married, we were struggling as a fourth-year medical student family with a baby on the way. Soon you'll be off to Europe representing our country. Now the important stuff; where are you going, and how long will you be away from us? I know it's important, but I do miss you so when you're gone." A look of concern replaced her smile as she took my hand in both of hers and squeezed, emphasizing her point.

Now it was my turn to frown. "The assignment is at WHO headquarters in Geneva. I'll be there for a month or two, depends on the work and how I do. It could be longer. Depends." Now my frown faded, replaced with a broad smile. "I'm sorry. I said that wrong. We'll be going to Geneva for four to six weeks," I said, pointing first to her then to me. A moment of confusion, followed by a broad smile that lit up her face.

"All of us? You, me, and Eric?"

"Yes. They're making arrangements for an apartment in Geneva for us. If you'd like, we'll be able to visit your family in Germany on the weekends, or you can spend some extended time with them if business takes me away from Geneva. I'm already committed to several trips to Paris, and I won't have any free time when I'm there."

"Paris. How wonderful. That might be when I visit family. But do you know enough French to get by for a week?"

"No. Just some high school and college French. The State Department is sending me to the Defense Language Institute in Monterey for a week's intensive refresher course. After that, they'll see if I need more."

"Monterey in California?"

"Yeah. Would you like to come along? We can fly into San Diego and visit your sister; then I'll go on to my school and either come back down and join you, or you can fly up to Monterey, and we can fly home on Sunday from San Francisco."

Grabbing my hands again in hers, she beamed. "Oh, yes. I can't believe the wonderful time we're going to have. A week with my sister in sunny California. Let Eric see the Pacific for the first time. It'll be his first experience with the sand and the ocean. Then off to Switzerland. I can't wait to tell my mother. Maybe she'll be able to go over for a little bit. She can meet me in Germany and then come back to Geneva for a few days. Watch Eric so we can enjoy Geneva."

The rest of the meal was a celebration. We ordered a bottle of Asti, the closest thing the restaurant had to champagne. When we got home, Monika checked in on Eric and then joined me on the couch. "Do you remember the first time we made love?" she asked as she sat down next to me, holding my hand, her head on my shoulder.

The mere mention of those earlier, less complicated times, when the only secret I kept from her was the hijacking of an airplane, allowed me to fall farther into the comfort zone that had been developing all evening.

"Yes. I do. You surprised me. I thought I'd die of semen backup."

She poked me in the side and laughed. "I wasn't sure until then. You were so mysterious, showing up at Energy for an indoctrination. You had no connection to any government agency. That usually means CIA, but you were just a medical student. I couldn't figure you out. Then I stopped trying, and when I did, I saw the real you."

I held her tight, feeling guilt creep back into the comfort zone. No room for guilt in the comfort zone.

"Then, when you got back to New Haven, I got the sense you were withholding a part of yourself from me, but I chalked it up to the pressure of your last year in school and the pressure of a family and starting a new career. It never really disappeared. There always seemed to be a part of yourself you were holding from me. You travel a lot, but I've never been invited."

This conversation was making me uncomfortable. I felt I had to say something but before I could, Monika snuggled closer, held me tighter, and continued.

"But now, all that mysterious zone is gone. You're taking me and Eric on a wonderful adventure with you. It'll be perfect. Come on," she said, standing up and pulling on my arm. "I need help getting out of these clothes."

When I arrived at the office the following morning, a lot of wheels had already been set in motion. My secretary Angela gave me a handful of pink "While you were out" call slips and an itinerary for my trip to Monterey and the DLI. The reservations had already been made for the three of us—me, Monika, and Eric—for San Diego on Saturday with a flight for me the following day to San Francisco. A car would meet me and drive me down to Monterey. Monika and Eric would join me in San Francisco the following Saturday and a return flight for the three of us to JFK on Sunday morning.

"Who made the decision we'd leave from San Francisco?" I asked.

"Don't know. The in-house travel department called when I got in this morning. I didn't even know you were going to California, Jonathan. If you've got an issue with someone, that someone isn't me." Angela was reacting in kind to the curt tone I had used on her. We had worked together for almost a year. She was a valuable colleague, and I usually treated her as such.

"Sorry, Angela. This trip came up while I was in Washington. Monika and I hadn't decided on the return trip. I guess I was annoyed someone had decided for us without asking."

"Do you want coffee before I ask you anything else?" she asked, half playful, half serious.

"Yes, please. My treat this morning." As I reached into my pocket for money, she held her hand up.

"Don't bother. There's still enough in the kitty for both of us. There's even enough in there for an 'I'm sorry, Angela' bialy for me. In fact, with you gone for the rest of the month, there's enough to treat me for the next week." I gave Angela twenty dollars at the beginning of each month to cover my coffee each morning from the cart that came up from the cafeteria. At fifty cents a cup, there was more than enough.

Angela came back with my coffee and a glazed doughnut. Placing the doughnut on my desk, she ended our minor dispute. "Eat it," she commanded. "Sweetest thing they had. Hope it works."

I took the hint and a big bite—unusual because I never ate doughnuts or bagels at work—chewed it noisily, and sighed. "Ah, perfect. I feel better already. How do I look?"

"Take another bite just to be sure," she said with a big grin. She sat in the chair in front of my desk and asked, "So what's up, Doc?"

Angela had reverted to the cartoon version of herself, so I knew all was well again. She was smart and a great secretary. A graduate of the Kathryn Gibbs Secretarial School, she knew how to be "proper" as defined by the almost-Victorian rules drilled into her at Katie Gibbs. But she was also a street-smart Italian lady from Queens. These street smarts gave her more maturity and self-confidence than the twenty-three years she listed on her driver's license. Of course, the whispered rumor her family had connections to the Mafia could be a reason for her self-confidence.

"The CDC has volunteered me to WHO for four to six weeks, and the company agreed. Think it reflects well on them. The CDC wants me to brush up on my French because most of the people at WHO headquarters speak it."

"Don't most people speak English these days? And where and what is WHO?"

I laughed. "That's funny!" I said. Angela just looked at me, trying to fig-ure out what was funny. I anticipated her next question and my response, and laughed harder even before she asked it.

"What's funny?"

"WHO's funny" was my laughing response. By now, my laughter had attracted attention. I shared Angela with John, who occupied the office next door.

John stuck his head in my door and asked, "What's so funny?"

I was still laughing when I answered, "WHO."

When John asked "Why?" I lost it.

I blurted out, "Why's on second."

Poor innocent Angela. She looked at John then at me and continued the skit without knowing what she was doing. "What?" she said, both hands going up, arms bent at the elbow, the equivalent of an Italian question mark.

John was in his early forties, already bald, a big nose and an even bigger sense of humor. He was a product of the public-school system of New York City twenty years before Angela and had an appreciation for the early days of televi-sion comedy that she didn't. When he smiled, his mouth widened, and his eyes got big as saucers. With no hair on top, it lit up his face and made his laugh infectious. "What's on second." Boom, he said it. I was laughing so hard I thought I'd pee myself. John was laughing now too. With the two of us laughing, Angela started laughing without knowing what she was laughing at. People outside of the office were staring at us, some smiling, others laughing. Not as hard as we were, but they were laughing. Angela got up and closed the door.

"What is wrong with the two of you?" she asked between laughs.

"Sorry, Angela," I said, trying to explain. "The conversation became a take-off on an old Abbott and Costello routine. It really isn't that funny. What makes it funny is how it fit into the conversation we were having. And then when John joined in. Well, I guess you have to be as old as we are to appreciate it."

Angela sat back down. "I still need an answer, and I'm not going to say any of those pronouns again."

"WHO is the World Health Organization in Switzerland," I offered.

"I've heard of that. Sounds like a big deal. What about the other thing, the CDC?"

Before I could answer her question, John offered, "You can't see the sea from there. It's Switzerland."

We both looked at him, understanding what he said and the intended joke, but neither wanting to continue the silliness. He put up both hands in mock surrender and opened the door. As he left, he turned and said over his shoulder, "I think it was funny, see da sea."

"And the trip to California?"

"That's where I brush up on my French, the Defense Language Institute in Monterey."

"Well, Boss. Looks like you're a rising star. Hope you take me along with you to the top?" Her statement had the inflection of a question.

Angela shifted in the chair, uncomfortable with her question going unanswered. "When do you leave for Switzerland?"

"Don't know. Someone else will decide it, like the California trip. You'll know before I do."

"What do I do while you're gone? Just work for John?"

"Yes, that makes sense, but I'll make sure you're here for me when I get back." That seemed to comfort her.

The itinerary for my trip to Geneva came in later in the day. I'd be leaving the second week in September. The delay was necessary to accommodate the August vacation schedule in Europe. Seems everyone in Europe took the month of August off, and business on the Continent virtually closed. The only commerce was providing for the vacationers.

Monika spent the next week making all the plans necessary for our visit in San Diego as well as for the family visits in Germany. Her mother, delighted to be invited, planned to spend four weeks in Europe, mostly with family in Germany but with flexibility to join us in Geneva when Monika wanted her.

Chapter 21

The trips to California and Geneva took on a sense of adventure and togetherness lacking since our move to New York. Monika and I decided to get into the spirit early and celebrate with dinner. She met me at the office just before six after I had spent the afternoon in a meeting. She didn't come to work often and seemed overwhelmed with my new office. On the sixteenth floor, it occupied the northwest corner with a spectacular view of midtown. The most predominant building being the Citicorp Building to the northwest on Lexington and Fifty-Fourth Street. The sloping roof line was an immediate attention grabber. To the southwest, the art deco spires of the Chrysler Building seemed almost within touching distance. As she looked to the east, straining against the north-facing window, she could see the United Nations Building.

She gasped at the sights, overcome by one then another as she moved from corner to corner, looking at the lesser buildings, seeing New Yorkers in their apartments living their lives, unaware, or not caring they were being observed. A man and woman sat on a penthouse balcony enjoying an early-evening dinner. Directly below, on the roof of a parking garage on the north side of Forty-Third Street, a film crew was dismantling a set they had used during the day to shoot photos of a hot rod, complete with a scantily clad model.

"Jonathan, how can you possibly have your office set up this way?" Monika stared out the window, her hands clasped just under her chin. Turning, she became animated, her arms stretched out, pointing to the skyline visible from my window. "The magnificent view is behind you with all those glorious, interesting things going on out there."

"That, my dear, is precisely why my desk faces the door. Still, I do find myself staring out the window at times. Too bad I don't do more negotiating in this office. The people who sit in the chair facing that view would be very distracted, and I'd win most of my arguments."

Monika sat in the visitor's chair and agreed.

"As nice as this view is, I'm sure there are others that are even better. Can you imagine an office overlooking Central Park, or an office at the top of the World Trade Center? In the upper level of the Trade Center, you can feel the building move in a strong wind, and you can see the planes landing at JFK on a bright, cloudless day. Imagine the thrill of being so high you can see airplanes that appear to be at eye level."

I watched Monika enjoy the view for a few more minutes and then reminded her we were already late for our early-dinner reservation at Bruno's Pen and Pencil. Exiting the building on the north side, we were only two blocks from the restaurant on Forty-Fifth Street, just east of Third Avenue.

Bruno's Pen and Pencil was one of the original restaurants known as "steak row," a group of steak houses that had become popular in midtown in the forties. Like the Palm, it catered to the newspaper and publishing crowd. The "Pen and Pencil" was a carefully chosen name reflecting their clientele. It remained one of the last independent steak houses of that bygone era, being supplanted by high-end chains like the Palm or Smith and Wollensky. Even the new Sparks, which opened this year on Forty-Sixth Street, had the potential to be a chain as the second restaurant opened by the owners.

Monika chose the restaurant after a careful review. She was driven by two primal urges. She considered herself a native New Yorker, born and raised in one of the five boroughs, so the restaurant had to be authentic New York City. Second, she was a meat eater. Despite her delicate appearance, she had a huge appetite, a fact I realized the first time we had lunch. Her preferred meat was beef, copious quantities of rare beef. In their Queens home, her father had built a fire pit and smoker in the backyard for smoking sausages but soon saw the benefits of the open fire for roasting meats. Monika grew up eating beef grilled over an open flame, something she couldn't enjoy on the fifth floor of a two-bedroom apartment on Roosevelt Island.

Entering the restaurant was taking a step back in time when New York City restaurants were supper clubs, often seeing the same neighborhood patrons several times a week. The place was small, again typical of the style in its heyday. The bar on the right as we entered was more of a service bar than a point of congregation. Only two stools were available. The maître d' welcomed us and took us to our table, one of twelve tables for four on the right side of the room, facing six tables for two on the left side. Mirrors covered both walls, creating the illusion of a larger space. Candles on the table reflected through multiple images in these mirrors added to the illusion.

"Jonathan, don't you love this place?" Monika asked as she reached across the table to touch my hand. "So elegant and yet so simple," she said, the slightest squeal of delight in her voice.

"Thank you, madame," said the maître d' in a humble tone, the tone a host would use if he were complimented on his home. Placing a napkin on Monika's lap, he asked if we cared for a cocktail.

"What was in when this place was popular?" asked Monika.

Humility still in place, he responded, "Madame, whatever the drink of today is. The Pen and Pencil is still a most popular place to dine. However, if you are asking what the popular drink was when there were several restaurants, the restaurants of 'steak row' of twenty-five years ago, I would suggest a daiquiri."

"A daiquiri it will be then, and thank you for understanding what I meant." A smile accompanied Monika's apology, and the maître d' left, replaced by our waiter, bringing rolls, butter, and water. He returned soon after with our cocktails.

Monika raised her glass, waiting for me to make a toast. It was simple and sincere, "For you, my love. The best is yet to come."

We both ordered Delmonicos, hers very rare, mine medium rare, a Caesar salad for two prepared tableside, and a bottle of Cabernet Sauvignon.

Lingering over a second cup of coffee and Bénédictine, we agreed the restaurant was a perfect setting, a step back in time for us, just what we needed before we set out on the future. We spent the evening enjoying each other's company without the distractions of work or parenting. It reminded us of the days when we dated. During the meal, we agreed to a date night at least once a month, just the two of us, no Eric, no double dates with friends.

By the time we left, darkness had descended. I suggested a cab, but Monika wanted to walk, feeling we could burn off some of the calories, but more important, allow the magic of our evening to last a little longer.

"Perfect. It's a short walk, only about twenty minutes to the tram, maybe a bit shorter. We can walk over to First Avenue, coming out near the UN, and then up to Fifty-Ninth." Monika took my arm in both of hers, and we headed east toward the river.

While I made this walk several times a week, I always started at Forty-Second and Second, walked east through Tudor City to First Avenue. Forty-Fifth Street wasn't as brightly lit as Forty-Second, and there were no people out walking. Monika held me tighter as we walked through shadows. I sensed a growing tension in her as we moved to the center of the block.

"You seem anxious. Let's turn around and go up Third and then across at Fifty-Ninth," I suggested.

"No, no. I'm fine. My friends and I used to walk around Queens all the time. I'm just so used to the small-town feel of Roosevelt Island."

Not convinced, her anxiety caused me to heighten my alertness. Monika was a city girl, tough as nails, but something was making her uncomfortable.

"Let's walk down the middle of the street until we get to Second Avenue. Then we can go up from there and not have another block of this to go through. The street isn't as nice as First Avenue, but it'll put you more at ease, and that's what's important."

Walking on the inside, she didn't speak but started to turn me between a car and panel truck parked on the street. I looked to her to say something calming when I saw a dark shadowy figure within the even darker shadow of a porch. It moved, and my eyes caught the reflection of something thin and shiny in his hand in the limited light. A glance to Monika's face, and I saw my concern turn her face to fear. Before either of us could move, the dark shadow emerged from the protective cover of the porch and moved toward us, the shiny reflection now clearly a knife. The figure, large and dressed in dark clothes including a dark ski hat, moved clumsily. I pulled Monika across me, putting myself between her and the approaching menace.

"Run to the street," I said as I braced myself for an attack. "Run down the middle of the street, and don't stop until you reach Third Avenue." My eyes had scanned the surroundings, looking for an accomplice before I sent her off. She skirted between two cars parked at the curb, and I could hear her start to run as I turned to face the attacker.

The shiny knife was now raised to chest level as he approached, and I focused on it. I put my right foot forward, standing sideways with my arms raised to my chest in a defensive position. He tried to get around me and run after Monika, perhaps thinking she was the easier target. As he did, I stepped again and brought my leg forward, raising both hands toward the knife in his left hand. Trying to charge past me, my move caught him off guard, and he tried to avoid me by moving to my right. This would bring the knife closer to me, but before he could bring it down, I used his mistake to my advantage, catching him while he was slightly off-balance. Old hockey instincts clicked in as I continued to push off with my left leg, propelling the right side of my body into a vicious body check. As I moved forward, I crouched, getting my shoulder under his arm, lifting him and pushing him backward, sending him to the ground. He hit hard, his butt and back first then his head. Most men wouldn't get up from a fall like that, at least men not wearing protective headgear. As he tried to get up, I kicked him in the face, not as hard as I could but hard enough to make his head snap back, hitting the sidewalk with a dull thud. The knife was still in his hand, and he swiped wildly at the air as he went down, trying to incapacitate me with a wound to my legs or groin.

While he was down, I hazarded a quick glance down the middle of the street toward Third Avenue to make sure Monika was safe. I didn't see her and panicked. The assailant was again trying to get up, angry, shouting, "You motherfucker. Now you're going to pay. You and your little bitch." This man was crazy or high on drugs. Twice his head had bounced off the sidewalk, and he was still trying to get up. There was no more time to waste on him; I must find Monika.

As he was raising himself on his elbows, the knife was no longer a threat, pinned to the ground by his hands assisting his moves. With his head no more than six inches in the air, his throat was exposed and vulnerable. I pivoted on my left foot and slid forward, my right foot at an angle like I was doing a quick stop after skating fast. The foot came down in the exposed portion of his neck. Even in the noise of New York City, traffic on Third and Second Avenue, horns from taxis and buses, the occasional squeal of brakes, I could hear the snap of his neck as the pressure from my foot overwhelmed the muscle and tendons holding the bones of his vertebral column together. Through the heavy leather of my Florsheim Imperial loafers, I could feel the grinding of the cartilage of his windpipe being crushed. The last noise he made was a death rattle gurgling through a mouth filling with blood.

Pivoting on my right foot, I strained to look up the street for Monika, caring little for the additional damage I was doing to our attacker's body. He was dead. I didn't see her in the street or up near the corner at Third Avenue where I expected her. My eyes followed the path I thought she took, down the middle of the street, focusing on the shadows and the spaces between the cars and trucks, hoping against hope she wasn't struggling with an accomplice. My panic rose as I scanned the street from the corner back to my position in the middle of the block. Then I saw her, not ten feet from me, between the two cars where I had last seen her running away.

Monika stood, both hands at her mouth, head bowed forward, fear, worry, and panic in her eyes. I moved to her, grasped her by the shoulders, and asked, "Monika, are you okay?"

She didn't answer at first. Then she dropped her hands and looked at me. "Jonathan, did you do?"

"Are you all right?" I asked again, this time firmer but not louder. She seemed in a daze. I shook her shoulders enough to get her to focus on me and what I was saying. I repeated, "Are you hurt?"

Her eyes moved to mine, "I'm not hurt."

"Good. Let's get out of here. Back to Third Avenue. Now."

She resisted momentarily then turned and let me lead her away. We stayed in the middle of the street, not convinced our assailant was by himself, and maximizing the distance between us and the shadows on the sidewalk. Reaching the relative safety of lights, crowds, and traffic of Third Avenue, Monika stopped and faced me.

"Jonathan, what just happened back there?" While her voice was calmer now, she shivered from fear on a warm New York evening.

I reached out to hold her close, to console her and to warm her, but she put her hand on my chest, wanting an answer.

"We were just attacked by a crazy guy with a knife. He was not a nice man, Monika. He wanted to hurt us."

"What did you do?" A concerned look came over her. A look that made me feel like she was looking at me for the first time and didn't like what she saw.

"I just reacted. I thought of him hurting you, or both of us. I thought of Eric left in the world without us, and just reacted."

"Have you been trained to fight like that?" she asked, deeper concern on her face, furrows forming on her brow and around her eyes, each probably representing another question, another doubt, another thought about this unknown side of her husband.

"No." An honest answer. I hadn't received any training in hand-to-hand combat except the basic stuff in Army Basic Training, and the only part of that I remembered was the "rear strangle take down," which I hadn't used there. Instead, my defense had come from years of playing hockey. The initial contact was a classic body check. "No. I think I just reacted. The things I did were things that became natural when I played hockey."

"Including stepping on his throat? Did you learn that in hockey?"

"No. That was personal. I didn't want him to get up. I didn't want to think about him coming after you or Eric." As I took Monika by the arm and turned her north toward Fifty-Ninth Street, the tram, and home, I remembered my first kill. It had been personal too, to protect Monika and our yet-to-be-born son, Eric.

Chapter 22

Monika and I walked home in silence. No need to talk. Both knew what the other would say. Had I been vicious? Yes. Why? Because I didn't want him to get up and hurt you. Did I kill him? Don't know, probably. Talk about what I had done would come later after we settled down from the assault. To discuss it now was futile.

After a restless night, neither of us sleeping much, lying next to each other careful not to touch, I got up at ten minutes to six. Eric continued sleeping soundly, and I was careful in my morning ritual of shower and shave to make as little noise as possible. Passing on coffee for myself, I prepared the coffee pot for Monika. All she had to do was turn it on.

At the island-side tram station, the only *Daily News* available was the bull-dog edition. Ignoring it, I walked to Grand Central Station and picked up the morning edition as well as copies of the *Wall Street Journal* and the *New York Times* and a coffee and headed for the office. Once there, I closed the door and started reading the papers, the coffee untouched, growing cold on my desk. On the fourth page of the *Daily News*, there was a small item, less than an inch of column, which reported finding a young, white male dead on the two hundred block of Forty-Fifth Street. No details and no speculation. Nothing in either of the other two papers.

I busied myself with routine work for the rest of the day, my mind occupied with what I might read in the afternoon papers or see on the news tonight. These thoughts were overshadowed by the image of returning to face Monika this evening. I left the office at four, headed back to Grand Central, and picked up the afternoon paper, the *Post*. Altering my regular route home, I went up the escalator and exited on Park Avenue. With more discipline than I thought I had, the paper remained unopened until I got past Fifty-Fourth Street and found a building entrance with planters and benches. A convenient, safe place to sit with a crowd.

Even after sitting, I resisted to urge to grab the paper and scan it for headlines and pictures. Instead, I took it, and like I had all the time in the world and trying to waste some of it, began reading it. Nothing on the first three pages, but on page four, an article expanded from the morning story in the *Daily News*. The afternoon paper repeated the description cited earlier and added the victim had a broken neck and crushed windpipe from apparent violent trauma to the throat. The police didn't have a motive as he had several hundreds of dollars on his person as well as his personal jewelry. They were seeking potential witnesses.

I sat for several minutes staring at the page, the words bringing to life my actions of the night before. I had acted on pure instinct, defending myself and Monika. While I had no formal training in fighting or self-defense, twenty years of playing hockey made me no stranger to violence. As a hockey player, I was aggressive, often described in my teens as the "baby-faced brawler" for my eagerness to drop my gloves and mix it up. But last night was different; the feeling was different. When Monika fled up the street and the assailant was on the ground, I could have followed her to safety, but I didn't. Instead, I moved in for the disabling blow and then the stomp on his throat. I knew his exposed throat presented a kill shot, and I didn't hesitate. The strike with my foot was vicious. And afterward, I felt no remorse, nothing. Nothing until I noticed Monika standing there horrified at what she had witnessed. Then, I had feelings of remorse, not for the killing but for the torment she went through witnessing what I did.

Now, I had killed twice with no remorse either time. Justified kills. Good kills. I wasn't a brawler anymore. I was an assassin!

Picking up my briefcase and the newspaper, I resumed my walk home, depositing the paper in the nearest trash. A street person grabbed it before it had settled, to resell in his quest to acquire the price of a pint of cheap wine.

When I arrived home, I found Monika sitting on the couch, the day's newspapers, morning and evening, spread on the coffee table, the local news on the television. Without a word, I sat beside her. Looking at me, she took my hand in both of hers.

"Jonathan, we must talk about last night. Not about the assault, but about you. I saw something in you last night that frightened me. You're a kind, loving man to me, to Eric, and to everyone we know. Yet last night you turned into someone or something, cold and ruthless, viciously beating that man." Her voice quickened. "I can understand your reaction to us being attacked and how you wanted to protect me, but I can't understand how you could be so cold about it, while you fought him and after..." She paused, looked down, and continued, saying the words that were difficult. "After you killed him. Even after, as we walked home, as I held your hand, my finger was on your wrist, and your pulse was normal. Mine was racing, but you were calm. I don't understand this, Jonathan. Help me understand," she pleaded.

What could I say? I had asked myself the same questions all day and again as I read the account in the *Post* article. I had no answer then, and I had no answer now.

"Monika, I don't know why I stayed so calm. Believe me, I've been thinking about it all day. I should be jittery. There should at least have been a sustained increase in my heart rate from the fight, but I could feel it become normal before we got to Third Avenue. I should have a sense of fatigue after the huge adrenaline rush during the attack and the fight, but I didn't, and I can't explain it."

"Jonathan, you're talking like a doctor, measuring pulse and heart rate. I'm frightened about what I saw in here," she said as her hand moved to my head, touching the forehead as if it were the site of emotion. "What do you feel now?" she asked, squeezing my hand and searching my face for some sign.

"Nothing. I don't feel remorse for killing him because he could have harmed you. It feels the same as when I was working the emergency service at Yale. Life-and-death decisions. Two people in a car accident. Both require immediate attention, and by immediate, I mean within seconds. There's only me, and I can only save one. Making that decision, I let the other die. Did I feel bad? Yes, but I saved the other." I looked at her for understanding. There was none.

"But, Jonathan, this was different. You didn't let someone die by doing nothing; you made someone die. You killed him."

At that moment, I had nothing to add, but I continued, "Monika, I know, it's crazy I don't feel anything, but I'm not even worried I'll be questioned by the police, or they'll suspect me."

"The police were here today," she declared.

"What?"

"That's the first real emotion you've had since we left the restaurant last night." She moved her fingers to my wrist. "Your pulse is up, not as much as it should be. I suspect if I checked it in another minute it would be back to normal. This isn't normal, Jonathan."

"The police were here! What did they want? What did they ask you? Why did they come here?" I remained agitated because I didn't have answers.

"Two detectives came here. The maître d' gave them my name because I made the reservation and had to leave a phone number. When we left, he saw us turn east on Forty-Fifth Street about the time of the"—she hesitated again— "the incident. As part of the routine investigation, the police questioned all the businesses in the area open last night."

Even at this intense moment, I admired Monika's thought process. She answered all the questions I asked in a clear, concise manner despite her agitation. "What did you tell them?"

"That we did turn left but saw there was a street light out halfway down the block and decided to turn around and go up Third Avenue, which was well lit. Then they asked if we saw anything, and I told them we saw nothing unusual around the restaurant, and of course the middle of the block was dark, so if there was anything there, we couldn't see it. We could see the lights on Second Avenue, but the block is long, and we wouldn't have been able to make out any detail if something was going on. They seemed satisfied and didn't ask any other questions. They didn't ask for your phone number at work, and they didn't say they'd be back." She sat up straight and looked at me. "There, that answers all your questions. Now it's your turn to answer mine."

"Monika, I don't know. There's nothing to add to what I've already said."

She sat staring at me for a long minute and then gathered the day's newspapers from the coffee table, straightened them, and placed them on the counter to take to the laundry room later. There, the janitor had set up a bin for newspapers and magazines. He'd collect them, bind them in stacks of about ten pounds, and take them to a junkyard near his home, adding several hundred dollars to his income each year.

Monika returned to the couch and stood in front of it. "That's the end of our discussion of the assault on us. If the police return and we're under suspicion, we'll have to tell the truth. It was self-defense, Jonathan. Of that there is no doubt. We'll only have to deal with the viciousness of your response. Even if we don't have to resolve that aspect with the police, we have to resolve it between us."

"Monika, I've already said what I can about it. Where it came from, I don't know." Despite my words, or perhaps because of my words, I was troubled. The look she gave me said she understood.

"There's more to this than just the vicious nature of your response. Back when we first met, when you came to the Energy department for your briefing, I was at once attracted to you, and I did a background check on you." She waited for a reaction from me, but none came. "The result took a few weeks to come back, arriving after you had moved on and after our weekend in Rehoboth. I ignored it for a while, but when I looked at it, it surprised me. Not at the content but rather at the time the security check had begun. I expected it to have been recent, perhaps during the last year. But that wasn't the case. Most of the initial documents were dated 1969, and one was 1968. I could understand the 1969 documents as relative to you starting at the Pentagon, but not the one from 1968. When I checked closer, even the 1969 documents predated your Pentagon assignment, and some predated you even being drafted. Somebody was checking you before you were a soldier."

This surprised me. "Is that unusual?"

"Very, and I didn't know what to make of it, and I couldn't ask anyone about it. I didn't want to bring attention to you or me."

"Would that be bad? Seems like you were just doing your job."

"With most people in my situation, you're right. But remember my background. My German parents survived World War II in Germany working for the German government. Then they came to this country. If whoever got alerted to my inquiry about your file did their job right, they'd do a background check on me and probably my family. My parents came to this country on a special pass from the Occupation Forces in Germany, sort of a gift for services rendered. The routine background examination wasn't conducted. This might seem curious to someone, and if they looked into it, it could be bad for my parents, and I didn't want to take that chance. Besides, by the time I had this information on you, I thought I'd never see you again, that you'd be someone else's problem. Then, a year later, you show up on my street, watching my house, looking for someone to share an ice-cream cone." At last she smiled. "How could that sweet young man be involved with anything? I let it drop, falling hopelessly in love with you. Did I make a mistake?"

"No."

"That's not all. I didn't sleep last night and thought about this all day. I was so worried, I thought we might have to get away, go into hiding. It was crazy, I know. You're innocent, you defended us, but I wasn't thinking clearly. The first thing I did was to call our financial advisor to see how much money we had."

"You called Jeremy?"

"Yes, and you know what I found." This wasn't a question. It was statement. I knew what she learned from Jeremy.

"Jeremy told me we had over three hundred thousand dollars in various accounts." She paused, waiting for a response from me. "That's more than two years' salary, and you've only been working two years. Where did that come from? What are you doing, Jonathan?"

This was the moment I dreaded, and it was worse than I had ever imagined because it was not only the money but the incident last night.

"Monika, you must trust me. I can't tell you anything right now. Let me see if I can straighten this out." I was lost for words. There was nothing I could tell her without violating my secrecy agreement.

"Did you steal it?"

"No."

"Are you selling drugs, taking bribes, skimming from the research grants, betting the horses? Oh, Jonathan. This is maddening."

"It's none of those things. Just give me some time and trust me."

"That's not enough, Jonathan. There's more." She paused, looking down at her hands folded on her lap now. A deep sigh from well within her and then a look that penetrated my soul. She continued, "I've spent the last twenty-four hours thinking about this, not just last night, but our life together. I realized there's always been more money than there should be. The other married medical students lived at a poverty level, even those whose wives worked. Yet we lived in a nice town house. We never struggled for rent, food, tuition, or anything. When I wanted to visit my mother, there was always money for a train ticket and spending money to take her to lunch. And, and I repeat, Jonathan, our bank account was growing all the time. This has been going on for a long time before we met. This has the flavor of government involvement. Are you working for the government?"

Chapter 23

✳   ✳   ✳

During the following week, Monika busied herself with preparations for the trip to San Diego, shopping for clothes for herself and Eric. "California stuff," she said although she had never been to California. It was the Queens, New York interpretation of West Coast-style based on what she had seen on television. I hoped she was right because she bought me casual wear for my day in San Diego and week in Monterey. Her mother gave her several gifts to bring to her sister, Jennifer, gifts she considered too big or too awkward to mail. When I saw the pile of stuff growing on the living room floor of our small apartment, I seized the initiative, took the bulky packages to work, and asked the boy in the mailroom to ship them ahead at my expense. Monika called her sister and told her not to acknowledge the gifts until after we arrive.

The flight to San Diego proved uneventful. Eric slept most of the way and didn't fuss until we started the descent. Probably his ears. We gave him a lollipop to suck on for takeoff but had forgotten one for the landing. Next time! Next time, Monika would be on her own on the flight to San Francisco.

The brief time with Monika's sister was pleasant. I had seen her only once, at our wedding. She scheduled a few days off during Monika's visit. She had a list of tourist activities for them with the zoo set aside as a day for Monika and Erica when Jennifer had to work.

With no direct flights from San Diego to Monterey, I canceled the earlier reservation and flew into San Jose, rented a car, and drove down to the DLI. With perfect weather, I enjoyed the ride.

San Jose's airport is close to downtown. There's not much to see that's different after driving away from most major airports in the country. Down Route 17, things started to change as soon as I left Los Gatos and approached the foothills of the Santa Cruz Mountains. From a distance, these hardly seemed like the mountains I knew from the East, the Adirondacks, the Green Mountains, or the Presidential Range of the White Mountains with majestic Mount Washington. These in this part of California were more like mountains named by people who lived in the desert. If they appeared in a painting, they would be described as primitive, not peaked but rounded as if deposited by a massive ice-cream scoop. Here and there a tree, but mostly barren of all but grass. A geologist could tell me the correct origin of these unusual formations, but I preferred my ice-cream-scoop theory.

As fascinating as the hills were, the road through the mountains was more so. It took the path of least resistance, meandering between the valleys of the rounded hills, following nothing more than the original game trail of eons ago. I passed through no towns of note, merely clusters of houses, some close to the road, others further back. I imagined early settlers staking a land claim, raising a family, and adding houses as children matured, married, and started their own families, staying close to work the common land. All these clusters of houses had clusters of old pickup trucks decorating the properties. In another place, these discarded vehicles would be called junk, but here they could only be classified as adding character. The contrast of these hillside communities to those I knew to be on the ocean less than ten miles away was stark. There was a peacefulness and sense of belonging to the land here that couldn't be manufactured or purchased. It merely was, and then it wasn't as I descended on the other side of the mountains and saw the majestic Pacific ahead of me.

In Santa Cruz, I turned north and drove what easterners called the Pacific Coast Highway, what locals called the Coast Road, and what is shown on the map as California Route 1. The afternoon was waning, and I had to be in Monterey soon, but I couldn't pass on the opportunity to ride this noted highway. I only drove as far as Davenport, a metropolis on this stretch of road at six city blocks long before I felt compelled to stop. Driving to the northernmost part of town, I parked the car and rewarded myself with a root beer float, which I took to the far side to the road as I enjoyed the view of the Pacific Coast.

The world is just a collection of dirt, rocks, water, and air. Put together in the right circumstances, they can support life. Evolution says life emerged from the combination of these basic elements. Those who believe in God need only visit this part of the world to see these components in their purest form, needing only man to marvel at their wonder.

The DLI campus was in downtown Monterey. When I worked at the Pentagon making assignments to the DLI, it had a code identifying it with Fort Ord, so I assumed it was at Fort Ord. Rather, it occupied several acres eight blocks from the ocean. The magnificent grounds resembled a college campus more than a military base. Even the starkness of army barracks and buildings couldn't detract from the beauty of the site.

After checking in at Charge of Quarters (CQ), I found my room, a college dorm-type with two beds, two dressers, and two desks. I had a roommate for the week! Unpacking took me less than five minutes, leaving me free to wander around the campus until a mandatory assembly at 1800 hours.

The DLI, now the DLI-FLC having become the Defense Language Institute-Foreign Language Center in 1976, appeared on local tourist maps, so the site had helpful plaques providing a more-than-adequate description and history. One of these plaques stated it was a sub-installation of Fort Ord, but to my mind it was much more interesting than Fort Ord. Officially, the Presidio of Monterey, it had been established as a Spanish fort in 1769. Ownership changed to Mexico and then to the United States, but during that entire time, it had always been called the Presidio of Monterey, a military installation under three different flags. Several buildings had a definite Spanish flair with adobe walls and red-tile roofs. The original chapel, now named the Royal Presidio Chapel, was the only building that survived from the original site. A chill went up my spine when I read it had been built by Father Junipero Serra, the famous Spanish missionary I had studied in grammar school. The chill disappeared when I read further that while the chapel had the distinction of being the only remaining building from the original fort, it wasn't within the Presidio. The original burned down just after being built, and Father Serra rebuilt it in Carmel-by-the-Sea, a few miles from here. Still, it made for a nice story.

With the time getting closer to 1800 hours, I made my way to the mess hall. I had limited experience with army mess halls, just three or four exposures, but a 250-year-old mess hall on a historic site with Spanish roots didn't look the same as the 12-year-old mess hall at Fort Dix. It was a small building, accommodating perhaps one hundred diners at a time. Not institutional, it had roughhewn timbers on the ceilings and forming arches around the doors and windows. Ceiling fans turned in the late afternoon with sun shining through the west-facing windows open to the breeze coming off the Pacific. Most of the tables were arranged to accommodate four diners with a few near the walls for larger groups of up to eight. Festive tablecloths of red-and-white checks adorned each table. Soft music, a classical string quartet I think, filled the room from speakers high on the walls.

It didn't smell the same either. Instead of the stale sourness shared by most institutional dining facilities, this "restaurant" bathed in the essence of the flora populating the grounds, the predominant fragrance being jasmine. I had seen dozens of midnight jasmine plants on my tour of the facility. The fragrant flowers closed, awaiting the setting of the sun until they opened to fill the air with even more of the pleasant essence. One of the plaques had noted jasmine was the first perfume used by man. Hopefully, they meant mankind and not my fellow testicle bearers, as the fragrance was definitely feminine.

A soldier at the entrance directed me to a corner of the room where others milled around two of the larger tables. Looking around, I saw no one I knew.

"Jonathan." The familiar voice sounded like it came from a loudspeaker in the hush of a group of strangers meeting for the first time, each unsure of the others or their own place in the pecking order of the assemblage. "A long way from home. Glad to see you."

I turned toward the voice. The shock of seeing Mike Allen connected to that voice wasn't lost on him. A broad grin preceded his advance toward me with an extended hand.

"Michael. I didn't expect to see you here. What—"

Before I could finish my question, Mike reached me and grabbed my hand, pumping it like we hadn't seen each other in years. Steering me away from the others, he continued talking. "I've asked to attend this course to brush up on my French because I have an assignment that will take me to Europe, and next to English, French seems to be the language most people share. I understand it's the preferred European language of the Middle East."

Still somewhat shocked, I asked, "You're going on assignment to Europe? Anything to do with me?"

"Everything to do with you, my friend. You don't think we'd, and I do mean we this time, would leave you over there without a lifeline."

The emphasis Mike had placed on his use of the word "we" was specific to an earlier request I had made of him to be more specific when he communicated with me. He alternated between "I" and "we," and I wasn't sure whether the instructions were suggestions from him or orders transmitted from his CIA boss. Mike would watch over me in Europe at the request of his boss, Mr. Anderson.

"It should be no surprise the assignment you have has high visibility at all levels, all the way to the top, although the top has plausible deniability. Besides brushing up on your French, there's other preparations needed and additional information you need. I'll take care of some of that this week. We're starting tonight." Mike looked around, nodding to other people. He seemed comfortable in this group of strangers.

Turning back, he said, "We'll stay for this greet and meet. I want you to mingle until the commandant gives his welcome speech. Don't mention your assignment. Nobody here will ask you, just as you've been instructed not to ask anyone else. I mention it only as a reminder. After the welcome speech, he'll tell us English should not be spoken for the rest of the week. Everyone is here for the French refresher course, so French will be the only language allowed."

None of what Mike said came as a surprise. I could no longer avoid the reality of the situation. I had started a mission that would result in the assassination of the Shah of Iran. For now, I only worried about whether I'd be able to get through a week of speaking only French.

"Then we'll duck out after the speech and go out for dinner. We need some time to talk."

Nodding agreement, I wondered how Mike got us special treatment on the first night.

"In case you're wondering how I got us off the site on the first night, I didn't. Mr. Anderson requested it. Actually, he didn't request it. He told the commandant (or is it 'commandantè' here at the Presidio?) we wouldn't be sticking around for the first meal."

When the speaker finished, Mike put his drink down and motioned we should leave. Outside, the scent of the local flora reminded me of the remarkable setting. We walked to the main gate, where a nondescript dark sedan idled. He indicated I should get in the rear passenger-side door as he moved around the car to the other side. No words were spoken to the driver before he drove away. Neither of us spoke on the short drive.

The car stopped at the Monterey wharf, a tourist area, abounding with attractions to separate tourists from their money. Mom-and-pop ice-cream stands, pizza places, T-shirt shops, and souvenir places dominated. There were several full-service restaurants, each boasting longevity on the wharf or seafood specialties, or both. Summer vacationers crowded the wharf, mostly families in search of an evening meal followed by an evening strolling the wharf and enjoying the ocean breeze.

Mike remained silent as we walked, arriving in front of a wood-frame building with lots of windows through which diners could watch the walkers or, if lucky enough to be on the ocean side, watch the sunset. The building distinguished itself from those around it by color, a greenish-blue probably meant to represent the color of the sea. An unfortunate choice. While it may have been the color of the sea once, years in the Southern California sun had faded it. At least it was distinctive, and that may have been the initial reason for the color choice.

The restaurant, Abalonetti's, had a long line in front. On the door, a sign declared "No Reservations." I looked around for other restaurants, seeking a place with a shorter line or maybe none at all. Mike moved to the front door, opened it, and held it for me. As I moved past the couple at the front of the line, the disgruntled man commented, "Hey, am I fucking invisible?"

Mike turned, first looking at the man, then to the right, and then back at the man as though he wasn't there. "Who said that? I swear I just heard something." Then, he looked to me and said, "I'm hearing voices that aren't there." It was a playful arrogance I'd not seen in Mike before, casual and natural. I liked it.

Inside, a hostess asked us for our name for the growing list she had on her hostess stand. She heard the exchange at the door and added as if to discourage us, "It'll be ninety minutes before a table is available."

Mike responded to her with the same aloofness he had used at the door. "Please tell Victor, Mr. Allen is here."

The hostess looked puzzled but picked up the phone on the stand, pushed three buttons, and relayed the information. Within two minutes, a distinguished-looking older gentleman presented himself to Mike. "Welcome. I'm Victor. So very glad to make your acquaintance. I've been expecting you and have the chef's table set up for you." As we left the hostess at the stand, her bewildered look followed us into the restaurant.

"Mike, the sign in front said it didn't take reservations, yet you seem to have one."

"Technically it's not a reservation. In most restaurants that don't take them, they set aside tables for special guests. Imagine if you would, the owner's mother decides she wants to have dinner on a crowded night. He wouldn't make her wait, so they set aside a few tables as chef's tables to accommodate these people."

When I said "And you're Victor's mother," I received an icy look. But when Victor finished seating us and asked to be remembered to Mr. Anderson, it became clear, and I added, "Mr. Anderson is Victor's mother?" This brought a smile to Mike's face.

Putting aside the menu, Mike said, "Tonight, we'll feast on California's best seafood and wine. The wine is available around the world, but the seafood is unique to California restaurants. We'll start with two appetizers. The first one is the sand dab, a small white fish, abundant in the Monterey Bay and seldom found in quantities large enough to fish commercially elsewhere. They'll serve it with head and fins removed but with skin and scales. It's a sweet meaty fish.

Then we'll follow with an order of abalone, which we'll share. The main course will be the cioppino, which is magnificent. Their interpretation of this classic seafood stew is the best I've had. You may pick the wine, but I would suggest a Napa Valley Chardonnay, preferably Wentè as its fruity buttery taste will complement the fish nicely."

Victor was replaced by Emily, our waitress, who served our appetizers. I looked at Mike for an answer. "I preordered just to make sure they saved some for us." Turning to Emily, he said, "Dr. West will order the wine. He doesn't need the list."

I ordered the Wentè Chardonnay.

Chapter 24

Michael's meal choice was superb. The tiny dabs were sweet, and I was pleased the heads were removed. With heads, they would have looked like bait on my plate. The abalone was so good, I ate the shadow on the plate. The cioppino was okay, but not to my liking. Too much New England in my blood. If you're going to have fish, have fish, not some clear, soupy collection of fish parts and sausage.

There wasn't much in the way of conversation during dinner, just comments on the food, the wine, and the beautiful California weather. For all the talking we did, we could have stayed on campus. Made me think Mike only wanted an excuse to have a favorite seafood dish at government expense. We finished the wine and passed on dessert, with Mike paying the bill. Outside, I turned left, toward shore and the town. Mike grabbed my arm, directing me in the other direction. We walked to the end of the concrete pier, past the last of the shops and restaurants to the area where retired men would gather in the morning to fish. With no one within listening distance, we stopped at the railing and faced the west. As the sun descended toward the horizon, the colors of the sky and ocean changed from the merely different shades of sky and ocean blue to the added majesty of orange, red, yellow, and green, made more breathtaking by the inverted reflection of the sky in the sea. The evening was silent except for the call of seabirds and the gentle lapping of the waves against the bulkhead, rhythmic like a heartbeat. Then Mike broke the silence. No foreplay but right to the point. "Jonathan, are you ready for this assignment?" He paused to see if I had a response. It wasn't his question that caused my momentary hesitation but the directness after a casual dinner.

"This assignment requires you to be the agent in the death of another human being. You'll be on the scene and make the final decision how his end will come. There'll be no outside help, and there may be others who may attempt to stop you, or if you choose a medical method, try to counteract whatever action you took. Before the time of the assassination, you'll get all the help you need, but when it happens, you'll be on your own. Let me repeat, are you ready?"

I knew the reasons the Shah had to be assassinated. The principal one being he was no longer a reliable ally. His erratic behavior could lead to significant unrest in the entire region. With his mind deteriorating, there was no telling what he could do. If he asked for help from the United States, we had an unresolvable dilemma. If we refused to come to his assistance, either to save his regime or his life, we would send a message to our allies we were unreliable. But if we assisted him, his enemies, now near neutral toward the United States, would become our enemies. The only solution was to eliminate the threat before it became a problem.

"Yes, I'm ready. I understand the need to eliminate the Shah in a way that appears consistent with the progression of his illness. If you ask me what I'm going to do, I can't answer you. I'll have to evaluate the situation and see what presents itself as an opportunity, and that can't start until I'm in Europe."

"Will having Monika and Eric with you present a problem?"

"No. Unless there are some very unusual circumstances, I don't see the assassination taking place during my assignment with WHO. Rather, I see it as an opportunity to become familiar with, to become involved with, and even trusted by those people treating the Shah. Maybe, if the opportunity presents itself, to initiate an interaction with the Shah. Monika and Eric will add an air of domesticity that should dispel any possibility of being perceived as a threat."

Christ! Did I say that? Was I considering, even subconsciously, using my family as a cover on this assignment?

"Good. This first assignment to WHO headquarters is a familiarization. We've arranged for you to meet the French physicians treating the Shah, and they'll know you work for American Pharmaceuticals. To make you more interesting to them, someone may have led them to believe you have access to experimental drugs useful in the treatment of the Shah. This suggestion was not overt, but very subtle."

"Why subtle?"

"The Shah is very sensitive to the word 'cancer,' so his physicians are limited in his treatment."

"But there's been limited success with chlorambucil or cyclophosphamide. Neither is perfect, but they're the best we have now."

"There's little doubt his physicians understand that, but the Shah is a difficult patient. Either of those two treatments cause side effects characteristic of cancer treatment, most notably hair loss, nausea, and vomiting. If he wants to deny the disease and hide it from those around him and the nation, these would be telltale signs. We suspect they're giving him subtherapeutic doses of chlorambucil, low enough to avoid the hair loss but enough to have the central nervous system side effects, including confusion and altered thought processes. Once the possibility of cancer came to our attention, we monitored him for signs. No hair loss but some bizarre behavior. That's our best educated guess, but in the absence of any inside information, it's the best we can do. The information is so vague, we haven't even alerted State or the White House."

"I thought you said something about everyone had been read in on this all the way to the top?"

"I said there is plausible deniability all the way to the top. That's all you need to know."

"You're that unsure?"

"No, we're sure. Just don't have the proof."

"That's where I come in?"

"Yes. Get in with his treatment team through WHO. While you're going over as an infectious disease expert, your dossier also identifies you as being on the cancer research team at American Pharmaceuticals. They'll seek you out to ask if there are any promising drugs in the pipeline and how far along before they might be used in humans."

"But American Pharmaceuticals doesn't have a cancer drug research program."

Mike gave me a look of frustration, a look that sent the message he knew that and knew I knew. "They know what's being studied in humans, but they don't know what's in research at American Pharmaceuticals, so they'll ask. The appropriate noncommittal response should be you can't discuss specific ongoing research interests of the company. They'll ask the question several ways, and you should have a number of answers, none of which says no but gets them to remain interested and ask more."

Mike had made it easy for me to become introduced to the Shah's medical team, and I understood what he wanted. "I'm not current on cancer treatment. The last and only time I studied it was during medical school."

"You don't have to get up to speed on 'cancer,' just chronic lymphocytic leukemia. When you get back to New York, I've arranged for you to spend time with Dr. Michael Weiss at Columbia, a leading cancer doc who can train you enough to get the answers we need from the Shah's docs. The time with Weiss should only be two or three sessions. There's not many drugs or treatments available for chronic lymphocytic leukemia."

"What if I screw this up?"

"You won't. This stage is information gathering. Confirm he has cancer, find out his treatment plan, and determine the prognosis. Not much chance you'll fail, but if you do, we'll go to an alternate plan."

I had this feeling during the preparation for the hijacking, and it had returned. "Or, am I the alternate plan?"

Even in the waning light, I could see the twinkle in Mike's eye that accompanied the wry smile sneaking onto his lips as he turned to face me. "There's the Jonathan I've missed. Thinking a couple of steps ahead, or is it thinking in the round, seeing all the possibilities? If you've asked, you've been wondering about it. What do you think? Are you plan A or plan B?"

"For this stage, it doesn't make any difference. While I'm probably plan A, I doubt I'm the only one trying to gather the information. It's too important to the second stage of the operation."

"Why do you think you're plan A for this stage?" asked Mike, now very pensive.

"I've got credentials that will play well with these guys, all of which you'll make sure they know before I arrive. I'm Ivy League educated. Work for a large, respectable international drug company with research interests all over the world. I'm credentialed by the CDC, an adjunct professor at Columbia, and have an assignment at WHO. All very impressive for a man my age. At the very least, they'll be curious."

"All true and on the mark, Jonathan. As you say, you are one of many gathering information at this stage and the one most likely to provide important intelligence. You'll succeed, of that I have no doubt."

"What about the second stage? Am I one of many? Am I plan A or plan B?"

Mike turned his gaze back to the sea, dark with night, reflective of the dark nature our discussion had taken. "This is an important mission for us. For the United States. The elimination of the Shah. If you look for the directive, you won't find it written any place. When we developed the policy for the future of the Middle East, it was obvious the Shah was the big unknown. No, that's not entirely correct. His usefulness for stability in the region was becoming a liability. I wouldn't say there was a wink and a nod, but the message was sent by the policy setters and received by those of us who carry out the dark side of policy. He will not go away, so he must be eliminated before he does harm. The White House and State don't know he has cancer. It was like a gift dropped into our laps." He glanced at me. "With cancer, we can do the minimum of collateral damage. We can make it look like the normal course of the disease, or an acceleration of the disease process. It may work to our advantage. To some, he'll remain a revered leader. To others, it will be good riddance. We can work both sides to our advantage."

Mike paused, pondering what he was about to say. Was it the words he was trying to choose, or the depth of the message he was contemplating? His foot came off the railing, and he continued, "The second phase of the operation has multiple plans and multiple assets involved in each. While there will be others evaluating and preparing for a medical solution and alternate plans, you will be our best chance. If a natural medical solution isn't possible, there are others. Accidents, collateral damage. Even a deranged dissident assassinating him. All those are complex—many parts, many participants, many opportunities for failure, or worse, discovery of our involvement. To answer your question. You are 'plan A' for the second phase."

The sun had set, and I had missed it. It only took four or five minutes for the big orange ball to fall into the ocean, but I was so involved with what Mike was saying I missed it. Maybe I'd get another opportunity during the week.

The week of study passed quickly. I was surprised at how the French I learned in high school and college returned. Within two days, I had little trouble understanding most of what was being said and became more comfortable speaking. By the end of the week, I enjoyed the challenge of eliminating my American accent and learning current slang.

There was also time to reflect on the discussion I had with Mike after dinner in town. Unlike our previous collegial interactions, he had changed, assuming the air of a boss. A boss who assumed his charge needed instructions on the basics. Of particular annoyance was his "lecture" on available treatments for CLL. I challenged him on this.

"Sorry, Jonathan. My role with you has changed as has the importance of the assignment. In the past, I was operating more as a coach, following instructions from Mr. Anderson. After more than five years now, he has stepped aside in the operational handling of you and delegated that responsibility to me. It's my first time in the role of an operational boss. If it helps you any, I was uncomfortable being made your boss. I'd prefer, and I think it works better, if we behave toward each other as we've done in the past."

"Thanks, Mike."

With a smile, he added, "But I am the boss."

Once I was back in New York, Dr. Weiss's office contacted me and arranged for three sessions to review current treatment options for cancer in general and chronic lymphocytic leukemia specifically. They provided three review articles on the subjects I had to read before meeting with Weiss.

I was impressed with Weiss from the start, a man much younger than I imagined. His reputation as a leader and authority in leukemia led me to think of him as an older wizened academic. Instead, he was young and dynamic, eschewing the academic club tie for an open neck denim shirt and lab coat. Personable with a big smile, a good teacher, I enjoyed my time with him, and felt well prepared for the task ahead of me. When we ended our last session, he offered to be available as a resource in the future should I need his help.

Chapter 25

Preparing for the trip to Geneva occurred at two distinct levels. While I took care of the things related to work, Monika managed the personal and family items.

I continued French lessons on my own, finding a young man from France seconded to corporate Finance Department for a year. We had lunch twice a week where I spoke only French. I continued meeting every other week with Weiss for tutoring in current leukemia treatments. He had spent a year in Germany at the Max Planck Institute and told me of the differences in European medical practices compared to the States. I had thought medicine was medicine, but it wasn't. Most of Europe was moving toward socialized medicine with England and Germany leading the way. This didn't change medical treatments as much as it changed the way physicians interacted with the patient. While everyone was supposed to be treated as an equal, gross injustices crept into the system. The better doctors shied away from the government system and formed private clinics for those able to afford it, leaving many patients in the hands of the lesser skilled physicians.

Weiss had experience with the pharmaceutical industry in Europe which differed from the companies working in the States. Because of socialized medicine, the government not only paid the bills, but also set the prices drug companies charged. These prices tended to be lower than in the United States and required an additional clinical trial not required in the States. To get a drug on the market and get it paid for by the government, the government required a comparative trial against a drug already used to treat the disease in question. To get on the government formulary, the new drug had to be better than an existing drug, and to get a superior price, it must offer a significant improvement. Usually, the formulary only allowed two or three drugs for a condition, not like in the States where there could be a dozen. On the surface, this appears to be an efficiency, removing duplicates introduced primarily for marketing. This was not always the case. The governments often decided to approve only on the efficacy of the drug, but some companies developed similar drugs just to reduce the side effects and deserved to be available for the patients who needed them.

My American Pharmaceuticals responsibilities couldn't be put on hold during my time in Geneva. Several other Medical Directors took over a portion of my work. The basic work, while easy to pick up, still required me to advise them on the unique aspects of the studies or the investigators to assure things continued to move ahead in my absence. As we prepared, WHO asked to have my stay extended to three months. The company agreed.

These things went smoothly because the company placed a priority on them, for several reasons. Despite this being my assignment, it was an honor for the company. Others in the company accepted the increased work load for the short term because it reflected positively on them, and might lead to something similar for them. Even if it didn't, it provided an opportunity to do a little more, always an asset in the promotion-minded corporate world.

Monika met with a person from the company personnel department who handled secondments. In any large international company, these two- or three-year relocations provided valuable experience for staff identified for future high-management responsibilities, and each company had people within the Personnel department to assist the move. The most important for us being the selection of housing in Geneva for the time we'd be there. Like most large cities hosting international businessmen, Geneva had a section where the internationals settled, and within it, a large American community, contiguous with the English and Canadian expatriate communities. The English-speaking neighbors gave a sense of "home" to those traveling abroad. Monika and I wanted to savor the experience of living in Geneva, away from the pizza joints, burger places, and other shops that made the neighborhood a little piece of America. We wanted to live "off the economy."

Switzerland, because of its position in Europe, had several distinct ethnic "flavors" that existed within their border. Three ethnicities dominated: French, German, and Italian. All were Swiss above everything else, but they also cherished their ethnic heritage, culture, and food and celebrated this within distinct communities. Geneva and other large cities in Switzerland reflected these same ethnic origins as neighborhoods, in much the same way large cities in the United States had a "Little Italy" or "Chinatown."

Once we agreed to make the secondment a family move, Monika thought it would be nice to live in a German neighborhood. It was an unusual request, and the company representative didn't have the experience with accommodations outside of the English-speaking compound. Instead, she put Monika in touch with her counterpart in WHO, Geneva. The young lady in Geneva was very pleasant and businesslike on the phone until Monika made her request. At once, she became more interested and, by the end of their initial phone call, considered herself to have a friend in America.

Within a week, Monika received dozens of pictures by mail of potential properties for us to consider, along with detailed description of each place, a description of the neighborhood, a map with each location noted, and the location of WHO headquarters clearly marked. She didn't know if I would have a car or a driver, so she identified public transportation points. Monika wasn't happy with any of the places offered. Unlike the northern part of Switzerland, Geneva had a small German population scattered around the city with no defined community. There was a concentration near the German embassy, but from our experience with the east side of Manhattan near the United Nations, they tended to be career diplomats who stuck together.

After another series of telephone calls, Monika's contact told her of the "Old Towne" section of the city, the Vielle-Ville. While not a German neighborhood, it boasted both a German bakery and a restaurant. She sent pictures of a flat, and we accepted it as our new home.

During all this, Monika got her passport updated to include Eric, notified the utilities we would be traveling, arranged for the building superintendent to check our apartment regularly, paid our condo fee in advance, and made the personal arrangements for family visits—her mother to Geneva and her trip with her mother to Germany. We also decided to stay in Europe after the assignment with WHO ended in mid-December and travel to Hanover, Germany, to spend the Christmas holidays with her family.

On September 14, 1977, we boarded Swissair Flight SR 23 from JFK International Airport for Geneva. The flight left on schedule at 7:25 p.m., arriving the next morning at Geneva's Cointrin Airport at 9:15 a.m., right on schedule to the minute. I later learned the Swiss regarded punctuality as much as they regarded their chocolate-making skills. Trains and planes were always on time, the exception being something on the order of an act of God. To arrive early was as offensive as being late and was an act of man, not God, and therefore never tolerated. Eric slept during most of the overnight flight. The company allowed me to fly business class and provided a coach seat for Monika. I used personal funds to upgrade her to business class. The extra room and attention from the flight crew made the flight much easier for us.

A car and driver were waiting after we cleared customs and immigration. I had studied the map of Geneva several times and recognized the roads the driver took. First south on the A1, then southeast on 101, or the Route de Meyrin. I'd have to learn the way the locals preferred to refer to these routes, either by number or street name. Route 101 merged with Route 1 at the bridge over the Rhone and became Route 102 on the other side. The simplicity of the pure mathematics of the two merged roads becoming the sum of the two could only happen in Switzerland, where precision and logic were part of their DNA. Was it by design or a coincidence? I'd have to follow up on this, watching where other highways merged.

Over the bridge was Vielle-Ville, "Old Town" Geneva. A quick right and the driver pulled to the curb in front of 12 Rue Bemont, arriving at our new home after a short ten-minute ride from the airport. The street was cobblestone and narrow. Two cars could get by each other, provided one put two wheels on the sidewalk. The buildings on either side of the street were separate but connected, like the brownstones in New York. All were five stories high, the limit on building height before steel infrastructure and elevators gave birth to skyscrapers.

As we exited the car and collected our luggage from the trunk, the front door of the building opened, and a young woman emerged with the doorman.

"Are you the Vests?" she asked.

I started to say no, but was interrupted by Monika, who asked, "Hilde?"

"Yes, Mrs. Vest. I'm so happy to at last meet you." They hugged and giggled like old friends who hadn't seen each other in a long time. "Ve have prepared for your arrival for two days, and ve hope you vill find things good."

"Please call me Monika."

I smiled at Monika. She knew I would correct Hilde, saying we were the Wests, not the Vests. I remained silent. In her country, I would adapt.

The small lobby reflected elegance of an earlier age. The granite floor was well worn and the mahogany panels on the walls dull from centuries of shellac. Decorations were minimal, perhaps an attempt to reduce dust collectors but more likely the result of accidents during its life. The building had been retrofitted with an elevator. From the looks of the contraption, a small cage of bronze and mahogany, it may have been one of the first in Geneva, accommodating only three adults at a time. Monika and I followed Hilde, leaving the driver and the doorman with our luggage. Monika had packed sparsely for the trip, only what we needed for a few days in case we got stranded. The rest, she had packed and shipped ahead.

The elevator began the ascent with a jerk and rose slowly with grinding and soft screeches of metal on metal. Any movement within the cage resulted in a countermovement of the cage reacting to the weight shift. Something else to adapt to—no sudden movements in the elevator. The arrival at our floor announced itself with an abrupt stop and a loud thud. We exited on the fourth floor. In Switzerland as well as the rest of Europe, they called the first floor the ground floor and numbering started on the second floor. The hallway shared the starkness of the lobby, the only difference being light sconces at the entrance to each of the four apartments, in addition to those at the elevator. A worn carpet's sole purpose seemed to be to deaden footsteps on the wooden floors, but nothing could silence the creaking of these ancient boards.

Hilde led us to a large wooden paneled door with a brass plate declaring it to be Apartment 401. She unlocked it, handed Monika the key, and gestured for us to enter. The welcoming brightness of the entrance hall leading to the interior of the apartment was in stark contrast to the elevator hallway. Monika moved further into the apartment with me following. As she entered the living room, she exclaimed, her hands together and at her chest, "Oh, Jonathan. Isn't it just perfect?"

"Yes" was all that was necessary because it was perfect. We had seen pictures, but they didn't do justice to the overall effect of the room. Thirteen-foot ceilings exuded grandness and provided tall walls in which large windows rose to within two feet of the ceiling and came down to knee level. The lower part of the windows had dense security bars, so we could be comfortable leaving them open as Eric moved around the apartment. The nicely appointed room had comfortable-looking furniture, mirrors that added more to the brightness of the room, paintings on the walls, and various odds and ends making it a home rather than a bland hotel. At the far end of the living room, a fireplace sat to the left of French doors leading to a small balcony. We stood breathless in front of these doors. Looking over the red-tile roofs of Vielle-Ville, the only thing that had changed in the last four hundred years being television antennas added to the chimneys. To the right, church spires dotted the cityscape. To the left, the river Rhone. But the main attraction was in front of us, a spectacular view of Lake Geneva and the mountains beyond.

Hilde broke the silence. "Monika, Vould you like to see the kitchen and the other rooms?"

"Oh yes. But this room, Hilde." She sighed, her feelings expressed in that simple gesture. "Thank you so much. This is wonderful."

I remained, enjoying the view, feeling I could stand here all day and not tire of it. Boats were on the river and the lake, pedestrians on the north bank of the river. As I looked out on the lake and to the mountains beyond, I promised myself a telescope, a good one. The view was captivating. A cloud passed across the lake and countryside beyond, changing the colors and contours of everything as I watched.

"Jonathan, come see the kitchen and the other rooms." Monika's cheerful voice broke my vista-induced trance. I joined her in the kitchen. It was nice, but it was only a kitchen. Maybe, I'd get into the French spirit of the region and learn to cook. Then I might appreciate it more.

We moved to a small bedroom, which Hilde had transformed into Eric's room with blankets, curtains, and toys shipped ahead. Eric was delighted to see familiar surroundings.

Hilde had transformed the master bedroom into "our" bedroom with items from the Roosevelt Island apartment. One item not ours drew my attention, a telescope, a big telescope. Looking out the window, I could understand why the owner had placed it here. The view included the magnificent St. Peter's Cathedral, a panoramic view of most of the Vielle-Ville, and the French mountains in the distance. I might look at them later, but the first use of that telescope would be from the living room toward the lake and mountains.

Hilde had dismissed the doorman and driver earlier and, after showing us the apartment, took her leave. She beamed the whole time because she could see we liked the apartment. She and Monika agreed to meet the next week for lunch.

Monika put Eric down for a nap while we unpacked and showered, separately, using the handheld shower spray in a cast-iron, claw-foot tub with an after-market shower curtain strung on a stainless-steel hoop. When Eric woke up, we went out to explore, drawn to the lake for our first stop. Between the lake and the Rhone was a man-made island, Rousseau Island Park, a beautiful, tranquil place to spend a quiet afternoon. But we weren't ready for that yet. We continued walking until overtaken by hunger and fatigue. The inviting green umbrella-covered tables on the outdoor terrace of the Angoletta Café in Place du Bourg-de-Four beckoned us, and we spent the rest of the afternoon eating and relaxing in the sun.

We used the rest of the weekend to settle in, stock the pantry shelves, and get ready for work on Monday at the WHO.

Chapter 26

O n Monday, I took a cab to work, leaving the car and driver for Monika. While not dedicated to our sole use, we had first call on the driver's services for the first two weeks in Geneva. After that, we had to schedule at least two days in advance or take our chances. Many expatriates, especially executives on short-term assignments, had a dedicated car and driver. The car service was a perquisite but also considered a more efficient use of time. An international driver's license was one thing, but getting a car and insurance proved troublesome. A car and driver also avoided those embarrassing situations when the executive got lost or parked in the wrong lot and had his car towed.

WHO headquarters was located outside the United Nations campus at the Palais des Nations complex in Ariana Park, north of Geneva. Palais des Nations was built during the 1930s to serve as the home of the League of Nations and became home to the United Nations in 1946. Switzerland has remained neutral even about the United Nations and is not a member. The buildings have a classic design, meaning they are big, box-like structures of light granite, much like the government office buildings in Washington. The WHO building was on Avenue Apia, about three hundred yards west of the main United Nations campus. In contrast to the UN buildings, the design was a modern interpretation of classicism I thought failed both as modern and classic.

Following the routine of checking in, getting a photo identification badge, and sitting through a brief orientation, I went to my office in the Infectious Disease Section on the fourth floor. There I met my section chief, Dr. Harry Kumkumian, a round little man, dressed in an impeccable black suit, immaculate white shirt, blue-striped tie, and shoes with a brilliant shine. A short man, a little over five feet tall with a belt size close to his height, who walked with tiny steps and a slight waddle. Blessed with a marvelous head of wavy jet-black hair, his blue eyes pierced you when he looked up to address you.

"Dr. West, welcome to the Infectious Disease Section."

"Thank you, sir. I'm looking forward to working here."

"Let's go to my office," he said as he turned. I followed. "I understand you and your wife chose an apartment in 'Old Towne' and not in the American compound."

"Yes. The housing office found us a beautiful apartment in Vielle-Ville. Monika, my wife, is German and wanted to experience living as a European. Hadn't heard about an American compound."

"It's really not a real compound, just an apartment building near here where the visiting Americans, Canadians, and Brits congregate. There's a big courtyard where they get together to celebrate all the holidays, theirs as well as their host country, and any other holiday they choose. That way when they get home, they can regale in telling of their European experience. If you like that sort of thing, I'm sure you can get an invitation. Most aren't worth the trouble, but Guy Fawkes Day and Bastille Day are unique experiences. Bastille Day has passed, but Guy Fawkes is coming up in early November."

"Thanks. I'll tell my wife. I'm sure she can get us an invite," I said, thinking of her lunch with Hilde. Hilde, someone who could get things done.

As we walked, Harry talked. "The Infectious Disease Section is one of the oldest within WHO. Some say it was the reason WHO was formed to treat the third-world nations, to teach them sanitary living habits, to avoid dysentery, all that. Others claim it was to study and treat blood diseases of the world, like malaria and later sickle cell. Doesn't make any difference, really. Most of the work WHO does is considered humanitarian now. The medicine disciplines are second to them and are, for better or worse, considered simply medicine."

"I wasn't aware of that."

"There are those who will deny those statements and point to a chart with multiple medical disciplines listed, but I would challenge you to find them in this building. At best, they exist as a dedicated spot on someone's desk." Harry shrugged. I couldn't interpret the shrug. Did it mean he didn't care, or did it mean he couldn't do anything about it?

"We've learned to adapt, and maybe, I say just maybe, we're better off for it. And more important, the people we treat around the world may be the better for it."

That was a curious statement after what he previously said. "How so?" I asked.

Harry walked to his cluttered desk. On the way, he cleared one of the other chairs of stacks of papers and books by moving them to the floor and indicated I should sit in the cleared chair. He took his suit jacket off, brushed it, and draped it across the back of his chair before settling in with a sigh. Even sitting was a chore for a man his size.

"The humanitarian do-gooders dictate a lot of the work we do now, except of course if there's a major disease outbreak. Then we take the lead, at least until the epidemic is under control. Here's how it works. Granted this is over-simplified, but it gets the point across. Someone in the UN decides an area needs clean water, or a school, or a nutrition program. Then, they develop a plan." He stopped talking and looked through the papers on his desk. After going through the pile in the middle, he stopped and began talking again. "I thought I might have one of their requests, but I guess it's in a different pile," he said as his arm moved in a wide circle indicating it could be in any of the dozens of piles strewn around his office.

"Anyway, they'd send us a detailed outline of the program they have in mind and ask us to provide medical staff for the assignment. If they were going to the Philippines to treat schistosomiasis, they'd expect an infectious disease doc, but because the disease is rampant in children, they'd want a pediatrician. Then, because of the young adult population, there'd be women of childbearing potential, so they may want an OB-GYN. We couldn't staff that kind of effort in the field, so we focused on infectious disease specialists who seem to be the most rounded in seeing all patient types. A bug doesn't have a single host, so the docs who treat bugs see all patient types. Makes it easy for us and better for the patient."

"But not all infectious disease docs have wide training like that."

"They do when they work for WHO. If they don't have it when they start, they learn quick."

"What about oncology?"

"Not much of a call for oncologists in the third world. A lot of the folks would be happy to live long enough to die of cancer. Oh, don't get me wrong, we see it, but not much we can do in the bush. Maybe operate if indicated, and it would do any good. Not much for drugs because it requires monitoring and dose adjustment. And certainly, no radiation, none. In the field, we use batteries and the occasional generator, nothing to support a radiation machine."

Harry reminded me of the country doctor of folklore in America. A realist, compassionate but pragmatic. "How do the infection docs get up to speed on something like oncology?" I asked, curious for the sake of understanding, but also trying to understand how I could become involved with the oncologists treating the Shah.

"There are seminars almost every day on some aspect of medicine here in our building. You asked about oncology. Let's see what's going on this week." He took a sheet of orange paper from his desk, put on a pair of Ben Franklin eyeglasses, and read. "You won't find this schedule printed on orange paper anywhere else but this office. I'm supposed to officiate at many of them, but I kept losing the schedule in this sea of paper. So they copy my schedule on orange paper so I can find it. I liked it better when I could lose it."

Harry continued reading, "Ah. Here you go. A hematologist from Paris is scheduled to give a talk on chronic lymphocytic leukemia." He paused. "See. We're making the physicians aware of these things. In this case, it would be helpful in the bush to recognize it as a cancer and not something else that has to be treated at once."

"I can see how that would be useful."

"You're scheduled to attend, to see how the subject is treated, you know, how it's made useful to the general physician in the bush. I know this man. Met him last year. I'll introduce you, and you can ask him all your questions."

It was that simple. Harry would introduce me to the French doctor treating the Shah who happens to show up in Geneva two days after I arrive. Was Harry part of this, or was this a coincidence orchestrated by Mike or Mr. Anderson?

Harry took me to my office, introduced me to the people around me, and left me on my own after saying he would take me to the seminar on Wednesday. The office was small compared to my office in New York. The view of the parking lot didn't inspire or distract me.

Monika bubbled with enthusiasm when I returned to the apartment in the evening. She loved Geneva. She took Eric for a long walk, exploring the main streets. On a side street, three blocks from home, she found a German bakery and had spent a pleasant hour talking with the proprietors, who gave her a list of other German establishments in town, the most notable being a restaurant with a beer garden. I agreed to Saturday lunch there, sitting outside while the weather was still nice, listening to her speaking German with strangers soon to become her friends.

Harry entered my office and announced we should leave for the seminar. I followed him to a large, half-filled lecture hall at the far end of the building. It resembled the large lecture halls at Yale able to hold 250 students on the tiered seating area looking down on the lecturer.

To make conversation with Harry, I said "Nice turnout."

He nodded and shrugged. "A little more than the usual. This guy has a good reputation, so some of the audience"—he waved his hand toward the seats—"might be from the university." He led me to the front of the hall, where a distinguished-looking gentleman was talking with several people. He spotted Harry and made his way to us.

"Dr. Kumkumian, so good to see you again. Thank you for the opportunity to share what I'm doing with your staff."

"Glad you could make it." Harry talked like an American with the pace and accent of a New Yorker. "Glad you" sounded like "glad jew" when he spoke, but he had another accent I couldn't place.

"This is Dr. Jonathan West from America. He's spending three months with us." Turning slightly, he said, "Jonathan, this is Dr. Jean Bernard." As each of us extended our hands, Harry left us and struggled toward the lectern saying, "Let's get this going."

Bernard smiled. "I've known Harry for over ten years, but you couldn't tell from that. It's just his way. A good administrator who used to be a first-class clinician. I consider him a dear friend." Still holding my hand, he continued, "We're not going to get much of a chance to talk before or after the lecture. I've asked to have a table set aside for us for a late lunch. Perhaps we can have a chat before I leave for the airport."

"That would be fine," I responded. "I'll wait around here until you've finished, and you can show me the way."

"Splendid." And he joined Harry at the lecture.

The seminar was boring. Dr. Weiss prepared me well, and I learned nothing new. I waited to the side until the last of the audience members had their private minute with Bernard. He smiled as he joined me. "Lunch?"

"Sure," I responded.

We ate alone in a private dining room to the side of the main cafeteria. In a room that could hold fifty diners, we were the only two.

"I'm curious to know if you learned anything from the seminar this morning?" he asked.

"Honestly. No."

"I didn't think so. The material is very basic and not much has changed in the treatment of cancer patients. Of course, with the recent success of tamoxifen in the treatment of breast cancer, I imagine many of the big companies are doing research on multiple compounds that may get into humans in the next year or so."

"I would imagine you may be right."

He played with his napkin, unfolding it and resting it across his lap. "Is your company one of those that might make advances that could put a drug in clinical trials soon?"

"Dr. Bernard—"

"Please call me Jean, Jonathan, if I may."

"Certainly, Jean. If you follow the literature and attend the medical meetings, you know we have nothing in humans, and you also know if we have something in animal studies, I can't tell you. The only way I could discuss anything like that with you is if you were one of our investigators, involved in a human trial. But seeing as we have no trials?" I let the point hang as a question.

"Ah. Yes, Jonathan. But if you are planning a human trial with a drug that is promising in animals, you would have to start talking with potential investigators. You can't wait. Am I right?"

"Yes, but as I said…"

"Jonathan, let me be more direct. I am interested in any new drugs your company may have to treat chronic lymphocytic leukemia. A colleague and I are treating a patient with CLL. Unfortunately, he is not responding as we would like."

I interrupted and asked, "Is he being treated with standard therapy, or do you have access to other experimental drugs from other companies?"

Bernard paused. "We're using only the standard treatments, chlorambucil and cyclophosphamide, but the case is complicated."

"How so?"

He looked off into the distance. "The patient, or rather his personal physician, won't let us treat him with the full doses of either of the drugs. Instead, he's insisted we use subtherapeutic doses of both, hoping the combination will be effective, but neither will be enough to elicit an adverse effect, especially hair loss."

"Really? Why the concern about hair loss?"

"Without going into details, all I can say is our patient is a public figure who cannot be perceived as suffering from cancer." Another pause by Bernard and a sigh. "And our patient is in denial."

"Then how does he rationalize he's being treated by an oncologist?"

"He doesn't need to. As far as he's concerned, we're hematologists who are treating him for a blood disease. Not an untruth, but far from the whole truth. It will get worse. The disease will progress, and his health will deteriorate, but part of our treatment includes prednisone. We are already seeing the early signs of high-dose prednisone treatment, mental confusion, which will lead to mental deterioration."

"Certainly, his wife, if he's married, must have some influence over him? Can't she convince him to get the proper treatment?"

"Yes, he's married, but she doesn't know. There are only three people who know the truth: his doctor, my colleague, and me. Now, with you there are four. That's why I need your help. If you can't help me, I'll approach other pharmaceutical companies for their help."

There it was. Bernard had laid it on the table: the patient, the disease, the request for help. If I rejected him, he'd move on, and I'd lose the opportunity to get close to the Shah.

"How soon do you need an answer?" I asked.

"Soon, perhaps a few months. I cannot wait until you return to the States. Time is becoming critical. There is perhaps six months before I must switch to more powerful treatment, but if you say no, I'll need time to seek help in other places. Fighting his disease, I have a timeline. Getting help is the unknown. If you were to say you'd have something to try in humans next spring, it would be fine. If you said you can't let me know until next spring, I can't wait. I hope you understand?"

"I do. Let me see what I can do. There's a WHO meeting in London next week with six international pharmaceutical companies to develop a plan to treat river blindness. My company will be there. I'll make inquiries and let you know when I get back. If there's anything in our pipeline, you'll need to sign a contract with us. It will contain an exclusivity clause preventing you from working with anyone else. Will that be okay?"

"Sure. If you have something, I'm willing to do that. I have no choice."

Back in my office, I called the secure number Mike Allen had provided and left a message.

When he returned my call within the hour, I told him of Bernard's request. Harry had already scheduled me to go to the London meeting, so Mike agreed to meet me there. He promised to have answers for me to present to Bernard.

Chapter 27

The flight from Geneva to London Heathrow Airport arrived at 8:15 a.m., gaining an hour due to the time zone change, which I'd have to pay back on the return later. A short ten-minute cab ride from Terminal 2 to the Hyatt Place Hotel on Bath Road got me to the meeting on time for the 9:00 a.m. start. The meeting room was small but adequate for the twelve participants and the staff from WHO. Long tables formed a large rectangle with the participants on the outside, facing each other. A smaller table was in the center of the rectangle with an overhead projector and a 35mm carousel projector facing a screen at the front of the room. Other chairs arranged around the walls provided seats for the observers and staff of the participants.

When I arrived, the participants were still milling around the breakfast buffet of pastries, muffins, fruits and breakfast beverages. I didn't recognize anyone and busied myself getting a Danish and coffee and took a seat at the table. As soon as I sat down, Mike Allen entered the room and took a seat at the back of the room, against the wall. We acknowledged each other with eye contact only.

The presentations in the morning session did little to add to the medical knowledge of the audience but were more of a formality for the media. The significant business took place away from the meeting room. When we broke for lunch, I left the building and took a walk on the hotel grounds. Mike Allen took a similar walk. We met at the far end of the park across the street.

Mike spoke first. "I'm not a physician, but even I know there wasn't much new in those presentations this morning."

"You're right. The formal presentations are just the backdrop that allows the speakers to get together and talk informally. In a few weeks or months, the organizers will release a statement containing the agreements made at the meeting. You'll wonder if you fell asleep during a critical part because you won't remember the agreement. Doesn't matter. That's how things get done. Speaking of which?"

"Over the past two days, we checked into current therapy and Bernard's and Flandrin's capabilities. There's nothing new being studied in humans. There are about a dozen drugs still in the labs being studied in animals. More on that later."

We had been walking, but Mike stopped when we reached a bench, motioning me to sit while he stood with one leg resting on the seat.

"Bernard is a smart guy. He's one of the physicians the French government has designated an 'expert' to review drug applications for cancer drugs. His partner, Flandrin, is in the same category of smart, but not an expert. Being the expert, Bernard knows what's in clinical trials. Him asking you to check was a test to see how cooperative you could be. His real interest is what's going to be available in the next year. While the treatment of CLL is limited, the course of the disease makes immediacy of treatment moot. But—and this is a big 'but'—he knows he's got to have something soon, like ten months. He doesn't want to be known as the oncologist who treated the Shah of Iran with subtherapeutic doses of effective medicines."

"That makes sense if he's the big shot you say he is. The thing I can't figure is why does he bother treating this guy if he can't treat him properly?"

"I've asked my people to consider that, but we don't have anything yet. They'll keep digging."

"What about the research pipeline? Is there any hope for something becoming available for use in humans sooner?"

"That's where we have something to talk about. Of the dozen I mentioned a few minutes ago, it looks like three or four could be ready to test in humans next year, maybe sooner, if the FDA allows a waiver. There's a lot to this, so bear with me." Mike sat and continued.

"As you know, American Pharmaceuticals doesn't have anything we can use next year. I've used my contacts to ask about other companies, and there are several that might be potential drugs but nothing for at least two years. Others are being worked on either by or under NIH or NCI contracts. The National Cancer Institute and the National Institutes of Health both have research facilities on their campuses and provide grant money to medical schools around the country." He paused and looked at me, to get a reaction.

"What about the three or four that could be ready for human testing next year?"

"One is in a major drug company, and the other three are at NCI or NIH, but none are of much help to us. If we go the drug company route, it would be very difficult to tamper with the drug. There are just too many controls built into the process by the FDA, and the company lawyers add another layer of complexity because of the fear of product liability. It's a little easier with NCI and NIH drugs, not much, but a little. However, the risk is much higher for us. They are government-sponsored agencies, and as such, 'the government.' If things went wrong with this assignment and the drugs traced back to either of them, the shit would most definitely hit the fan. No, the risk is too high."

"So you drew a blank?"

"Yes. So far, but we're still looking. What have you learned in the last two days?"

"I've learned of another site with a series of drugs being developed for CLL."

Mike stood up again, excited. He took one step and turned. "Where is it? How did you find it? Was it somebody here or in Geneva who told you?"

"The drugs are at Roswell Park." My turn to be smug.

"The UFO place in Arizona?"

"New Mexico," I corrected.

"The drugs are at the UFO site in New Mexico?"

"No. The Roswell UFO place is in New Mexico. The drugs are at Roswell Park Memorial Institute in Buffalo."

"And they're developing multiple drugs for CLL? Multiple, like how many?"

"Could be dozens."

"Why do they have so many compared to the rest, and why didn't they show up on my list?"

"They have the most comprehensive cancer program in the country. Back in the 1890s, they became the first institute of its kind dedicated to the research and treatment of malignant diseases. They've developed multiple disciplines to attack the disease. While some cancer centers focus on the treatment of patients, trying different things and relying on others to supply the drugs, Roswell goes looking for and designing drugs. They also have a collaboration with the medical school in Buffalo and work with the medicinal chemistry department to modify drugs. And there, Michael, lies the beauty of what Roswell has for us."

I had his full attention now. "How so?" he asked.

"Most drugs up to now have been hit-or-miss types of discoveries. There are minor exceptions, like the antibiotics, but for the most part the chemists make a lot of drugs with not much of a goal in mind. They give them to pharmacologists who screen them for activity. The promising ones warrant more thorough research. At Roswell, they're taking a different approach. They've seen a drug like chlorambucil has activity in CLL. They've then designed new chemicals where they change one part of the chlorambucil molecule. Sounds easy, but a complex drug like chlorambucil can present them with hundreds of options, and all of them must be tested. They've found some that have better anticancer activity but far more severe adverse effects."

"What can be worse than cancer?"

"A sudden heart attack for one."

"Point taken."

"They've gone one step further. Are you aware of isomers and enantiomers?"

"Yes. Isn't that like the mirror image of a drug?"

"Close enough. You have the concept. Besides the chemical changes, Roswell's discovered some of these drugs have isomers or enantiomers. That's not a surprise because most chemicals do. What was exciting was they found some of these enantiomers aren't stable; they switch back and forth between one form and another, in a dynamic chemical reaction. If one form is used up, the other form switches to it."

"Why's that good?"

"Let me give you an example. If form A is the good form, and it gets used up, you want to be able to assure all of form B gets switched to form A. And vice versa. If A is the bad form, the one that gives the heart attack, you want to prevent it from switching."

"Okay. I understand the basics, but why is that so exciting to you?"

"With all the chemicals they've made, they have hundreds of combinations. What if they have one that causes all the normal side effects of cancer treatment, like nausea, vomiting, blood changes, and hair loss, but very little or no anticancer activity?"

"Ahh, I see where you're going. But wouldn't a smart oncologist see the drug wasn't working and stop?"

"Yes, but what if one of these was an enantiomer that had the side effects in form B and the beneficial effects in form A. You could start the patient on the mixture. The oncologist would see the side effects and know he had an active drug, and in the short term, he would see an improvement from form A component. Then, if you added another chemical that accelerated the conversion from form A to form B, he wouldn't see it until it was too late."

"Brilliant! Do they have one like that?"

"Don't know, but it's something they can look for."

Mike paused, looking at me with a puzzled look. "You figured this out in two days?"

"Yes."

"By yourself?"

"I had some help."

"Who?"

"Dr. Weiss at Columbia."

"So what do we do now? Call up Roswell, and ask for one of those magic isomers that switches the way we want?"

"Enantiomers."

"Whatever the fuck it is. What do we, or you and Dr. Weiss do now?"

"Weiss has contacts at Roswell. Over the next several weeks, he'll renew those contacts, make them more current. He'll engage them in light conversation, let them drag some information out of him. He'll tell them he's working with a loose consortium of oncologists and research scientists exploring animal and test tube models for testing oncology drugs. The models are based on receptor theory, which fits well with the isomers and enantiomers they have."

Mike interrupted, "What's receptor theory? Will Bernard know what it is? Does he need to know what it is?"

I looked at Mike, disappointed he asked the question. My disappointment must have been reflected in my face.

"What?" he asked.

"Yes. He'll know what receptor theory is. Everybody knows what receptor theory is. Well, almost everybody. Receptor theory for drugs has been a research tool for over fifty years to describe how chemicals act in the body. It's described as Lock and Key in some textbooks. The drug being the key that fits into the unique receptor, the lock, that lets the chemical work." I still got a blank look from Mike. "In the 1950s, a scientist in England discovered a drug that fit the lock but didn't produce the effect that the natural chemical did. He called the lock the beta-receptor and the drug that blocked the lock, the beta-blocker." Still nothing from Mike.

"You never heard of this?" I asked. "It's been written up in *Scientific American*, *Life Magazine*, and maybe even *Reader's Digest*."

"No. Why would they write about it?"

"Because the drug the scientist found, the beta-blocker, was approved by the FDA earlier this year to treat a form of heart disease. There's another receptor-based drug in clinical trials that will be used to treat ulcers. That's the reason for the write-up in popular magazines."

"Okay, so Bernard will know about it. What happens then?"

"The scientists at Roswell will probe and ask more about the models. Weiss'll say it's too early. That he needs a couple of drugs with a similar structure to see if the models can distinguish between them. If he does it right, Roswell will offer him a couple of drugs."

Mike asked, "What if they don't offer?"

"Then he'll ask."

"What if they say no?"

"Then we're back where we started and we'll develop a new plan, but Weiss is very confident they'll offer some drugs. He can ask for the characteristics of the drugs, what makes them different. Why aren't they in development? That's when we'll get the one we need. One that starts working has the desired effect and the undesired effect and then stops because of the form A and form B switching."

"You seem pretty confident, Jonathan?"

"I am. The science is straightforward. In a few years, most drugs will be designed this way. The plan will work because we're out ahead of the learning curve on this with cancer drugs, so most people won't understand what's going wrong. Especially, if we don't tell them the drug the Shah will get is an enantiomer."

Mike had no more questions. Content, he suggested we get lunch before the afternoon session convened. We continued talking through lunch, but in vague terms only we could understand. It was getting him to understand the switching between the various forms of the drug. Once he understood it was just an elegant utilization of basic chemistry, he became more comfortable our way forward was secure.

I left the meeting when they took the afternoon break and grabbed a cab to the airport to catch my early-evening flight back to Geneva. I settled into my seat as the plane flew into the blue-black sky of night that had already engulfed Europe, alone with my thoughts, and content we had a plan to accomplish my assignment. Little did I know the next month would disrupt those carefully laid plans.

Chapter 28

For the next two weeks, I tried to establish a routine that allowed me to get my work done, both jobs—a secondee to WHO and assassin. It meant rising early with Eric. He watched me shave and dress; then we had breakfast together before we woke Monika. We all enjoyed those early mornings—time with my son and an extra hour of sleep for mom. I arranged for a car each day, having the driver take me to work and back home. Having an office schedule forced me to fit my work into an allotted time so there would be family time. During the second week, I went to Paris to meet with Bernard to discuss progress of his patient's condition and update him in vague terms about a potential experimental drug. But it was all talk. Nothing would happen until after the first of the year at the earliest.

Monika spent her days enjoying Geneva and introducing Eric to European culture. She was a regular visitor to the German bakery and met several other Germans through the proprietors. Each night, she beamed as she told me what she had done during the day. As a child and young adult, she had learned of her German heritage through her family, through stories, and through traditions they practiced as Americans. With her new friends, she was seeing a different version of those traditions, and it made what her parents did much more special for her.

Monika kept the weekends for family activities: a picnic at the park, the zoo, or trip to the mountains or another city. We could use the company car and driver for these trips, but we chose the rail service. In fact, we planned our trips so we could take the train, much to Eric's delight.

In mid-October, any thoughts I had of a continued idyllic stay in Geneva evaporated. News reports came out of Iran of violent anti-Shah demonstrations, which escalated to riots. Young men, many university students, filled the streets with chants, slogans, and banners calling for the removal of the Shah. Many of the chants and banners were written in English, a clear sign the audience was not only the Shah, but the West, particularly the United States, which supported him. Just so there was no ambiguity, there were anti-American chants and signs. I was watching this on Sky News one evening when I got a telephone call from Mike Allen telling me he would come to Geneva on the overnight flight, and I should meet him at the airport for breakfast. He asked I forego the car and driver and take the train to the airport.

In the United States, being asked to meet someone at an airport for a meal would be a hardship. The meal is just not worth the difficulty encountered in getting to the airport. Not so for Cointrin in Geneva. The airport is less than three miles from the center of the city and takes about ten minutes regardless of the mode of transportation. An Olympic-class runner could make it in less than fifteen minutes. Once there, the traveler can choose from several patisseries and bistros. Mike was due in on the overnight Swissair flight from JFK, arriving at Pier C in the main terminal just before eight o'clock.

The airport has a unique location. Part of Cointrin is located in France, and as part of the agreement between the Swiss and French when the airport was being expanded to accommodate a longer runway, the French retained one gate, Pier F, considered the French Sector and used exclusively for flights to and from French cities.

Arriving before Mike, I took a table at the Café Cointrin in the courtyard near the arrivals area and ordered a coffee. Mike showed up with only a briefcase before I finished my coffee. The waiter took our order before he spoke.

"Sorry I had to drag you out here, but I couldn't take the chance of a telephone call. The WHO is not a secure location. Everyone there shares information. All that crap about working for the benefit of man, and we know the Soviets, and some of our allies have ears there. Little tidbits of trivial information when added to other tidbits can provide valuable intelligence."

"And we know that how?"

Mike smiled, unapologetic. "Because we have ears there listening for tidbits."

"Understood."

"We couldn't meet at the embassy either. Too many eyes. We'd have to build you a cover story for going over there. This seemed the easiest, and it's best for me. After we meet, I'll jump on the return plane to the States."

"I thought you had plans to stay here for a while. Didn't you brush up on your French?"

"Things change."

"Why the urgency to talk? Is it the anti-Shah demonstrations in Iran?"

"Yes. There have been demonstrations in the past. Remember the Shah is not a popular ruler. His opposition comes from all sides. This one isn't much different from the others. Maybe a little larger and more vocal, mostly students. But this is the first time we've seen what appears to be a coordinated effort."

"And by that you mean?"

"This wasn't spontaneous. Someone planned this demonstration. The signs in English and the anti-American twist are the giveaways. The Shah responded as he had in the past: break it up, arrest a few, impose a curfew. The demonstrators broke up, but I get the sense this was a test."

"A test? Of what? By who?"

"Don't know yet. I'll know more after our people in Tehran nose around a bit. It feels like outsiders. If so, they could merely be testing themselves. How to organize, get a feel for the response, plan their next move."

"What's their next move?"

"Don't know, and that's a problem. We haven't alerted State or the White House because they'd ask the same questions, and we'd have the same answers

I gave you—we don't know. They'd put it aside. If I were manipulating this, I'd do the same thing they did. The next time, I'd ramp it up a little. Make the crowd a little larger, a little louder. Maybe, I'd have it happen in more cities rather than just Tehran, or involve more than students. But above all, the ramp-up would be small. And then, there'd be another with another ramp-up. If we tell the White House and State about each of the ramp-ups, they'd only see a small incremental increase, and without answers to their questions, they'll ignore it. No, we must use this time to find out what's going on and who's behind it. Then, somewhere down the line, the demonstration won't be ignored. I just hope it doesn't go too far before we get a handle on it."

"Do you think it's the Soviets?"

"They may know about it, but I don't think they're behind it. They don't have a lot to gain for such a risk, especially the anti-American stuff. Might be the religious right, but there's no one in Tehran strong enough to plan and run it. The Ayatollah is still in exile in Paris. He might be running something from there, but most of the clergy in Iran welcomed his exit, so I'm not sure where his local support is. They didn't like his mixing of religion and politics. But his son just died, so who knows what he'd do."

"You came all this way and brought me out to the airport to tell me that?"

Mike raised his eyebrows as he took a sip of coffee. He put the cup down and motioned to the waiter for a refill. I didn't need more coffee. I needed an answer.

"No. You need to get Weiss moving on the drugs to treat the Shah. With the anti-Shah demonstrations in Tehran, he might get rattled, shake him back into reality. If reality means facing his disease, he may decide to change doctors and seek oncologists, not the hematologists Bernard and Flandrin claim to be. If that happens, we lose the opportunity to have you on the inside."

"Yeah, I see your point."

"But even if he stays in denial, the unrest could force us to take action before we know who's behind it. The anti-American banners could force us into this fight to bolster his position, defend ourselves. We don't want to do anything like that."

"Two events are moving forward over which we have no control: the progression of the Shah's cancer and the political unrest in Iran. And you think if we get a drug to treat his disease, it will solve the problem?"

"No. If we have a drug from Weiss that does what he claims it will do, I can tell State and the White House the Shah will die. When he dies, our problems go away with him. But without the drug from Weiss, I'd have to tell them I don't have a solution. Then, they'd have to take more overt action, and possibly traceable back to us."

"If I'm reading this right, Weiss is a contractor just like me. Why don't you call him up, or meet him at an airport and tell him? Why do I have to do it?"

"The more layers of deniability we can put between us and the drugs, the better."

"Yet I can call him on an open line and talk about this?"

Mike shrugged. "Yes. You're talking about a screening assay. You're not mentioning human use, and you're not mentioning the Shah by name. Stick to those rules, and we're okay."

Mike paused to listen to the overhead speaker announcing his flight. He picked up his paper cup, crumbled the napkin into it, and stood. He extended his hand and said, "Today would be better than tomorrow to call Weiss. Yesterday would have been best."

I shook his hand and assured him I'd call Weiss as soon as I got into the office. Then I left, taking the train back into the city, and transferred to the northbound line that would take me to the Palais des Nations. Even with this nondirect route, I was in my office within thirty minutes.

I called Dr. Weiss at Columbia as soon as I arrived at my office. Trying to sound casual, I inquired about the weather back in New York.

"It's a fine fall day in Manhattan, one of the best we've had in a long time."

I feigned interest for a couple of minutes, describing the weather in Geneva, which was delightful. Lake Geneva acted as a heat sink, keeping the area warm late into the fall, and it was far enough from the Atlantic it didn't have as much rain as England and France. Being on the lee side of the mountains of eastern France added to the pleasant weather.

"You're a busy man, so I won't hold you, but did you get a chance to contact our colleagues at Roswell?" I asked.

"Yes. I spoke with one of them this morning. We had an interesting discussion. He's willing to offer a series of drugs we can use in our screening experiment. He told me he could send me six by the end of the week. I asked if they had been fully characterized, and he said, yes, both chemically and pharmacologically."

"That's great he got them together on such short notice."

"In ordinary circumstances, I'd agree with you, but all six are active compounds with varying degrees of activity. They differ in the adverse effects. I told him we needed a mix of compounds, some that are active like he has, but to fully test the screen and avoid false positives and negatives, we'd need a few that didn't work, but had the adverse effects." Weiss understood what we needed, and equally important, he maintained the ruse of the screening experiment in case the phone call was being monitored.

"Can he get some of those too?"

"He thinks he can include them with the batch by the end of the week."

"Great!"

"He has one condition," Weiss added.

"What is it?"

"He wants a contract with the consortium that gives Roswell use of the screening method for two years if it works."

"Tell him he's got it. I'll get a contract drawn up, and we can have someone deliver it to him."

"He wants the contract before he sends the first compounds."

"Okay. We'll have the contract sent by courier tomorrow."

"You can get a contract that soon?"

"Yes," I said, knowing I'd pass the pressure for the contract to Mike. He'd get it done. "I'll let you know when it's on the way."

After I hung up with Weiss, I called Mike's secure number. I left the message about the contract, hoping his people knew what was going on with Roswell. At the very least, Mike would get the message when he landed at JFK late this evening.

Mike called in the morning telling me he sent the contract to Roswell by courier. I passed the information to Weiss, who readied himself to receive the sample compounds and send them to Fort Detrick, Maryland, where a clandestine laboratory group would analyze the samples to confirm the activity reported by Roswell. After they confirmed everything, I'd select the one I'd give to Dr. Bernard to use on the Shah. After my selection, chemists at Detrick would synthesize more of the drug for our use. It would be important we account for all the drugs sent from Roswell, so making more for our own use was essential. It would take six or seven weeks at the earliest before a drug would be available for Bernard to use. In the meantime, I'd talk to him about the exciting new drug I had for him to use.

The rest of October went by in what I would like to call a normal manner. The work at WHO was mostly familiarization with the programs running around the world and providing input about those in development. This planning aspect of the job didn't differ much from the planning I did for the clinical trials in the United States. It was coordinating the activities of personnel from WHO, both headquarters and on-site, getting drug and other medical supplies ready for shipment, and reviewing the reports sent back by medical staff. The experience I had at American Pharmaceuticals allowed me to make suggestions to improve the WHO processes.

On the personal side, I enjoyed the weekends with Monika and Eric a great deal, more so than I did back home. We had a limited time in Geneva, and we wanted to make the most of it. Because our weekend time was so special for us, Monika shortened her trip to Hanover to a Monday through Friday. Her mother met her in Germany but remained in Hanover for the weekend, joining us the following week in Geneva. We had been in-country long enough to see several things, and Monika shared our favorites with her, especially the German bakery, which became their breakfast spot.

Her mother was with us for the Guy Fawkes celebration at the English-speaking expatriates' compound. The Brits oversaw everything, even the weather. It could have been worse, but then it probably would have been canceled. With the official celebration starting after sunset, which in November is late afternoon, it got colder as it got darker, and I couldn't see the puddles of mud that had accumulated after a full day of chilly rain. The organizers provided carnival rides for the kids and carnival food, most of which wasn't what I was used to from American carnivals. There were no hot dogs or hamburgers and no cotton candy. There were fish and chips and mushy peas and pasties—a heavy pastry filled with an assortment of ingredients including egg and sausage, bacon, and a curry-based mixture of vegetables. And beer, lots of dark, warm British beer. Many people wore Guy Fawkes masks, which gave the festival an air of a late Halloween. The highlight of the evening was a five-minute firework display, where a roman candle soared into the sky every twenty seconds, giving the audience fifteen seconds to cheer as it sputtered back to earth. Eric had a great time as did his mother and grandmother, and that was all that mattered.

On the world stage, there were misleading signs of peace. Israel welcomed Anwar Sadat with a twenty-one-gun salute as he addressed the Knesset, the first Arab leader to speak to the Israeli congress. At the same time, President Carter welcomed the Shah of Iran in Washington, and anti-Shah demonstrators had to be dispersed with tear gas. The Shah returned the favor, without the tear gas, when Carter visited Iran in December, and the president toasted Iran as an "island of stability." World politics at its best!

Chapter 29

✳ ✳ ✳

I finished my assignment at WHO in mid-December, and we took the train to Hanover. In many respects, it was the highlight of the trip for Monika. We purchased a first-class compartment on the right side of the train. I preferred the right side traveling north as the left side tended to get hot in the afternoon sun, even in the winter. It also allowed us unobstructed views of the countryside as well as a quiet place for Eric to nap. Monika became quieter when we crossed into Germany. She was seeing parts of her homeland for the first time.

As we went through the larger cities of southern Germany, I found the hundreds of "kleingartens" small gardens, on the side of the railroad fascinating. These were small parcels of land, usually about ten by twenty meters, lined up side by side for hundreds of yards, each fenced with a small shed on the property, some elaborate, some just basic walls and roof. Monika didn't know what they were, so I asked a porter. These were parcels of land that became popular after the war when food was at a premium. Families were allotted the land to grow food. When the economy improved, the gardens stayed. Now they were a refuge for nearby apartment dwellers, who continued to use them to grow food or in some cases merely flowers. There were a few with neither vegetables nor flowers, only grass—a weekend retreat where a more pastoral life could be enjoyed.

We both became silent on a stretch north of Frankfurt where the train came close to the East German border. My choice of the right side of the train allowed us a view of "no man's land," the cleared space between two barbed wire fences separating the East from the West, and an unobstructed view of an East German guard tower where a soldier with a weapon was on duty, which sent a chill up my spine.

Christmas in Germany was wonderful, a collection of memories that would last a lifetime, reminding me of my earliest holidays in the years before television and the mass marketing of the holiday.

Monika's extended family lived in the northern part of Germany, some in Hanover, but the majority, including her grandparents, on the Steinhuder Meer, a lake twenty miles west of the city. A small lake and shallow by my standards, only thirty-five miles around and four feet deep, it is the largest lake in this part of Germany. The gentle hills surrounding the lake reminded me of the Finger Lakes region of New York State. A snowstorm enhanced the natural beauty of the area the day we arrived, and continuous dustings of the white powder maintained the wonderland image for our entire stay.

The Schweer family, Monika's mother's family name, were eel fishermen, having worked the lake for three centuries, the first two under an exclusive license from the government. Now they shared the lake with others, but everyone considered them the best at what they did, including smoking the fresh eel.

The family business included a fishing fleet of two small boats and a lake-front shop, where they smoked and sold the eel. The home sat several blocks inland. And what a house! A cousin, overhearing my wonderment, proclaimed, "The house is older than your country." A seventeenth-century farmhouse with the ground floor that originally served as a barn for livestock in inclement weather. The upper floor contained the living quarters with a loft for sleeping above. The home had been modernized several times, moving the livestock out and adding amenities like indoor plumbing and electricity, yet it still retained the quaintness of an old Saxony farmhouse.

Steinhuder celebrated the Christmas holiday season with several festivities including a "Holiday Bazaar" in the center of town with decorated shops, holiday foods, and a Christmas pageant. All meals at the Schweer home included smoked eel, something I didn't like at first but grew fond of by the time we left.

It was a nice family vacation, but all too soon it ended, and we returned home.

Back in New York, I got back into the routine of work as if I'd never left, my time in Geneva becoming a distant memory. Developments in Iran required I also attend to the business of preparing for the assassination of the Shah.

The Shah remained quiet after putting down the demonstrations in early November, but he didn't stay inactive. Convinced the Ayatollah Khomeini was behind the anti-Shah marches, he became further outraged by sermons Khomeini gave, charging the Shah with corruption. The Shah took his revenge in the form of an article he published in an Iranian newspaper in early January 1978, alleging Khomeini was a homosexual, British spy, and drug addict. Clerics, including those who had earlier opposed Khomeini mixing politics and religion, became outraged. During an anti-Shah demonstration, the following day, they demanded the Shah retract his allegations. Instead, he sent his army to squash the rally, killing twenty people. Emboldened by this renewed support from the former hostile clerics, Khomeini returned to Tehran three weeks later to meet with the Imam. Hundreds of thousands of the faithful traveled to Tehran to give support to the holy man and show their opposition to the Shah.

Beginning the second week in January, I was either on the phone or meeting with Mike or Dr. Weiss daily. The State Department and the White House now had the Shah and Iran on alert status and asked Mike for regular updates. Mike, in turn, pressed me for updates and accelerated action on the drug we would use on the Shah. The domino effect then forced me to put pressure on Weiss, who put pressure on the scientists at Fort Detrick.

By the end of December, we identified a compound meeting our criteria. It had low anticancer activity but all the side effects of chlorambucil. The chemists could synthesize enough to treat the Shah for six months and for testing to assure the compound's properties remained as originally designed. Roswell shipped the compounds from their labs to graduate students and junior faculty members in medical schools around the country, asking for help in developing a screen for anticancer activity. The modest stipend of $10,000 assured the project would reside with the graduate students but remain visible to the faculty member in case it led to something that could become a major contribution to medicine and a major research grant. The next step was bringing Dr. Bernard fully on-board. I had held off giving him any solid information, fearing he would talk to the Shah. When he convinced the Shah he needed a better treatment, I wanted to give him our compound immediately and not have the Shah shop for a different drug or different doctor.

Bernard was eager to begin treating the Shah with the new compound. He came to New York in late January for an international hematology conference but spent most of his time with me or Weiss, or both of us. He remained vague about the identity of his patient, saying only he was well known and lived in the Middle East. In response, I remained vague about the exact date the compound would be available. This caused him a great deal of anxiety, and he finally took me into his confidence when we were alone.

"The patient is the Shah of Iran," he said, pausing to let the full impact sink in.

"Holy shit," I responded, feigning surprise. "There are so many questions, I don't know where to begin."

"I can answer several by telling you he is in denial. His physician in Iran led a team who told him his condition in 1975, but he refused to believe them, insisting they find someone more knowledgeable. The primary physician came to me because we went to medical school together. He's a good doctor and a good man. I know him and his family quite well. He met his wife in Paris when he was a student."

"But if he's such a good doctor, why isn't he treating the Shah appropriately?"

"I asked him the same question. The Shah considers himself invincible, almost godlike. He read a textbook about cancer, and because he's lost no weight, he thinks his doctor is wrong and he only has a rare blood disorder. He gave his doctor the chance to redeem himself by getting me to assist in his treatment. I agreed, only after being convinced if I didn't, he'd kill my friend and his family. I don't know if he would, but my friend thinks so, and he's terrified. So where are we with the drug?"

"We are almost there," I lied. "A promising compound has come to our attention. Right now, it's being characterized."

"If you have it, give me it now."

"Dr. Bernard, you know better than that. Characterization takes time. In addition to quality and purity, all its chemical properties must be documented, and they have to synthesize additional drug so we have enough to treat the patient, the Shah, for as long as he might need it, and we have to put samples aside for stability testing to make sure it doesn't deteriorate. All these things take time."

"How long?"

"I'll check with the chemists when I get back to the office, but we're fortunate because his disease seems to be progressing slowly, so we have time. Better to be right than be quick."

Bernard thought for a minute and then spoke in a soft, measured tone. "You've seen what's going on in Iran—the anti-Shah demonstrations and his response. Now Khomeini is back in Iran, and the clerics are turning from the Shah to support Khomeini."

Why was Bernard concerned about the political unrest? "What does that have to do with treating him for CLL?"

"I've been treating the Shah with chlorambucil, together with full doses of prednisone. There are those who believe prednisone may have a therapeutic value in cancer by bolstering the immune system. I don't know, but I am convinced the bizarre behavior exhibited by the Shah is a side effect of the prednisone."

"Yes. I'm aware of the wording in the package insert and the literature on the subject. Again, why the concern now?"

Bernard looked uncomfortable, playing with a paper clip, uncoiling it as he spoke. "Please don't get me wrong on this. If I had a lot of time, I'd fully explain my position, but I'll give you the condensed version. I was sympathetic to the Shah when he started the modernization of his country, but as time went by, I realized, my comfort came from thinking as a Westerner, and I was happy he was moving toward a way of life I appreciated. With time, I've had several young doctors from Iran work with me. During that time, I've learned there is another side to the story. One of these young doctors posed a question. 'How would you feel if someone came into power in France and tried to destroy centuries of French culture, replacing it with another currently in vogue but foreign?' My immediate response was typical, and I responded to the issue in Iran rather than the question he asked, citing it was better. With time my view changed as I moved about my life, enjoying those things that are French. Just take wine. In Iran before the Shah, alcohol was forbidden. With the Shah, he looked the other way. Using the example of France, it would be like someone making wine illegal here. It changed my thinking about the man."

Bernard was sharing a lot more than was necessary to answer my question, but I was fascinated and listened, eager to understand this complex man and his comprehension of unfamiliar cultures.

"When my former colleague called and asked me to help on the case, my professional ego took over, and I wanted to bring Western medicine to this land I perceived as backward but emerging. But there was something else, two things actually. The first was a sense my friend was in trouble and came to me for help, not for his patient but for himself. Later I learned of the threat to him and his family, something he already understood. The other thing was the arrogance of the Shah. A knowledgeable doctor had correctly diagnosed his condition, but he refused to accept the diagnosis. Not only that, he insisted he had a less serious disease."

Bernard looked at me for understanding. I gave him a noncommittal stare, indicating he should continue as his story was not yet at an end.

"I agreed to the sham of an unknown blood disease. How did I justify this as a physician? Easy. If I gave the Shah currently acceptable medical treatment, it was not a guarantee of cure. The disease is advanced, so the chance of success is low, maybe less than fifty percent. I treated him with prednisone. While not a cure, it may stimulate the immune system and have an effect. But most of all, continuing to support the treatment recommended by my friend maintained his credibility with the Shah and assured the continued safety for him and his family until I could do something else. What that something else could be, I didn't know."

"And you feel the need to do something more now. Why?"

"The political climate in Iran. I see it in the newspapers, and my friend tells me of his concerns regularly. When I reflect on the things the Shah did in the early seventies, they are in sharp contrast to what he's doing now. The suppression and killing of the demonstrators and the bizarre letter about Khomeini disturbed me most."

My concern grew. I could see multiple ways this could go. Bernard could back out, or he might consider ways to extricate his friend and his family from the situation they were in by helping them escape from Iran. Neither of those were good for me. If Bernard or his friend weren't treating the Shah, neither was I. There was only one way good for me.

Bernard continued his plea. "You need to offer the Shah a cure, something that allows him to stop taking the prednisone, and you need it in a hurry, preferably now."

"I don't know about now, but I'll see what I can do about soon. Is that okay?"

"Yes. Thank you, Jonathan, for understanding."

Mike Allen knew I met with Bernard and awaited my call. I went through the conversation without interruption and then paused for his response.

"Good job! Nothing changes other than the timetable. If we give him the drug, Bernard may be more committed now because of the immediacy of the threat his friend faces." He paused. I heard him breathing on the other end of the phone; then his voice became muffled, like his hand had gone over the mouthpiece. When he returned, he said, "Okay, I'll contact the folks at Fort Detrick and tell them we need the drug now."

"What about Weiss? He was our contact at Fort Detrick. Won't they be suspicious?"

"I won't be talking to the same people."

"What if they object?" I said, knowing scientists don't like to violate an established protocol, and full characterization of this drug had a specific protocol.

"Then someone else will tell them we need the drug, and we'll get the drug a few hours later."

"I'm impressed, Michael."

"Call me back in two hours. Then you'll be able to impress Dr. Bernard," he said and hung up.

I waited two hours and called him back.

"Call Bernard and impress him. He can't take it back with him. Could be a problem if it shows up in a random customs search. Can't ship it either for the same reason. Find out when he'll be back in his clinic. We'll send it to Paris in a diplomatic pouch on tonight's Air France flight. It'll be in our embassy an hour after the plane lands. He can't pick it up, so we'll deliver it when he can personally receive it."

"Will do, and thanks."

"All in a day's work, Jonathan, or in this case, two hours."

I relayed the information to a relieved and delighted Bernard. He wanted the drugs delivered in two days, Wednesday, and asked if I could meet him in Paris on Friday to discuss the breakthrough therapy with the Shah, scheduled to have his monthly treatment on the weekend. Without hesitation, I agreed.

Chapter 30

*   *   *

The Thursday-night American Airlines flight to Paris was full and noisy, every seat booked with European businessmen and women homeward-bound after a week in the United States. Many tried to work through the night, preparing reports so they could spend fewer hours in the office on Friday and leave with a clear conscience after passing the paper work to their bosses. Bernard sent a driver to meet me, so I avoided the long wait for a cab. I looked forward to at least an hour's nap in the back seat of the car during the ride to the Pasteur Institute in the center of Paris.

Before I had settled in the car, the driver pulled into the private air terminal on the edge of Charles de Gaulle airport and stopped at a guarded gate, where he exchanged words with an armed soldier. The brief exchange they had told me nothing, merely a statement of fact. "This is the passenger Dr. Bernard is waiting for." The guard saluted and raised the barrier. Once inside, the driver proceeded across the tarmac and stopped beside a white Falcon 20, the popular French business jet. I got out of the car when directed by the driver, who moved to the trunk to get my luggage. Then I saw the figure of Dr. Bernard at the open door of the plane, his friendly face and toothy smile beckoning me aboard.

Once inside, he directed me to a plush leather seat in front of Dr. Flandrin, the only other passenger on board, as the attendant secured my luggage after closing the door. The engine noise as the plane started moving eliminated any conversation. I buckled my seat belt.

Once aloft, the engine noise abated a little, just the sound of the wind against the fuselage causing a momentary flashback to that Thanksgiving eve of 1971 on another Falcon 20, flying through the night to bring me home. This plane was rushing into the unknown.

"Jonathan, would you care for breakfast? The plane has a full galley. The trip over must have tired you, but if you need something to eat?"

"Thank you, no. I had a light breakfast on the plane. That's all I need in the way of food, but I do need some answers. I thought we were meeting in Paris to examine the Shah and discuss his new therapy."

The toothy smile returned. "My apologies. Perhaps my English is not as good as I think it is. I always go to Tehran to treat the Shah. I invited you to meet me in Paris so we might travel together in more comfort than a commercial carrier. It is a long trip from New York to Tehran, and there are few direct flights. I thought this would be better. And there will be no record on your passport of visiting Tehran. I don't know if you would want that. It might be difficult to explain."

"Is this the Shah's plane?"

Bernard looked around and smiled before he spoke. "No, Jonathan. This is not the Shah's plane. While elegant by our standards, it is much too common for his tastes. He has a modified 727 with all possible amenities. No, this belongs to a man who is merely rich. He is another patient of ours," he explained, nodding to Dr. Flandrin, "and the public reason for our trip to Tehran. Dr. Flandrin and I will visit him this evening at the university hospital where many people will see us. You will stay in the hotel, where no one will see you. Tomorrow, a private car will take us to the palace where we will meet and treat the Shah." He smiled, more to himself than to me. "I like that, 'meet and treat.' Perhaps I'll say that tomorrow. The Shah has a sense of humor. He'll appreciate that."

I yawned, and Bernard saw how tired I was.

"Jonathan, the flight to Tehran is a little over six hours. Why don't you stretch out and sleep? I'll wake you when we're an hour out. Then you can freshen up and have a refreshment. That seat reclines almost flat. Quite comfortable. I've slept there many times. We'll stay quiet, so we don't disturb you."

"Thank you. That sounds great. What time do we get into Tehran?"

Bernard looked at his watch. "It's nine a.m. now, six hours of flight and two-and-half-hour time difference…we'll touch down around five thirty this afternoon."

"Did you say two-and-half-hour time difference?"

"Yes."

"Is that possible? I never heard of a half-hour time zone."

"An interesting aside for you to contemplate before you go to sleep. Before the railroads, there was no need for time zones. Nothing traveled faster than ten miles per hour. In your country, trains traveled vast distances at speeds up to thirty or forty miles per hour, allowing hundreds of miles a day. Of equal importance, the trains ran to a schedule. In your prairie country, the early train lines were one track with sidings to allow for oncoming traffic. To allow these trains to pass, schedules had to be established. With time, it became apparent daylight lasted longer as the trains moved west and shorter when they traveled east. Solution was acceptance of time zones. Our friends the British had a great deal to say about the time zones in the parts of the world they ruled and made certain adjustments to accommodate their needs. Needs that have not survived history, so we don't know why they did it, but three areas of the world are half-hour time zones relative to the rest of the world, all in former British territories—central Australia, western India, and most of Iran."

"Maybe their trains were slower," I joked.

Bernard laughed. "Superb, Jonathan. I must find a way to introduce this into the next conversation I have with a British colleague who is spending time with us at the institute. Besides being an excellent researcher, he is an avid railroader who took a two-week vacation in India to ride one-hundred-year-old, un-air-conditioned steam locomotive trains in the hinterlands. When he returned, he wore a shirt from his trip with dozens of burn marks from the cinders thrown from the smoke stack. With that bit of trivia, I bid you a pleasant sleep."

I drifted off and awakened from a dreamless sleep after four hours. A trip to the lavatory for a pee and quick wash and I felt ready to go. I now had an appetite. Returning to my seat, Bernard asked if I was hungry.

"Yes, famished."

The steward brought a selection of meats, cheeses, vegetables, and fruit.

"No alcohol I'm afraid. Not even a California wine. The owner is a strict Muslim and makes no concessions, even for this world-renowned doctor who is saving his life. You may eat your fill here, or try room service at the hotel. I would recommend this fare if you've not familiar with the local cuisine."

As I ate, Bernard remained silent, reading in his seat. "Are you studying the Shah's case?" I asked him.

"No, just reviewing some poetry."

"The world-renowned doctor reads poetry?" I chided.

Removing his glasses, he looked across the aisle at me. "No. The world-renowned doctor writes poetry."

"No shit! Sorry. That just jumped out of my mouth. I mean, here we are getting ready to treat a world leader for a terminal disease amid public demonstrations, and you prepare by writing poetry. Amazing, Doc. Just amazing.

"Does the Shah know?"

"Yes, and he likes my work."

I liked this man. Brilliant, humble, and a sense of the world. A renaissance man. A sense of humor as well. "Must be the half-hour time zone thing."

Bernard looked at me without reacting. He didn't get my joke.

"Was that a joke, Jonathan?"

He got it but didn't find it funny.

The plane started its descent into Tehran. With the shroud of intrigue around this trip, I wondered if we were going to the main airport or a more isolated private strip, or we could even land at a military base. Bernard said his patient was rich, which didn't exclude him from being in the military. I couldn't see any markings on the buildings when the plane taxied to a stop, so it remained a mystery.

As we made our way to the cabin door, Bernard told me the ground rules for the next fourteen hours. A car would take us directly to the hotel. The driver was a member of the Shah's security detail. He would check us in and accompany us to our rooms. I had to stay in my room. If I needed anything, there would be a guard in the hallway who would get it. We would leave for the palace at eight o'clock the following morning, where we would have breakfast. If I needed coffee before then, ask the guard. I was to talk only to the guard.

The first sensation I had when I exited the plane was surprise. Expecting hot dry air, cool rain greeted me as I descended the steps to the waiting car.

Bernard, noticing the look on my face, commented, "Not what you were expecting?"

"Not at all. I was expecting it to be hotter."

"That was my expectation the first time I was here. One of many misconceptions about the city. News broadcasts and pictures in the magazines show tan as the predominant natural color, so we assume it's desert. The city sits at almost four thousand feet, which accounts for the temperature. The tan is real, making it a high desert. This is the start of rainy season, the bulk of which is next month. If you come back in August, you'll get your hot and humid."

After an uneventful evening in the hotel, I retired early and awoke at 6:15 a.m., craving coffee. I opened the door and looked to the guard. He said, "Coffee?" to which I nodded yes. He spoke to his wrist, and ten minutes later, he delivered a pot of a rich, aromatic blend. I sat in the hotel robe enjoying the coffee and watching a French news broadcast on the television until it was time to shower and shave. A knock on the door at eight o'clock told me it was time to meet the Shah.

The ride to the palace took only ten minutes, but we didn't arrive at the front entrance. Rather, we drove underground and got out at an elevator that took us to the Shah's living quarters. His personal aide greeted us and ushered us into his private dining room.

The room was not to my liking. It reeked of unapologetic wealth. Window treatments were ornate tapestries of silk and gold. There were thick Persian carpets covering most of a polished granite floor. All the light fixtures were gold, with a huge chandelier hanging over the dining table. Six liveried attendants stood against the walls while another four waited to serve us at a gold coffee service set up between two windows. Unlike mornings at home where I needed the caffeine of several cups to get started, the two small cups at the hotel supplied enough caffeine for the day. I wanted another cup of coffee, figuring if the hotel coffee was great, this must be even better.

"May I have a decaf please?"

The attendant looked unsure. Before he answered, a swarthy gentleman with curly hair and an aquiline nose was at my side.

"To decaffeinate the coffee of my country would be as bad as taking the alcohol out of the wine in France." He turned to Dr. Bernard, who stood on the other side. "Surely, that would be an abomination, would you not agree?"

Bernard nodded his head in agreement and began to introduce me, but before he could, the gentleman interrupted him and said, "This must be your esteemed colleague from America, Dr. Jonathan West. Only Americans ask for decaffeinated coffee after having two cups in the hotel."

And there he was, Shah Mohammad Reza Pahlavi, the Shah of Iran, extending his hand. A slight man about five feet eight inches tall, his hand cool and weak as he grasped mine. He was pale for a native of the Iran, no doubt a reflection of his illness.

I took his hand and shook it, saying, "Excellency, forgive me. You are correct. I had two cups in the hotel and can feel the jolt. I thought—"

"Nothing to forgive, Dr. West. However, you have made the mistake many Westerners make. Yes, there is a little more caffeine in each drop of coffee, but there are fewer drops in a smaller cup." He smiled, his lips forming a crescent, but the smile was not in his eyes. It was a practiced smile, the smile of a diplomat. "So, my friend, you may drink as many cups as you normally do with no expectation of ill effects." He waited as I took the offered cup from the steward and tasted it.

My eyes lit up when the rich sweet blend touched my tongue. "Ah," I said. "That's wonderful. Do I detect a hint of cardamom in it? More Persian than Turkish."

"Of course," he responded. "This is Persia. You are knowledgeable about coffees of the Middle East?"

"Yes." And I told him of my coffee house meetings in New Haven as a medical student.

He told me he was pleasantly surprised to hear an American had taken such an interest in an aspect of Persian culture. Thinking for a minute, he said, "You have gained a unique insight to the diversity of the Persian cultures through something as simple as the way we prepare coffee. You are a student, Dr. West, and I look forward to our day together."

As we talked, he moved us to the table, seating me to his left and Dr. Bernard to his right, and his personal physician to the right of Bernard. Breakfast was a full meal—a combination of American with eggs and pancakes, no sausage, bacon, or ham; French with baguettes and croissants; and Iranian with breads, cheese, and fruits with an emphasis on dates and walnuts. The Shah explained that breakfast in Iran is a simple meal consisting of locally available food, the exception for many being English tea, Earl Grey. He preferred the coffee as did I.

The Shah ate little, a small piece of bread, a bite of cheese, and a few dates, confirming his earlier statement of breakfast being a small meal, but the clinician in me saw it as a sign of his deteriorating condition, the wasting associated with cancer. He waited until we finished eating before he stood.

"Come, Dr. Bernard. Let us see if Dr. West can impress me with his knowledge of the new drug as much as he impressed me with his knowledge of Persian coffee."

Chapter 31

* * *

The Shah led us down a short hallway to a bright white room containing a vast collection of medical equipment, an examining table, and a staff of two doctors and three nurses, all male. The large object in the corner of the room drew my attention.

"Is that what I think it is?" I asked.

The Shah responded, "If you think it is the latest version of the ACTA machine, you are correct."

"ACTA?" I asked.

Dr. Bernard added, "Automatic Computer Transverse Axial. The newer term is 'CAT scanner.' It's the latest version from Pfizer, the 200 FS model, FS for fast scan."

"A whole-body scanner." I'd heard of these but had seen the smaller model that could only x-ray the head. "There are less than two hundred of these in the United States. There's a wait list of months, and you have one," I said, turning to the Shah.

"Dr. Bernard mentioned it might be necessary to do a body scan as another means of monitoring the progression of the disease." He turned from Dr. Bernard. "Or to monitor the success of therapy in overcoming the disease. So I brought one here."

Bernard added, "It surprised me he had one. An interesting aside. Rather than call one of the dozen companies selling them, he had someone go to the inventor, Dr. Ladle, a dentist in the greater Washington, DC, area, and told him that the Shah wished to buy one for the hospital here in Tehran. Impressed, Ledley worked with Pfizer to get him the latest design. When Ledley delivered it to the hospital, he asked the Shah why he chose the model he designed. The Shah responded that he heard the Ledley ACTA was 'the Cadillac.'"

At this the Shah laughed and said, "Dr. Bernard. Must you tell that story?"

Bernard nodded and continued, "Ledley explained the reason he called it 'the Cadillac' was because when he finished making the prototype with a mechanic friend, it looked a mess, so he took it to the local Cadillac dealer and had them paint it."

The Shah turned to Dr. Bernard and said, "Shall we begin?"

Bernard led us to a small conference room to the side of the treatment suite and invited us to take seats around the table. The Shah indicated he wanted me to his left and Bernard to his right, the same seating as breakfast.

There were papers and reports on the table in front of each of us. Bernard shuffled through the papers and spoke. "Yesterday, the Shah's private physician and his staff conducted a series of routine tests: a standard physical, modified to emphasize the diagnosis; a panel of clinical chemistry tests including liver enzymes; a complete blood count with differential; platelets; and a urinalysis. White cells remain elevated with the same percentage of immature lymphocytes as the last visit. I'll take a sample of blood back to the institute and look at the B cells. We don't know a lot about them now, still learning, but it's worth a look." He said this as a statement but looked around for confirmation, which we gave, including the Shah. "As always, Your Excellency, your name will not be on the sample."

I was getting an inside look at the relationship of this expert and his famous patient. They trusted each other, a trust gained over time.

Bernard continued, "Platelets and hemoglobin are both reduced, not below the limit, but low enough to be a concern. We should give you a unit of platelet-rich packed cells. That'll remove any concern about potential bleeds, and the packed cells will give you a boost of energy. Make you feel more like your old self."

"I know I am older than anyone in this room, Dr. Bernard, but you shouldn't remind me," the Shah responded. "Perhaps you mean I'll feel more like I used to feel before I got this wretched disease?"

Bernard was right. The Shah had a sense of humor. "Yes, Your Excellency. That is a better way to say what I meant."

The Shah sat up, head and shoulders square, looking healthy and regal. "Now it is time for Dr. West to tell me about the new treatment he has found for me."

I adjusted the papers in front of me, the ones left by his staff, and pushed them to the side, and brought mine in front of me.

"A colleague at Columbia brought several compounds to my attention."

"Who is this colleague?" the Shah asked.

"Your Excellency, I prefer not to share his name with you, just as I have not shared your name with him."

His wary eyes pinned me to the seat; then he nodded, and I continued, "The drug is part of a series of drugs developed taking advantage of the isomers of chlorambucil and the emerging receptor theory of drug action."

The Shah interrupted again. "Dr. West, I am well read in this area of isomers, the left-hand and the right-hand models, and receptor theory, so talk as you would to a colleague."

"Thank you. That will make it easier. Besides the basic isomers, they developed racemic mixtures of enantiomers and diastereomers of chlorambucil. I won't bore you with the chemistry, but as it relates to the receptor models, if you consider the left- and right-handed isomers as hands, and the gloves as receptors for these hands, it's easy to see that a left-hand cannot fit into a right-hand glove properly. To work, the drug, the hand in this case, must fit the receptor, the glove, precisely. To simplify the enantiomers and diastereomers for this example, consider a left hand with a finger turned around, bending the opposite direction. The hand will fit into the left-handed glove, but it won't work, or will work inefficiently. So too, with these engineered drugs."

The Shah wasn't getting all this, but the hand and glove examples made it easy for him to grasp the concept.

"Now, here's where the brilliance of this work comes in to treat cancer. While receptor theory has been used to design drugs that fit the receptor, they focused on the efficacy of the drug. With cancer drugs, we have a lot of very potent drugs, but inherent toxicity limits their use. The chemists designed this series of chlorambucil enantiomers to reduce the side effects, so more of the active part could be given with the same level of side effects. Absolutely brilliant!"

"But, Dr. West, I don't understand. If they could do this, why don't they develop a drug that has no side effects?"

"Excellent question. Maybe someday they will, but right now, this drug is the best they've got. This gives us the ability to give a fivefold multiple of the current dose but only elicit the same level of side effects."

"If the current dose of chlorambucil is therapeutic, why not only give one-fifth the dose and reduce the side effects dramatically?" he asked.

"The current dose of chlorambucil is not the most therapeutic, merely the most tolerated. This new mixture allows us to approach the ideal therapeutic dose."

"So I will still get the nausea, vomiting, appetite loss, and hair loss as I have with the current dose?"

"Yes, but—"The Shah cut me off, waving his hand in the air like a meat cleaver, slashing my words out of the air. "If my condition is not progressing rapidly with the standard dose with the full range of side effects, does it not make sense to double the dose and enjoy the benefit of increased efficacy with a reduction in the side effects I would experience?"

I paused for effect. Now I knew I had him. He accepted the logic of the argument, and he would accept the new treatment.

"Yes, it would make sense," offered Dr. Bernard, "but there is something else Dr. West and I discussed that we've not shared with you yet. You are also taking prednisone to augment your immune system. There is a concern in the medical literature that long-term treatment with prednisone can impair the mental processes. With everything you are facing now, not just the CLL, I wonder if this should be a consideration? If it is, I would agree a dose of five times the current one might not be necessary. I would want to see a dose of two-and-a-half times or perhaps three if we remove the prednisone."

"Dr. Bernard and Dr. West, I applaud you. You are skilled and inventive physicians beyond the norm. The suggestion to remove prednisone is excellent. I've noticed my ability to concentrate for extended periods of time has diminished. I will agree to two-and-one-half times the standard dose for the new drug. When do we start?"

Bernard was sitting straight in his chair already but sat even more so before he began. "Sir. I would like to start the new treatment at once, but you must take it daily for four to six weeks. You cannot miss a dose. In the past, you've not adhered to the daily dosing but skipped doses when you needed to be free of the nausea for a public function."

The Shah lowered his eyes. "Dr. Bernard. Thank you for your candor. As you spoke, I had a flashback of my father saying, 'Mohammad Reza, you must show more diligence in your studies if you are to be a great leader of Iran.' I accept your advice, but I cannot start now. My security team tells me they must analyze the drug before I take it. They will get the specifications and test it."

The Shah stood as he continued, "Next month, the rainy season starts. I usually take the month at my resort on the Caspian Sea and continue my duties from there. This year, it would appear the rains have come early, so it won't be unusual if we move to the sea early. My protocol chief will send an announcement to that effect. When we are there, I will start the treatment, away from the eyes of Tehran. You will accompany me?"

Bernard didn't expect this. "Excellency, your physician is very capable of administering the drug and monitoring your progress. I would be happy to visit regularly, but it's unnecessary."

"And you, Dr. West. Will you go with me to the Caspian?"

"No sir, I won't. I agree with Dr. Bernard that your staff can and should handle your treatment. I have a full-time job in New York, and as you requested, I have not made public my involvement in your treatment. Of course, I would like regular progress reports, so I can let my colleagues know how the new drug is working."

"Very well. I expected such answers from both of you, but I had to ask." He moved to the intercom on the table, pushed a button, and spoke to an aide. "We will leave for the Caspian next week."

When he finished, the Shah remained standing. "Gentlemen, thank you for coming all this way, but more important, I thank you for the help you have given me. Not just help, but hope. Hope for me and hope for my country that I may continue my work, a stronger and clearer thinking leader for the people of Iran. The plane will be ready to return you to Paris anytime you wish, but I hope you'll be able to stay for lunch. Dr. West, to answer your unspoken question, even if you left now, you would miss the last flight from Paris to New York today. So relax and enjoy the rest of your stay. Perhaps I will see you on the Caspian where the weather is always much better."

Bernard and I didn't speak much on the flight back to Paris. He busied himself with his poetry, but I caught him several times staring into space. I doubt he was pondering the next verse he wanted to write because his book was upside down.

The next month passed with the weekly progress reports being my only contact with the Shah. His white blood cell count was holding without further elevation, and his hemoglobin and platelets, while still low, stabilized. Dr. Bernard went to the resort once to examine the Shah. He asked if I would like to accompany him, but I declined. There was no sense in making such a trip. It was a two-and-one-half-day trip—an overnight flight to Paris, the private jet to the Caspian, a quick examination followed by an early flight back to Paris to catch the last flight back to New York. For what? To say the results are encouraging?

Then that call from an excited Dr. Bernard in mid-April.

"Jonathan, wonderful news! He's in remission."

"Who?" I asked, knowing Bernard was treating the Shah and the "excuse" patient, the rich Iranian who provided the plane and the reason to visit Iran regularly.

"The Shah, of course."

My mouth said, "What wonderful news," while my brain screamed, "What the fuck!"

Chapter 32

✳   ✳   ✳

An ecstatic Bernard said, "Yes, wonderful. The white count is down, and his platelets and hemoglobin are up, not much, but enough to almost put them into the normal range. We'll have a better picture when I see the results in another week."

"That's a good approach, checking in a week. Don't want to tell him and get his hopes up if it's just an anomaly," I replied.

"He knows. In fact, he knew before I did. His physician told him as soon as the results were available. You should be here to share the excitement."

I could imagine the joy of not only the Shah and Bernard, but also the local physician, who could breathe a temporary sigh of relief, knowing he and his family were safe for the time being.

"I've agreed to examine him in two weeks, and he wants you to come over. The Shah holds you in high esteem and credits you for the new drug. I'm embarrassed to say I'm jealous of the number of times he mentions you, but we are a team, and I know what he means."

"Remind him you found me."

"I did, but rather than thank me, he thanked Allah for helping me find you."

"I'll check my schedule, but it makes little sense to spend all that time in the air for a handshake."

"And a kiss," added Bernard. "The chaste cheek-to-cheek thing the Shah is fond of doing."

"Sorry, my friend. That doesn't change my mind." I was feeding his excitement, but I had to get off the phone and contact Allen. This was not the news we expected.

When I called Allen, he duplicated my response. "What the fuck? How can that be if he's not getting any drug?"

"Mike, settle down. It's not what we planned for, but now that I've had time to mull it over, it might work to our advantage."

"Tell me please how a remission can work to our favor."

"It's not unusual a patient responds to a change of therapy in a positive way for a brief time. While it's unfortunate, the patient believes they're in remission on bogus treatment, it's more devastating to other patients who hear of the remission and forego accepted treatment for the phony one. This anecdotal endorsement keeps people from getting proper treatment."

"Okay, I understand, but how does it help us?"

"With anecdotes, people hear of a so-called cure and want to try it. No, they insist on being treated with it. Here, the person with the anecdotal cure is the patient. The Shah's on it and thinks it's a miracle. Two things in our favor. He's admitted to himself he has cancer, and he believes he's being treated with a drug that will cure him. So he won't seek other drugs or doctors. He's ours."

"And that's good why?"

"Because we know he's not getting a drug; it's a placebo. You can't cure cancer with a placebo, period. He'll stay on the drug thinking anything other than a cure is merely a setback."

Mike didn't respond.

"We have him until he dies. And die he will of the normal progression of the disease. He told Bernard Allah sent me and the drug to him. He'll stay with it. It's Allah's will."

"Can we speed up the progression of the disease?"

"Jesus, Mike. We've come a long way. You asked me to assassinate him and make it look like he died of natural causes. You can't get a better scenario than we have. If I try something, Bernard may get suspicious."

"Okay, okay. I get it. Forget about speeding up his end. That was just me being me. This is the best thing we could have hoped for. How long does he have?"

"Six months to two years."

"Six months would be nice," said Mike. "Two years would be okay if he dropped out of sight, stepped down from being Shah. Then we wouldn't have to support anything his regime did. If the regime changed, and we didn't like what was happening, we could back off, saying our support was for the democratic process the Shah brought to the country. Blame everything on the new guys as being counter to our democratic beliefs."

"I don't see him stepping down. Do you?"

"No. Did you say he admits he has cancer?" Mike asked.

"Yes. Bernard told me he admitted it."

"Do you think he'd admit it to the rest of the world?"

"Don't know. Why?" Mike was thinking, but I didn't know where he was going. The best I could do was answer his questions.

"If he announces he has cancer, he'll be viewed as weak. His supporters will rally around him, but his opponents will see the illness as an opportunity. Then his loyalists might see the future with him gone and support him less vigorously. With no one to follow him, he's no longer a leader. As a leader, he'll be dead before he's in the ground."

The week passed slowly as I waited for the results of the next checkup for the Shah and the results of the blood tests.

Bernard called from the Shah's resort on the Caspian Sea. He was to skip the weekly visit and only review the blood results from Paris. As soon as I heard him speak, I could tell from the tone of his voice he had unwelcome news.

"Jonathan, I have the new blood test results." There were no pleasantries, not even "Hello," just straight to the results.

"I take it they're not good."

"The white count is up again with an increase in immature cells. Hemoglobin down slightly as are the platelets. The increase we saw last week didn't last. Not what we expected. The good news is the Shah is still positive. He wants to increase the dose to five times the standard dose as you suggested. He had a moment where I thought I saw a hint of remorse for not paying attention to the recommendation of the young American doctor sent to him by Allah."

"Is that what you'll do, increase the dose?"

"Yes. I'm confident he's taking the drug as he's supposed to. His hair is starting to fall out, and he's taken that as a positive sign the drug is working. He's isolated here, so his public appearances are limited. He's a vain man, so he's prepared for this with a half dozen high-end hair pieces. I think we're okay for the time being."

There was a hidden message in Bernard's words. Besides the obvious reference to the treatment of the Shah, should things go bad, the well-being of his medical colleague in Tehran concerned him.

"All right. There's nothing I can do from here. With the increase in the dose, I'll make sure we have enough for the next six months. We'll reassess drug needs regularly."

"Good. Thank you again, Jonathan, for the help you've provided." Again, the double meaning.

Bernard called me on Monday following his return to Paris.

"Jonathan, passport control detained me when I returned from my trip. Apparently, they've been monitoring my travel. I'm afraid I got sloppy on this last trip, flying into Ramsar rather than Tehran. Tried to avoid a long, dusty trip by car from Tehran to the Shah's summer palace."

"Why should that be a concern to passport control?"

"I had a cover for my trips to Tehran with the rich man I was supposed to be treating there. The patient remained in Tehran, but I went to Ramsar. Customs asked why, but they already knew the answer. The Shah."

"What now?"

"I spoke with the Shah, and he's prepared to let the French government announce that two French physicians are treating the Shah for cancer. Yes, he's willing to announce to the world he has cancer. With his belief he's in remission, he'll say he's conquered the deadly disease because Allah has favored him. Feels it will strengthen his position as the leader."

"What do you think?" I asked.

"I'm his physician, not his political advisor. I don't know what it'll do for his standing in the country."

"What about me? Will the announcement refer to my involvement?"

"No. The government wants to have all the credit go to me and Doctor Flandrin, French miracle workers. The Shah agreed with that as I'm sure you do."

"Yes, that's my preference, and I won't get into trouble with my government for getting involved without their permission. Thank you and thank the Shah for his consideration."

"It had nothing to do with any of that. The Shah is selfish. He was afraid your government would be upset and forbid you from treating him. He wants you to stay on board, so he'll stay quiet about you as long as you agree to continue in his treatment."

"I will."

It wasn't until September when the French government informed the United States and the rest of the world the Shah was dying of cancer. Washington feigned surprise and sorrow for the Shah but secretly pleased the melodrama was playing itself out on the world stage, and support for the Shah's regime could shift to support for the Shah's health.

There had been rumors about his failing health when he moved to his resort on the Caspian and disappeared from his daily duties. Although denied by the seaside palace, they persisted. The Shah even made one attempt to show himself as the robust, healthy man of his youth by arranging a photo op on the beach. A photograph of him appeared in the Irani press showing him strolling on the beach, long pants and long-sleeved shirt to cover his wasting body. In actuality, two aides escorted and supported him on his walk. The photo was carefully posed and edited to remove the aides, so his supported arms seemed to be in a vigorous stride. It would have worked except the alteration failed to remove the footprints of the aides in the sand.

The Shah's mental condition deteriorated to the point he wasn't making any decisions at all. His wife pleaded with him to leave Iran and seek medical help someplace else. She even offered to serve as his regent, running the country until his return. He refused, and his continued presence as the head of state led to chaos in the country. Because he had set up a government that required his input on every decision, his incapacity meant no decisions could be made. There was no backup plan.

Nowhere was this more evident than on September 8, 1978, a day that would come to be known as Black Friday, when thousands of anti-Shah zealots gathered in Tehran for a religious demonstration. The military didn't know what to do when the demonstrators refused to disperse, so they did the only thing they knew how to do; they opened fire on the crowd, killing many and seriously injuring others. That was it; the revolution started. Opponents saw the Shah as weak, incompetent, or ruthless dictator, or all three. There was no turning back.

Through all this, I was in contact with Bernard and Mike Allen. Washington was silently elated. Their problem would soon be gone, either by revolution or by cancer. There would be a different regime to deal with without the baggage of the Shah and the allegiances of the past. A fresh start! As a physician, Bernard was concerned with the continued decline in the health of the Shah and asked for assurance the drug used for the early remission was still being used. I confirmed it was. As a humanitarian, he worried about his former colleague and friend. Only if the Shah left Iran could he and his family be safe. If he stayed, the next regime may seek out all those who aided the Shah and prosecute them, and in Iran, they prosecute with a Damascus sword.

In October, the Shah continued the self-destruction of his regime when he granted amnesty to all the dissidents he had expelled from the country, allowing for the return of the radical cleric Ayatollah Khomeini.

Publicly, Washington continued to support the Shah, but privately they knew he was doomed. The only question was whether he would stay in the country and be prosecuted or flee. His personal physician made plans to leave. On the pretext of taking a short holiday in Paris to celebrate their wedding anniversary, he took his family and left in November.

With his friend's family safe in Paris, Bernard informed the Shah he could no longer travel to Tehran to treat him; he considered it unsafe. The Shah gave assurances, but an adamant Bernard told him that he would not return to Tehran. The Shah was still insistent on receiving the drug. We considered walking away from him but feared he would seek a different doctor who might discover our ruse, so we agreed to continue the drug supply.

For the rest of the year, the Shah's physical and mental health continued to decline. He became obsessed with the idea the revolution against him was a conspiracy fostered by Britain, America, and the Soviet Union while all around him the country was collapsing due to strikes. He was incapable of handling these problems, and they escalated to the point when in January 1979, the Shah turned the country over to the prime minister and fled.

The departure of the Shah from Iran reduced the pressure on Mike and me from the White House and State Department. Reduced but not eliminated. While they focused on establishing new and different diplomatic relations with the new leadership in Tehran, they still wanted the Shah eliminated as a potential threat. After all, he had been in exile before, only to return to power. Our mission remained the same. The Shah must die of natural causes, or apparent natural causes.

Chapter 33

From January 1979 to September, the Shah traveled to countries he considered friends. After stops in Egypt and Morocco, he realized his hosts' interest didn't come from any sense of friendship, but rather greed. These hosts wanted some of the estimated two billion dollars he took from Iran for the privilege of staying in their country.

During his first stop in Egypt, I traveled there to treat him and assure him I'd continue to support Dr. Flandrin. Bernard was trying to distance himself from the Shah, and Flandrin now had the responsibility for his treatment. I wanted to make sure he came to me when he had a question about his treatment and not someone else. While in Egypt, his hair loss stopped, which made him question the potency of the drug. I assured him not everyone suffered from hair loss on chlorambucil, and his hair loss may have resulted from worry about the civil unrest in Iran, merely coincidental. The Shah accepted my explanation. The stop in Morocco was so brief, I didn't have to go there.

Fed up with the greed of his supposed friends, he moved to Paradise Island just over the bridge from Nassau in the Bahamas, where I made two trips to examine him. The beautiful pristine beaches and tropical vegetation were a welcome change from Iran. The Shah rented a villa in the Ocean Club, a high-end resort. I declined staying with the entourage at the hotel on the grounds, opting instead for a room in the Holiday Inn at Pirates Cove.

The stay on Paradise Island was supposed to be a pleasant interlude while the Shah waited on a petition seeking asylum in the UK. He chose the UK for the schools for his children, tolerating the cold, damp climate for their future. Perhaps he also understood the cold would only be temporary, a welcome respite before damnation to hell's fires for eternity. The British denied his request, fearful that granting asylum to him would place their diplomats remaining in Tehran in jeopardy. The Shah became deeply troubled as he learned of the mass execution of his supporters who remained in Iran. This was a defining moment for him with no doubt remaining; neither he nor anyone in his family could ever return to Iran.

The rejection of his request for UK asylum came during one of my visits to the villa. After hearing the dreaded news, the Shah excused himself, claiming fatigue, and left me with his wife. As I got up to leave, she asked me to stay.

"Jonathan, the Shah and I are very grateful for all the help you've given him. He feels you are the only one who has stayed by us during this ordeal. President Carter has been very kind to the Shah, welcoming him to the White House last year and saying such pleasant things. The president too understands what we were trying to do in Iran. The Shah and I would like to acknowledge your service."

"Majesty, that is very kind of you and the Shah to consider honoring me in such a way, but I must ask you to refrain. I don't treat patients directly, but I've sought to fulfill my Hippocratic oath as an employee of a large international drug company, so I may serve many. Similarly, my company lends my services to the WHO, where many of the poor can benefit from the work I do. The exception is the Shah, but I consider it an extension of the work I do working for the company, for WHO, and for the personal satisfaction I get. But as with our friends in the UK, I must ask you not to disclose my participation in the treatment of your husband. American Pharmaceuticals wouldn't like the attention for the same reasons as the British and may forbid me from any further involvement. So for the sake of your husband and the safety of my company colleagues who remain in Tehran, please let this remain our secret and my gift to you and the Shah."

"Jonathan, I am humbled by your selfless act. As we have seen in the last few months, there are those who offer their assistance to the Shah but have selfish motives. These hosts want money for their help. Yet you, a gentle healer, seek nothing, not even recognition for the work you do. You sacrifice notoriety for the safety of others. Jonathan, you are a noble man worthy of the name healer and friend."

The empress reached across and took my hands in hers, brought her lips down, kissing them. When her head came up, tears had welled up in the corner of her eyes, ready to stream down her face. Did I feel like a shit? Most definitely. Mike would be elated I had worked myself into her confidence. Between this and the hijacking, maybe I should consider a career in acting.

The Shah was content for a brief time until he tried to buy Paradise Island, offering a price the government considered an insult. With that and the UK denying his request for asylum, he lost his enchantment with the Bahamas. On short notice, he announced he and the family were moving again, this time as guests of Jose Lopez Portillo, the president of Mexico, in Cuernavaca outside Mexico City.

There was a brief period when I felt sorry for the Shah. The man had been forced to flee his home country and suffered through short stays in several countries only to learn he wasn't welcome there either. When I reflected on why he wasn't welcome, the pity didn't last long. It didn't extend to his wife either. She knew or should have known what was going on and the harsh way he treated his subjects. I did feel sorry for the kids, four innocents whose only crime was getting half of their genetic material from him.

The stay in Mexico proved the most troubling for me and my assignment. Mike and the CIA wanted me on-site with the Shah regularly, which meant two days every other week. I was to stay alert for an opportunity to shorten his time on earth. Once the Shah settled in, he received visitors. Former president Nixon showed up with Dr. Benjamin Kean. Nixon took an interest in the Shah; perhaps being a fellow reluctant exile had something to do with it. He got Kean to examine the Shah and evaluate his treatment. The Shah agreed to this, but insisted Kean discuss everything with me, his plans and his findings. After I got over the celebrity of Nixon, I realized Kean presented a potential problem.

Before examining the Shah, Kean interrogated me about the Shah's treatment. He was arrogant and authoritarian until the Shah entered the room, stopping in the open doorway. I stood to acknowledge his presence. Kean looked bewildered, not knowing what to do.

The Shah spoke. "Jonathan, even in these unfortunate circumstances you know the protocol when the Shah enters the room." A look to Kean was all that was needed. It said, "You don't, but if you want me to cooperate, you better."

Kean stood, bowed at the waist, and said, "Your Excellency. An honor. I was just getting briefed on your treatment."

"It sounded as if you, a guest in my home, were interrogating my trusted physician about the treatment Allah revealed to him. Both Allah and I might be offended if that was the case."

Kean, now humbled, responded, "Excellency, that was not my intent. Forgive me, but in my enthusiasm, I was too eager and may have come across in a disrespectful manner. Let me assure you, I have the highest regard for the counsel and treatment Jonathan has provided."

The Shah corrected him, "The treatment Allah has revealed to him."

"Yes. Of course. The treatment Allah has revealed to him."

The Shah remained a political animal, albeit an ill animal. He now desired asylum in the United States, and insulting Kean, a friend of Nixon, was not the way to endear himself to those he might need to assist him. Now, more reluctant, he allowed Kean to examine him.

After several examinations, Kean confirmed the cancer, citing in a private message he thought it had progressed as evidenced by the appearance of hard tumor nodules in the neck area. He also noted a swollen spleen, worsening jaundice, a possible infection of the biliary tract, and gallstones. He recommended immediate surgery for the gallstones, surgery he would conduct at the university hospital in Mexico City. We debated the need for surgery.

"Benjamin. Please consider what you're recommending to the Shah. He'll ask me what I think, and I'll have to tell him he is so weakened now surgery presents as big a risk as no surgery, especially here in Mexico City. Convince me the risk is warranted, or I'll have to recommend a less radical course of therapy."

"Such as?"

"If you think there is a cascade of ailments leading to his overall conditions, one of them being an infection of the biliary tract, I would suggest we treat the infection for a few days, watching and waiting. Use the time to find a top-notch medical facility for the surgery if it's needed later."

"I can see you have a great deal of pull with the Shah. No matter how right I am, if you disagree, he'll go with your recommendation. There is no choice but to do as you suggest. Let's start a regimen of penicillin and metronidazole. There's no time to collect a sample for a culture and sensitivity, so we'll treat him empirically for both gram-negative and gram-positive pathogens."

I concurred.

Kean continued, "During the wait, I'll inquire about other medical facilities where we can do the surgery if necessary."

"Don't bother with anyplace in the UK. They've denied him asylum for fear of retaliation from his enemies. They'd probably feel the same about treating him."

"Anyplace else?"

"He doesn't seem to have any friends in Egypt or Morocco anymore."

"Neither do I, so that's not a problem," said Kean, as he showed a smile for the first time.

Only after Kean left did I realize the error of my thinking. I was behaving like a physician rather than an assassin. The Shah was a poor surgical risk: older, a significant number of concurrent diseases, platelets and hemoglobin low. He could bleed out on the operating table. I should have agreed with Kean's assessment for immediate surgery, preferably in the salmonella department of a Mexican mushroom farm, using surgical instruments from the local humane society spay and neuter suite. He should close the wounds with chewing gum from the underside of cafeteria tables in a tuberculosis ward. Stupid me!

Or I could have argued for no surgery at all, but to let him stay in Mexico where he was incorrectly being treated for malaria. The Mexican doctors didn't treat his cancer because the Shah neglected to tell them he had it, and they didn't look for it. The Shah continued to self-medicate with the altered chlorambucil I provided. His condition deteriorated as evidenced by a profound loss of weight. Chances were he wouldn't last a month if we did nothing.

Kean found a reputable hospital in Switzerland that agreed to the surgery. Switzerland being neutral, it had no political reservations, but the triumph was short lived. The Shah rejected the Swiss, instead insisting on having the surgery performed in the United States.

The Carter administration didn't want the Shah in the country for any reason but couldn't withstand the onslaught of Nixon cronies, including Henry Kissinger, who lobbied on the Shah's behalf. Despite the State Department warning of reprisal by the Iranian regime, including the potential seizure of the American embassy in Tehran, Carter allowed the Shah to enter the country.

At this point, I realized Kean was a formidable opponent. He was using all the skills he had to keep the Shah alive, and these included using influential friends. If he suspected the chlorambucil wasn't as effective as it should be, and if he gained the Shah's confidence, he could change the treatment and prolong the Shah's life. At least I had cancer on my side.

They admitted the Shah to Cornell Medical in New York City. Mike thought this was an ideal opportunity for me to speed up the demise of the Shah. I disagreed. In the other places the Shah received treatment, I was just one of the favored foreigners tending to him. Once through the outside barrier of security, I was free to come and go as I pleased. No one asked to see my credentials. Everyone assumed I belonged. Not so at Cornell.

Security was intense at Cornell. Besides the Shah's normal staff, the US State Department was all over the place. They didn't want a dissident assassinating the Shah in the United States. Security existed as a series of concentric circles, each getting more rigorous as the center of the circle, the Shah, was approached. In addition, as an adjunct professor of medicine at Cornell and Columbia, I had to sign in every time I walked in and always wear my name tag. While it afforded me access to the inner circles, it also served as a record at every checkpoint I passed through. The number of people allowed direct access to the Shah was closely monitored. I was on his list for close access, but no one could be alone with the Shah. It was impossible to be the assassin. I was limited to being a healer.

The new revolutionary regime learned the Shah was being treated in New York; they demanded his return to Iran. The State Department denied the request stating as a partial reason the Shah's deteriorating medical condition.

This was met with disdain in Iran, and demonstrations broke out, resulting in the take-over of the US embassy in Tehran on November 4, 1979, and with it the beginning of the Iranian hostage crisis.

I met with Mike the week following the take-over of the US embassy.

"Mike, how could that happen? Didn't we know what was going on in the country and the risk to the embassy?"

"Yes. We knew. At the operational level, we had the information and heard rumors of the potential for an action against the United States, even the storming of the embassy. The information was in reports within the CIA. The problem was, it never got the attention of the senior people in the Agency."

"Why not?"

"Several reasons. Since the early 1970s, the government's been trying to shift from hard assets collecting information in the field and building a network of informants to relying more on computers to collect information from open sources. Academic-type analysts convinced them there was a wealth of information in the public domain that could be used to predict behavior. They used models based on information sources in the United States and Europe, collecting information on activities in the United States and Europe. Budget-conscious bureaucrats welcomed the opportunity to reduce head count and money spent. Problem was, in Iran they don't put announcements for student protests on the bulletin boards. Everything is quietly planned and quickly executed, and the perpetrators fade into the shadows."

"That's fucking ridiculous. How could that be possible?"

"Tight budgets were only part of the problem. The political climate was right too. Most of the government has been distracted since 1971 and Watergate. Even after Nixon, the country stumbled through the Ford administration, focused on the problems within, rather than those we faced overseas. Then came Carter, and now we're distracted by what he's doing with Egypt and Israel."

"How so?"

"That's a hard question to answer in a few words. The best I can do is tell you there are still many very bright dedicated people working around the world, collecting information, analyzing it, and identifying threats. Reports get sent up the chain of command where, for any number of reasons, they sometimes get filtered before being passed to the next level. Sometimes this information has been so sanitized by the time it gets to the top, it has no intrinsic value and is discarded." Mike paused, looking at me for understanding.

I recalled my first summer of indoctrination with Frank and the State Department. He had described the same scenario, but at the time, it was hypothetical. "I understand," I said.

Mike continued, "Could that have happened with intelligence about the seizure of the embassy in Tehran? Yes. It's possible someone thought the information might upset the delicate balance of the Carter–Middle East peace meetings and sanitized a report. Who knows? We have to deal with it now."

"We?" I asked. I didn't want any part of trying to free the embassy prisoners. I had enough to do with the Shah.

"No. Not the you-and-me we. The collective we of the US government. They."

Following the initial surgery, the Shah suffered many setbacks, but there was no opportunity for me to intercede in a negative way. Kean hovered over the Shah, leaving his side only for meals or to rest in a room down the hall. The setbacks resulted from conflicting medicine being performed by several, mostly unwilling, feuding participants. Dr. Flandrin had accompanied the Shah to New York but got pushed aside despite protestations from the Shah.

He had a second surgery to remove his gallstones in late November and then whisked away by the US Air Force to the hospital at Lackland Air Force Base in Texas. Perhaps they chose Lackland expecting a return to Mexico. Regardless of the reason, everyone at Cornell Hospital felt relieved when he left. They no longer had to run the gauntlet of Iranian student protestors, who showed up for the entire Shah's stay in New York chanting, "Death to the Shah."

President Carter felt the pressure for the hostage situation in Tehran and allowed the Shah to stay in Texas only long enough to have emergency removal of his gallbladder.

Mike sensed my frustration about this time and said, "Jonathan, I appreciate the effort you're making on this, but you must speed up the process. Killing him by removing one organ at a time is taking too long."

Throughout his stay in Texas, the Shah asked for me, but I remained in New York. The risk of being discovered visiting the Shah was too great. He remained drugged for most of the time, but when lucid, they told him I had been there and gone. Were that the case, I might have been able to expedite his demise because if people were willing to tell that lie, they'd be willing to let me stay with him without supervision. After nine days, the Shah left Texas for Panama, where he recovered at the villa of the US ambassador on Contadora Island.

Mike insisted I visit our patient in Panama. The Shah's security force formed his inner circle and made it easier for me to access him than within the States. They knew me, trusted me, and let me pass. The Secret Service agents assigned to guard him in New York trusted no one, not even his wife whom they stopped every time she attempted to visit him. It was also easier for me to travel outside the United States than within. I went to Mexico under the cover of a meeting with a potential clinical investigator, and then a private plane took me to Panama where a car met me on the tarmac, avoiding customs, and drove me to the Shah. The Shah's people arranged for my ground travel through his Panamanian security force led by a local army colonel, Manuel Noriega.

Noriega met me as I exited the car in the gated courtyard. A nasty-looking little man, he made up for his lack of any redeeming physical attractiveness with arrogance. He was short, stocky, greasy skinned, with a puffy face scarred by childhood smallpox. He was the embodiment of what every school yard bully dreamed of becoming as an adult. His lips formed a snarl as he turned to the driver of my car and ordered him to change the radio station. The driver pushed a button on the radio and Jethro Tull singing "Too Old to Rock-and-Roll; Too Young to Die" was replaced with quiet, a mere pause between songs on the new station.

In the brief silence, Noriega turned and said, "I hate that fucking song."

The pause on the new station ended, and the sound of Clash belting out "I Fought the Law" echoed in the courtyard. He turned again to the driver, screaming this time, "Turn the fucking radio off. Now! Your music sucks. That's even worse than the Bobby Fuller version. Don't turn it on again until you're five miles from here."

Turning, he said, "You, get over here. Lean against the gate and spread."

I looked at him in disbelief. He was angry about a song and took it out on me. "I've treated the Shah in five different countries. Never have I been subjected to a search. His security team knows me. Ask them."

"They ain't around. I am. So lean and spread them, or you wait here."

Fuck him, I thought. I'm not giving in to this shit-for-face bully. "I'll wait. Let's hope the Shah doesn't need any medical attention while I do." Actually, I hope he has a massive medical emergency. Then I'd be rid of the Shah and this pimply faced prick.

I stood, hands in my pockets off to the side, leaning against the now-silent car I had arrived in, humming my version of the song he hated, "I fought the law, and fuck you Manuel," my fingers touching the cool glass of the blue Vacutainer, where I had combined the sodium citrate from six other Vacutainers—the real reason I didn't want them to search me.

Chapter 34

✳ ✳ ✳

Noriega checked with the head of the Shah's security unit and confirmed my clearance to visit the Shah. An aide came and got me. As we left, I stared down this bully and whistled the Clash song he disliked. A truly despicable man.

The Shah was glad to see me, perhaps just a familiar face, or, as his wife said, he trusted me more than the others, believing I had been sent by Allah. I examined him and checked his chart. The man was wasting away due to the cancer and concomitant illnesses but also because of a small internal bleed.

"Jonathan, I hate this dismal country. I long for my own country, but I know I can never return. Even my friends in Washington won't let me return to their country, to live or die with dignity. They chanted for my death during my recovery in New York. They let Nixon stay and keep his dignity and everyone despised him."

"Excellency, please do not judge my country harshly. The protestors in New York were not Americans, rather foreign students sympathetic to Khomeini. Mr. Carter regrets placing the innocent hostages in jeopardy by allowing you to be treated in New York. Sir, you are a very visible pawn on the chessboard of the world. The president cannot let you return. His focus now is the return of the hostages."

"So tell me, Jonathan, when will I be well enough to be a voice of reason?"

"The cancer is not in remission but appears to be in check. With the splenectomy and removal of your gall bladder, I expected you to rebound, but that's not the case. The lab tests say the opposite. The low hemoglobin and platelets aren't a good sign. There's also evidence of a small internal bleeder we can't get to in your weakened state. Flandrin has recommended packed cells to help with the low hemoglobin."

"Packed cells?" the Shah asked.

"Yes. It's a way of increasing the number of red blood cells where we take a unit of blood and separate off the plasma, giving a more concentrated infusion. It addresses the low platelets to a certain degree. Blood transfusions must have an anticoagulant added to keep the blood from clotting. If we give a lot of blood, there's also a lot of anticoagulant, which with your low platelets and internal bleeder is a bad combination. Hence the packed cells."

"Good. I hope it works, and I start feeling better."

"Yes, then we'll only have to deal with the cancer."

The local doctor arrived with the packed cells. While they had been at room temperature for thirty minutes during the packing process, they still had a chill from the refrigerator and needed another thirty minutes before the Shah could receive them. He left me alone in the room, a trusted friend and healer.

The Shah slept most of the day now, not a deep sleep but out. As he slept, I removed the Vacutainer tube from my pocket and took a disposable syringe from the supply in the cabinet. Vacutainers are the test tubes used to collect blood in the doctor's office or at the bedside. Each contains a different chemical to keep blood from clotting, depending upon the test ordered. Sodium citrate was one of these chemicals, and I chose it because it would be nondetectable in the blood even if looked for. The body contained sodium and citrate, although not in combination, and there was no routine lab test for sodium citrate. This Vacutainer had six times the normal amount of anticlotting agent. It was the perfect weapon for this assassination. There was no chance of discovery at this stage. The Shah received multiple medicines by direct injection or by addition to the IV bag hanging beside his bed. Accountability for the syringes was nonexistent with used syringes thrown in the waste basket after cutting off the needle.

I withdrew the large dose of sodium citrate from the Vacutainer and injected it into the port on his intravenous line, cut the needle off, and threw the used syringe in the waste basket, the entire process taking less than a minute.

Today, this dose of sodium citrate was not enough to cause any visible harm, but it would circulate within his body. In his condition, with low hemoglobin and low platelets, his physicians kept close track of the amount of blood or packed cells he received. A delicate balance had to be maintained that provided the lifesaving red cells but didn't reduce the ability of his blood to clot due to the anticoagulant in the transfusion. This was particularly important because of the small bleeder he had. With the added sodium citrate from my injection, I upset that delicate balance, and tomorrow, I would upset it a little more, until he bled out.

On March 10, 1980, I left Panama and returned to the United States. I could only spend so much time in "Mexico," interviewing "investigators" before some-one at American Pharmaceuticals got curious and asked questions or made telephone calls. Mike Allen had enough contractors to cover for me, but extended absences from the office with little to show for my efforts wasn't a clever idea. While in New York, I met with Mike. I briefed him on the anticoagulant strategy I had implemented.

"How long?" he asked.

"How long for what?"

"Before that sodium stuff works and the Shah bleeds out?"

"Hard telling. If it was only me treating him, I'd say a week. He'd get his packed cells, which would increase his blood pressure a little and put more pressure on the little internal bleeder. Because of the reduced ability of the blood to clot, the internal bleed will get a little bigger. Then the process would repeat itself until it was out of control."

"Why did you qualify your response with 'only you treated him'?"

"Because there are about a half dozen specialists running around. Can't ignore the possibility someone will see the bleed getting worse and change treatment."

"Like what?"

"Too many things for me to counter. I think there are enough opposing views down there that there will be a debate about treatment, and a debate means time, and that's to our advantage."

"Who's in charge while you're back here?"

"Flandrin and Kean seem to be the dominant voices, but the locals want a say and a hand in his treatment. Every time Kean wants to bring in another expert, the locals object and offer two of their own. I'm glad I'm here and not there."

"Why so? The bickering and power struggle?"

"Not just that. A Panamanian thug is in charge of the local security."

"And?"

"And I don't like him." I then described my run-in with Noriega, including the almost-comical episode about the music.

"What were the names of the songs?" Mike asked without looking up from the pad he was taking notes on.

"Why's that important?"

"Jonathan, in intelligence, you don't know what's important until you need it. That's why these reports are so detailed. Someone may find it useful to know songs that irritate Noriega."

Thinking this was a useless detail, I changed the subject. "Mike, can we talk about my time with the Shah?"

"Sure."

"I'd like to limit my travel to Panama, or wherever the Shah is being treated, to the weekends. I can't keep misleading my company. You may cover for me with the right call from the right person at the right time, but that's just senior management. It wouldn't cover my colleagues. I need their trust and the trust of the people who work for me. Let me do my job for the company during the week and do the job for you on the weekend."

"Is that okay with Monika, you being away on the weekend?"

"It was her idea. She'll have me home most nights, and she understands this situation is short term."

"What about the Shah? Will he go for his super doc only working weekends?"

"I've touched on this before with his wife. Told her I need to stay out of sight or my company and perhaps even my country will pull me off the case. She understood, and she'll explain it to the Shah."

"Okay by me, if we're in the final stages."

On March 14, I received a call from Dr. Kean advising me he had admitted the Shah to the hospital in Panama City for an emergency splenectomy. Luckily, it was a Friday and coincided with my plans to fly down to Panama for the weekend.

During my short absence, the local medical team brought in a blood expert, not just any blood expert, but Jeane Hester, a specialist in the separation of various blood elements, in this case platelets. She recognized the problem with clotting and planned to treat it by infusing massive quantities of platelet-rich plasma. Based on the data she had, she had no reason to believe her treatment wouldn't work. The increased sodium citrate went undetected. More important, the platelet-enriched infusion wouldn't reverse the damage that had already occurred.

The surgery didn't happen. Internal bickering among the medical staff gave the Shah too much time to think about his enemies. He feared extremists from Iran had made their way to Panama and would kill him, perhaps on the operating table.

Kean called me again on March 23 at the Shah's request to tell me the Shah left for Cairo at the invitation of President Anwar Sadat. They rescheduled surgery for the evening of March 28, a Friday. He told me the Shah wanted me at his side. I put in for a vacation day and left for Cairo via Paris on Thursday evening. Also in the air on a separate flight, was Dr. Michael DeBakey, a cardiac surgeon chosen by Kean. The local doctors had refused him permission to operate in Panama, but he would lead the team in Cairo.

During my trip to Cairo the previous year, the palace staff recognized me as a friend of the Shah and allowed me free access wherever I wanted to go. I hoped they'd grant me the same privileges on this trip. Being alone for thirty seconds with the Shah, his transfusions or anything hung on his IV-drip tree, was all I needed to inject the sodium citrate from a preloaded syringe.

When I arrived, the Shah had increased security in response to the paranoia he developed in Panama, but I still passed through to the inner circle. Once there, the number of people administering to him dumbfounded me. DeBakey brought a full surgical team to assist in the splenectomy, and they were all busy prepping the Shah for the surgery. It was unlikely I'd get the privacy to dose him. I only hoped to get access to one of the IV drips they'd use in surgery, but the small pharmacy area was under heavy security. The Shah might die this weekend, but it wouldn't be by my hand.

After surgery, security lessened, and I had my opportunity. I injected the sodium citrate into his post-surgery transfusion. I avoided sterile technique and, quite the opposite, encouraged a nonsterile environment by running my finger across the injection site. The Shah regained consciousness Saturday afternoon. He was pleased to see me, smiling faintly with his eyes. While he wanted me to stay, he understood the delicacy of my situation having had it explained to him by his wife. I agreed to visit him in the evening before leaving on an early flight back to the States.

That evening, I entered his half-darkened room with only him and a male nurse present. The nurse recognized me, finished working on the Shah, and left us alone. I checked the hallway, and except for a guard at the entrance to the corridor, all was quiet. I noticed all the rooms on the corridor were empty when I arrived. The Shah was in isolation. Was this a medical precaution or security? It didn't matter. Either suited my purpose. I took the syringe from my pocket and pierced the rubber cap of the delivery line of his IV, injecting another large dose of the anticoagulant. The process took less than twenty seconds. When I finished, the Shah was awake, staring at me.

"Jonathan, have you stolen back my treatment from these bickering specialists? If so, you must share your secret with Dr. Flandrin. He seems to face obstacles at each turn."

"No, Your Excellency. I was just assuring there were no air bubbles in your IV line. I'm afraid I have no secrets to share with Dr. Flandrin except perhaps to visit you when the rest of the medical team is at dinner."

He smiled and tried to say something but drifted off to sleep again. I looked around, found the waste bucket that had the used syringes, and disposed of mine. One last look at the Shah and I left the room, hoping I'd not see him again.

At Heathrow Airport, I called Mike through a connection he set up with the CIA office in London.

"Not much to tell you. I gave him two doses of the anticoagulant. He's weak. Despite the team he has assembled around him, I'd be surprised if he lasted the weekend."

"We can only hope. Safe home, Jonathan."

"Thanks," I said and hung up the phone.

Back in New York, I expected to hear Kean's or Flandrin's voice every time I answered the phone. It occurred to me they might be busy with the Shah's remains if he passed, and I might hear it first on the news. There was a magnificent old walnut-cased Bang and Olufsen radio in my office. After tuning it to an all-news station, I waited.

Mike called on Tuesday. "When you said you doubted he would last the weekend, did you mean last weekend or this coming weekend?"

I kept my frustration in check and responded, "Mike, from everything I know, he should be dead. If he made it, he did so because of some brilliant medicine by his team. Too clever for me. He should have bled out or gained a sepsis. In his weakened state, either of those would kill him."

"Fucking guy thinks he's superhuman. Maybe he is. What's the next step, Jonathan?"

"I'll call Kean tomorrow. See what's happening. Ask if I should come over this weekend. Chances are he's fed up with all the people over there and will tell me to stay home."

When I called Kean on Wednesday, I expected him to tell me the Shah was failing.

"Jonathan, it's not the best news, but it's not the worst. The Shah got through the surgery well. While not on the road to recovery, he seems to be holding his own. His platelets remain low, so low I didn't think he'd get through the surgery, but DeBakey and his team deal with these difficult cases all the time and knew how to handle it. There were multiple nodules on his spleen, probably cancerous. As a precaution, we took a liver biopsy, which shows cancer, so we have metastases from the primary. Not all the news is bad. We're planning on starting him on more aggressive chemo on Monday."

"More aggressive?" I asked.

"Yeah. We'll change the meds and give him a combination of drugs, not just the chlorambucil."

"Great," I said. Shit, I thought.

Chapter 35

K ean remained in Cairo, overseeing the start of chemotherapy. The Shah responded well and was discharged, moving into the royal palace as the guest of President Sadat. Once there, he started down a path of deterioration confounded by confusion.

This was a grim time for Americans traveling to the area. Carter had authorized Operation Eagle Claw to rescue the fifty-two American hostages in Tehran. The rescue failed, and the reputation of the United States suffered.

Near the end of April, an x-ray showed a buildup of fluid around the Shah's lung. Kean summoned all the physicians to Cairo—Flandrin from Paris, DeBakey from Texas, me from New York, and several others from Egypt and Europe. Although not treating him, the Shah insisted I be present, that "special messenger" thing I guess.

The result proved disastrous for the Shah but worked to my benefit. Each being an expert meant each had to have "the answer." The consensus focused on an infection, but the site and specifics debated constantly. That is all except DeBakey, who thought the deterioration was due to the chemotherapy weakening his system. DeBakey reduced the dose, and we all waited.

No one asked me. I was the Shah's pet, a mere paper pusher. Unqualified in the eyes of all but the Shah who asked me about everything they did. "Jonathan, my dear friend. Do they know what they are doing?"

"Your Excellency. You have the finest physicians in the world taking care of you. No one could ask for more."

"I understand that, but do they know what they're doing?"

Despite his weakened physical condition, he still retained his sharp mind. The Shah recognized the confusion around him and perhaps even the bickering. Sure, they were smart men, but did they know what they were doing? Very astute of him to use the collective they, not each individual. Of course, they, the individual, knew what they were doing, but the drove of docs as a group behaved like a group of clueless first-year residents, each trying to impress the other with a carefully constructed diagnosis. This is the part of medicine I didn't miss. The part where the physician ego must be salved before the healing salve for the patient could be administered. During my first year at Yale, a teaching assistant put it in perspective when an eager gross anatomy lab partner acted like a prima donna or perhaps a prima doctor. "Remember," he said, "you're not learning how to become a damn doctor God; you're just learning to be a god-damn doctor." Those words rung true as I watched the battling egos.

"Are they looking for the wrong thing? Perhaps they should look for bubbles in the tubing." With his eyes still clear, his voice strong, he was alert and composed. While his eyes stayed fixed on mine, he raised his hand and summoned me nearer.

Approaching with apprehension, I felt the Shah knew my intent, had seen me inject the sodium citrate. Confusion clouded my thinking. That happened weeks ago. This man had ordered the deaths of thousands. If he harbored doubts about me, I should be dead, not being summoned nearer his death bed. Maybe he didn't know, and it was just my paranoia. But why the reference to the bubbles in the tubing?

"Jonathan, come closer, please." His hand remained extended, and as I got near, he took it. "Sit," he asked, an ask, not an order.

"As a trusted friend, I will ask you a question, and I want you to answer me honestly. Do you agree?"

I dreaded the question. If he suspected my intent, and I lied, he'd have me executed. If he had lingering doubts, and I answered truthfully, I was dead. They're wrong about one's life passing in front of you at the moment of death.

I experienced that now: my childhood, my parents, my years as a student, a hockey player. The descent on a parachute in the dark, cold November sky passed in a flash. Mostly, I saw the future I would be denied, a future with Monika and Eric, growing old together, watching Eric grow up, holding grand-children—all crystal clear and unattainable. Or they weren't wrong, and this was the moment of my death.

The Shah's cold, dry hand took mine in his. A slight tug as he pulled me closer. His fetid breath expelled the smell of the rot inside despite the glycerin mouth swabs used.

"Jonathan," he said. Here it comes, the question. "Can they save me from the cancer?"

Not the dreaded expected question. My body deflated with relief, a sigh, audible in the quiet room, the only other sounds being the life-support equip-ment humming, pumping, beeping, and hissing. The question hung in the air.

"No, Excellency. They cannot stop the cancer. It's too far along and vigorous."

He smiled. "I can't imagine anything vigorous left in this body."

Sighing, he continued, "When you first arrived many months ago, I believed Allah led Dr. Bernard to you. Since that time, I continue to believe Allah has sent you, but now I think it is not to save me from the cancer but to serve a more noble purpose. A purpose much larger than me or Iran. A purpose known only to him."

The Shah loosened his grip on my hand like he was loosening his grip on this life.

He continued, "I have fought the cancer, fought for life. Now I think I was wrong. I should give up and accept the fate planned for me. A fate you will have a hand in." He closed his eyes, and a calm fell over him. The respirator con-tinued to pump air into his lungs, but was it a mechanical exercise aerating an already dead man? I leaned closer, taking his hand again, probing for a pulse. As I felt the vein pulsate, his eyes opened.

"You must help me leave this life. It is what is necessary. It is my destiny. Will you help me?"

"Yes, Excellency."

"Good." With that he fell into a calm sleep, his face serene and relaxed, the wrinkles less apparent.

An alarm on a monitor over his bed sounded. Before I could look up to see which of his failing systems set it off, the room became crowded with men in white coats, all rushing to the bedside to administer to the Shah. Pushed aside, pushed further back from his bed to the periphery, I became an observer. Orders were being shouted in three different languages: English, French, and presumably Egyptian. There may have been more, but all the non-English and non-French sounded the same. The alarm quieted, and calm descended on the room again.

Flandrin approached me. "The Shah had difficulty breathing, and his temperature is elevated. I think it's that abscess. Can we now agree to go in and drain it?"

"Ask them," I said, pointing to the rest of the medical team.

The bickering continued as I left and returned to my hotel.

When I got back to New York, I called Mike in Washington and told him of my conversation with the Shah with emphasis on the Shah's reference to the bubbles. Mike's reaction was unexpected. Rather than a concern my mission had been compromised, he was elated.

"So. Now the end is near. How soon can you go back and finish him, or did you do that before you left?"

"It won't be easy. He had at least a dozen physicians in attendance, all vying for dominance. The Empress is an enthusiastic fan of Flandrin and upset by the conflicting egos which she thinks are responsible for the Shah's continued decline. She sent them away, but they fell back on their reputations and refused to leave. President Sadat got involved and supported the wife, putting Flandrin in charge, and anyone who disagreed could leave. If they didn't leave and continued to cause problems, he'd expel them from the country. Worse for us, he increased security around the Shah claiming such prominent physicians should be more in agreement, and disagreement could be an attempt to assassinate the Shah through incompetence. Might be more difficult for me to get to the Shah. More important, Sadat implemented total pharmacy accountability in the

Shah's unit. All meds are signed in and accounted for. Called it 'chain of evidence' like the preservation of evidence in a criminal case. The order included all equipment used on the Shah, including syringes."

"You have to be kidding! We want the Shah to die. The Shah wants to die. He's got a shit load of illnesses trying to kill him, and now we have the President of Egypt keeping him alive. Why?"

"Don't know. I don't think he cares. Might be the Shah's wife got to him and he's doing it for her. She is very convincing, or she has something on him."

"So, what's next for you?"

"I'll go back over, bring a syringe loaded with sodium citrate and contaminated with bacteria, but I'll leave it in my hotel until I'm sure I can get it past security. I may need the Shah to intercede for me."

"Good thing he wants to die."

"Yeah. I'm helping a patient commit suicide."

I remained in New York through the end of June as the Shah underwent surgery to drain the abscess from the former surgery. The long time between the original splenectomy and the drainage procedure had been one issue debated and argued by the docs in attendance. No one offered a good reason for the delay. After the drainage procedure, a Cairo newspaper reported that during the original surgery to remove the spleen, the pancreas had been compromised. Flandrin reexamined the pathology slides from the splenectomy and found pieces of pancreas present. This started another pissing match between DeBakey, the original surgeon, and the others, including a finger-pointing contest without parallel by physicians and surgeons who were sloppy, incompetent, or had a malevolent intent.

During July, I made my final trip to Cairo arriving late Friday, July 25, on a private plane from Geneva. Mike covered my travel with American Pharmaceuticals by setting up an emergency in WHO that required my attention. I didn't try to see the Shah until Saturday morning but sent a message to his wife of my arrival. As a result, she arranged for an aide to meet me at the first security barrier and escort me through to the Shah's bedside.

With his condition listed as critical but stable, he was sliding toward death. In his room, a dozen medical staff, mostly physicians, all men, including Kean and Flandrin attended him. Awake and talking to his wife, he saw me enter, and motioned with his eyes for me to approach his bed. The medical staff in the room stopped their ministrations as the empress made room for me at his bedside, the Shah's fair-haired doctor.

"Jonathan, I'm so happy you could come to see me today," he said in a wispy voice barely perceptible even though I stood two feet from him.

Nodding, I accepted his outstretched hand. He looked terrible, on death's door—his eyes sunken and the skin on his face drawn taut pulling his lips back, exposing his teeth and gums in a deathly grin. His eyes were bright, illuminated by some glow from within.

The empress commented, "Jonathan, you always bring peace to the Shah, and with it a look of serenity. He told me earlier he wants to be alone with you for a few minutes. I've made the necessary arrangements with the medical staff and with President Sadat's security. They objected, but a word from the president, and he granted the Shah's wish. He's been awake for about fifteen minutes, so now would be an appropriate time. He usually stays awake for about a half hour before nodding off again."

I looked to the Shah, and he nodded his head ever so slightly. The empress saw this and ushered everyone out of the room. She became animated, speaking sharply and waving her arms as if she was herding sheep or children from a playground.

The Shah pulled me even closer, knowing his voice was weak. "Jonathan, it is the middle of Ramadan and time. I had a vision and was told a place is waiting for me today. Help me leave this world and go to the next. It is his will, and you and I are his servants."

The final act was here. I took the syringe from my pocket and removed the protective cap. It weighed heavy in my hand, heavier than I remembered. As I injected the sodium citrate in the intake port of the intravenous line, I remembered the hijacking. This act could also change the course of history. Unlike the hijacking, today there were victims, the Shah and me, neither of us innocent. The Shah watched me as I pushed the plunger of the syringe, expelling the anticoagulant. We were doing this together. When finished, I put the cap back on the syringe and pocketed it, and turned to the Shah. He closed his eyes. No good-bye. No thank-you. Better that way. I stood and watched as the antico-agulant coursed in his vein back to the heart, diluted by the blood there before being pumped out to the rest of his body. The drug would do the most dam-age in the intestine, already compromised by multiple surgeries and the small bleeder no one had yet found.

As soon as I opened the door to leave, the nervous medical staff rushed in to resume doing whatever they had been doing when I arrived. The empress stood alone at the door as I emerged. She held out her hand and whispered, "Thank you." Did she know? Had he told her it was time to go and I was the hand of God sent to deliver him? Or was she merely thanking me for being there in his final hours? A trusted friend or an assassin of God?

Walking back to the entrance of the palace, I passed the elaborate gar-dens framing the portico. Alone, no escort for my departure, I took a left and walked to the edge of the balcony and looked out over the acres of grass, trees, flowers, and fountains. It was midmorning by now, and the silence in the garden stunned me. There were no birds chirping, no insects buzzing, no sounds of workman tidying up the place. Not even the distant sound of traffic on the streets of Cairo. Just the almost-silent breeze of the air moving around the building behind me. The quiet hung like a pall over the natural signs of life around me. Now would be a good time for a cigarette, but I didn't smoke anymore and had none. I wanted to linger for five minutes, no more, no less. I felt a compulsion to do something while I lingered. So I counted the cypress trees aligned to the left of the reflecting pool, seven-teen. There were cypress trees to the right of the pool. I counted them too, eighteen. Why were there more trees on the right than on the left? Had I counted wrong? I counted again. No. Seventeen to the left and eighteen to the right. I pondered this discrepancy for five minutes, turned, and contin-ued to the palace entrance.

The car was waiting when I arrived at the door, no doubt alerted by some-one deep within the confines of the palace. I had left my bags in the car this morning, sure I would not stay another day. "Airport, please."

The driver took me back to the Falcon-20 with no tail markings waiting on the tarmac. The flight crew was ready when I arrived.

"Where to, Dr. West?"

"Amsterdam, please. Can you call ahead and get me on the late-afternoon KLM flight from Schiphol to Kennedy? Seem to recall it leaves around five twenty."

"Yes, sir."

As the 747 began its climb, fighting the grip of earth, the tension left me, a tension born months before when I received the assignment to assassinate the Shah. As the tension lessened, my mind grappled with the act I had just performed. Was it murder, or was it an assisted suicide? Was there a difference when measured against my oath as a physician to be a healer? My thoughts turned to the fifty-two hostages in Tehran. I took comfort knowing the sacrifice of this one evil man would free a nation to choose its own fate and free the United States from a bond that made it look the other way as a despot imposed his will. I took solace there were no impediments to the release of the hostages now, and these innocent people could return to their loved ones. After an hour of thought, I justified my action. While morally gray, the assassination of the Shah was closer to the white than the black, closer to good than evil. I fell into a sleep for the rest of the flight, not a deep sleep but a sleep that shut my mind down.

As I slept at thirty-seven thousand feet above the Atlantic, the Shah's condition deteriorated rapidly. Being Ramadan, most of the physicians attending him had left to break their daylong fast and have their evening meal. As they rushed back, Flandrin, who had remained on-site, suspected a massive internal hemorrhage and started the first of eleven units of blood the Shah would receive in four hours. All the administered blood contained the standard amount of anticoagulant, but on top of the large dose of sodium citrate I injected, the Shah's blood had no ability to clot. He survived the night and had time to say good-bye to his family, who gathered by his bedside, before dying midmorning the following day.

Sadat arranged a huge funeral for the Shah with dignitaries from all over the world, including former president Nixon, in attendance. I didn't attend.

On Monday, after my return from Iran, Mike called and asked me to meet him for lunch at the Palm on Second Avenue, the place where this had all begun that evening with Anderson two years earlier. I would have preferred to have spent the evening with Monika, but it was an order, not a request.

Mike sat in a rear corner, his back to a wall, facing the door as I entered. I walked to his table and took a seat opposite him, an Amstel Light already there. He hoisted his glass and toasted me. "A job well done, Jonathan. The Shah died, and from all accounts, he died of natural causes. The medical staff have started to point fingers at each other, saying he got too much blood, and it compromised his clotting mechanism. They say he should have had a direct transfusion."

I touched his glass of amber liquid of what I presumed was his favorite, Bushmills, and accepted his congratulations.

After our toast, Mike said, "I'm told the amount of anticoagulant in his blood was so high, he was still bleeding when they put him in the casket. They had to bury him wearing a diaper."

Mike leaned forward, his hands surrounding the tumbler of Bushmills in front of him. In a low voice, he started our dinner conversation and the need for the meeting. "Let's talk about your next assignment."

In the weeks and months that followed the Shah's death, the medical community argued the Shah's medical condition was not managed properly. They cited the interference of conflicting specialists, poor diagnosis, and the political environment having more to do with his treatment than medicine. Some claimed, if properly treated, he could have lived another ten years. Not once was there a mention that the Shah's death was a deliberate act that took advantage of the serious, but not life-ending, medical condition he had. Nor was there any mention of the Shah's fair-haired American doctor.

About the Author

A retired pharmaceutical executive, William J. Kennedy lives in Rehoboth Beach, Delaware. He is the author of the Jonathan West trilogy, which he launched with his debut novel, *First Kill*. *Morally Gray* is the second thriller in the series.

Kennedy invites readers to contact him at consultkennedy@aol.com.